DECEPTION

ALSO BY JOHN ALTMAN

A Gathering of Spies
A Game of Spies

ECEPTIONDECEPTIONDE

DECEPTION

John Altman

G. P. PUTNAM'S SONS/NEW YORK

G. P. Putnam's Sons
Publishers Since 1838
a member of
Penguin Putnam Inc.
375 Hudson Street
New York, NY 10014

Library of Congress Cataloging-in-Publication Data

Altman, John, date.
Deception / John Altman.
p.   cm.
ISBN 0-399-15040-4
I. Title.
PS3601.L85 D43   2003   2002036818
813'.6—dc21

Printed in the United States of America
1   3   5   7   9   10   8   6   4   2

This book is printed on acid-free paper. ∞

BOOK DESIGN BY AMANDA DEWEY

For Margaret

Inevitably, chance does occasionally operate with a sort of fumbling coherence readily mistakable for the workings of a self-conscious Providence.

ERIC AMBLER
A Coffin for Dimitrios

PROLOGUE

The suntanned man behind the front desk glanced up, recognized him, and looked back down without a word.

Of course. The killer had let himself be seen in the hotel lobby twice over the past two evenings, walking in approximate lockstep with the Epstein couple as they returned from dinner. As a result, the night clerk assumed he was their son. From a short distance, after all, he appeared to be just another spoiled child of rich American tourists—wearing his tacky T-shirt emblazoned *Venezia, Mi Amore* and carrying his rolled-up magazine.

After satisfying himself that the desk clerk hadn't taken any special notice of his arrival, the killer strolled through the lobby with his eyes cast down. He climbed the staircase to the third floor and came out into the dank, quiet hallway. On his earlier forays into the hotel, he had continued down this corridor and left the hotel via the rear exit. This time, however, he came to a stop before the room marked 33. He put his ear to the wood and strained to hear.

At first came only shuffling noises. Then a toilet flushed. At roughly the same instant a television came on: CNN.

Then the woman's voice. "Café Lavena tomorrow?"

The man grunted, from very close to the door. That was good; for the killer wanted to confront the man first.

There were two objects secured in the waistband of his Bermuda shorts, concealed by the loose hang of the T-shirt. He looked to either side, confirming that he was alone, then reached down and withdrew the object on the right: a seven-inch tube of black metal, which he fit into the rolled-up magazine.

He knocked on the door with his left hand, raising the weapon with his right. On the magazine's cover was a truncated bit of the *Rolling Stone* logo, wrapping back on itself—a curlicued *ing Sto*.

"Who's there?" the man's voice said.

"Room service," the killer said, in the lowest register he could manage.

"Room service," the man said. "Did you order something?"

"Order something?" his wife said.

The door cracked open. "I'm afraid you've got the—"

The killer raised the tube inside the magazine, tugged on the cocking rod, and pulled on the firing lever. Inside the device, an ampule of acid was ruptured; a cloud of gas discharged directly into the man's face.

As his features registered surprise, the killer pushed forward. He dropped the magazine and withdrew the second device from his shorts: another short tube, this one six inches long and silver.

The woman was sitting on the bed, rubbing her bare feet and facing the TV. She turned her head and blinked dumbly at the sight of the child who had entered her room. Her husband was still on his feet, swaying slightly.

As the husband's knees buckled, the killer moved past him. He pulled the retractable garrote from one end of the Peskett, stepped to the woman's right—she was still looking at her husband, not understanding—then whipped the cord around her throat and threw his weight back.

From this angle he could see only her temple, and the soft curve of her cheek. There were small, downy hairs on the cheek. The temple was laced with transparent veins. As the killer kept pulling, the veins turned blue, then angry violet.

After thirty seconds, it was finished.

The door was still ajar. He crossed the room, pushed it closed, and shot the bolt. He picked up the poison-gas gun which had fallen from the magazine, carried it to the bed, and set it by the Peskett.

It had been nearly silent; he had time in which to conduct his search. That was another good thing, for Keyes had not been able to tell him exactly what he was looking for. A scientific formula, yes, but in what form? Microfilm, a scrap of paper, an audiotape, a digital device, a pack of playing cards with certain corners bent—anything was possible.

He began the search, moving quickly but calmly.

CNN was doing a piece on Palestinian refugee camps. From time to time, he glanced at the screen as he worked, mildly intrigued despite himself.

There was no obvious scientific formula in the couple's luggage, on their bodies, or in the man's wallet. He went on to the next series of usual hiding places: under the bed, taped behind the mirror, tucked inside the toilet tank. Nothing. He came back into the center of the room and considered.

The man was—had been—a differential geometer. A mathematician. He should not have been terribly familiar with more sophisticated methods of concealment. He would be more apt to play clever games, bending the corners of playing cards, and so forth. But he had been working for Applied Data Systems and so he may have met people; he may have learned things.

The killer would proceed on the assumption that he had learned things.

He went through the change on the dresser top, inside the corpses' pockets and the lady's handbag. None of the coins were hollow. He inspected the woman's hairbrush, which contained no secret compartments. He unscrewed the telephone receiver and discovered nothing inside but machinery. He screwed it on again, looked absently for a moment at CNN—an advertisement for toothpaste now—and then continued.

The man's shaving brush and shaving cream were only what they seemed to be. There was no laptop computer anywhere in the room. The only piece of electronic equipment was a CD personal stereo, which was simply a CD personal stereo. The killer took out the batteries and tapped the casings with his thumbnail. The batteries were only batteries.

A worm of apprehension began to wriggle inside his stomach. He did his best to ignore it.

He moved back to the man's corpse, sprawled faceup in the small foyer, and knelt beside it. He repeated his search, paying closer attention this time to the body itself. Neither eye was artificial. Neither leg was hollow. There was no scientific formula concealed on the man's body.

He stood again, crossed the room, and searched the woman for a second time.

Nothing.

The worm in his stomach wriggled again, more forcefully.

He returned to the dresser and flipped for a second time through the man's wallet. *Steven Epstein,* the credit cards read. Visa, Master-Card, and American Express; a full complement. He peered closely at the numbers on the plastic, searching for signs of manipulation. He set the wallet aside and moved to crouch beside the luggage. He reached for the camera, removed the film, and slipped it into his pocket. Perhaps the man had photographed the formula and then destroyed it. He found himself studying the couple's airline tickets. Something might be concealed in the mundane figures here: the seat assignments, the flight number. But everything seemed ordinary.

He fingered the tickets, and something tickled his mind.

Steven Epstein, flying first class, aisle seat. What about that seemed wrong?

Then he wondered: Where were the documents for the cruise?

According to his information, the couple had been intending to board the cruise ship the following day. That had been his reason for acting tonight. Yet there were no documents pertaining to the cruise.

He opened the tickets again. The flight back to New York was scheduled for two days hence. Had they changed their plans?

As he stared at the ticket, the something tickled again. He set the ticket aside, reached for the man's passport, and opened it. Name: Epstein, Steven. Nationality: United States of America. Date of birth: 21 October, 1947. Then again to the wallet. He stared at a Montana driver's license, and frowned. The error had been so glaring that at first it hadn't even registered. *Montana?*

Suddenly he was clawing through his pocket, digging past the film. Keyes had instructed him to dispose of the photograph after memorizing the face, but the killer hadn't trusted himself; so he had bent the rules.

The man in the photograph was at least ten years older than the man who had answered the door.

The killer looked at the two dead people in the room. He swore softly.

The bellboy had given him the wrong room. The wrong Epstein.

At length, he stood. His knees popped dully, like wet firecrackers. He spent one more minute looking at the two dead people. Then he swore again, jammed the photograph into his pocket, collected his gear, and left without looking back.

PART ONE

ONE

I.

The stateroom was ten feet square.

The walls were plain white plasterboard; a single lithograph hung above the bed, picturing six turbaned men on horseback. The carpets were a bristly, artificial blue. Opposite the door was a large, round, tinted window—*a porthole*, Hannah Gray supposed, although it was much bigger than she had thought a porthole would be.

Beneath the porthole was a low redwood table featuring a lamp, a vase of lilies, and a bowl of fruit. Against the left-hand wall, when Hannah turned back to face the door, were a small desk, a wall-mounted television, and a refrigerette. Against the right-hand wall were a single twin bed, a standing lamp, and a teak dresser. Atop the dresser was a clock radio, blinking *12:00*.

Inside the refrigerette she found a bottle of champagne, two chilled glasses, Evian water, a jar of macadamia nuts, and a package of double-A batteries. Inside the end table she found two packets of Bonine motion-sickness pills, a plastic bracelet, a pair of foam earplugs, and a condom labeled *Transderm Scop*.

She picked up the condom, and turned it over in her hands.

After a moment, she replaced it, shut the drawer, and continued her inspection.

The bathroom was small and tidy. The entire cabin was small and tidy. Within five minutes, she had seen all there was to see; she dropped down onto the bed. The ship was rocking softly in the waves by the dock, making her stomach roll.

A loudspeaker behind the bed crackled to life and then emitted the voice of the cruise director, replete with false cheer:

"Ladies and gentlemen," the cruise director said. "Welcome aboard the beautiful *Aurora II*! As we look out our windows at the palace of the Doge of Venice, we see much the same thing that the envoys of the Comte Thibaut would have seen in April of 1201, when they first arrived to secure transports and warships for what would eventually become the Fourth Crusade . . ."

Hannah didn't move. *Windows,* she thought.

Not portholes after all, but *windows.*

She felt a funny little flicker of disappointment.

She'd had *windows* back in Chicago.

2.

Two hours later, the cruise director stood behind a podium in the lounge of the *Aurora II*, repeating her speech into a microphone almost word for word.

"As we proceed in the footsteps of the Crusaders, the past will come vibrantly alive. We will experience this remarkable journey much as it was experienced by these men so many centuries ago. When presented with the Hagia Sophia or the mosaics of St. Mark's, keep in mind the impression they might have given to these traveling rogues in the summer of 1204—"

The lounge sparkled: glimmering hardwood floors, shining silken wallpaper, and rows of portholes—*windows*—looking out onto the sun-dappled Mediterranean. At one end was the dining area, with glass chandeliers, lace-edged tablecloths, and ornamented bars built into the corners. At the other was the podium, set before a baby grand piano and a rack of stereo components.

An elegant, high-cheekboned woman of about seventy-five was introducing herself to Hannah. "Renee Epstein," she said in a stage whisper, and offered her hand.

Hannah took it. "Vicky Ludlow," she said, and smiled pleasantly.

The cruise director was still talking, filling her other ear:

". . . reach the island of Methoni early tomorrow morning. This is only one of several spectacular islands we'll be visiting over the course of the upcoming week. We'll spend the day at Methoni and pull out tomorrow night, and on the morning of the eighth we'll be arriving at Valletta, Malta . . ."

Renee Epstein was asking something; Hannah had missed it. "I'm sorry?" she said.

"Oh, I hope that's not too forward. I do have a way of putting my foot in my mouth sometimes. But it's a mother's prerogative, isn't it? To try to find somebody right for her son. He's a periodontist, my Charlie." She leaned in closer; her pitch dropped even lower. "Very comfortable," she said.

Hannah kept smiling. The woman reminded her of her grandmother—a New England blue blood, hair dyed black but with a single streak of gray near one temple, a calculated admission of age. Tight skin around the temples pulled the eyes into catlike slits.

"I hope that's not too forward," the woman said again.

"Not at all," Hannah answered. "But I'm afraid I'm taken."

"Oh! I didn't see a ring."

"No, I—"

"The *Aurora II* is two hundred and seventy feet long," the cruise director said, "and forty-six feet wide. She accommodates eighty passengers in forty-four staterooms, all with ocean exposures. She's equipped with stabilizers for smooth sailing—although it's very common to experience some seasickness, especially in the first few days; I'll get to that in a moment—and she meets the latest international environmental and safety standards, including those of the U.S. Coast Guard and the U.S. Department of Health."

She paused to take a breath. "I had an accident in the hotel," Hannah said quickly. "My ring went right down the drain. Straight into the canals, I bet. Gone forever. My husband's going to kill me."

"Oh, dear," Renee Epstein said. "What a pity."

"During our voyage, you'll want to make a point of taking advantage of the many luxuries on board the *Aurora II*. There are five decks on the boat. At the bottom is A Deck, housing the crew's quarters and the doctor's office. Above that is the Main Deck, with the passenger quarters and reception area; and above that is the Boat Deck, so named because it's the deck with the lifeboats. Also on the Boat Deck you'll find some more passenger quarters, as well as the salon, the library, and the auditorium. Then comes the Upper Deck, where we are right now, featuring the kitchen, and of course"—with a sweeping, inclusive gesture—"the dining room and lounge area. Finally the Sun Deck, accessible only from the outside stairwells, featuring everybody's favorite—the pool."

A ripple of laughter moved through the crowd.

"It may seem like a lot to absorb all at once," the cruise director went on. She was a handsome woman of about thirty, with twinkling eyes and an auburn wedge of hair, wearing the standard Adventure Dynamics staff outfit of navy top and tan slacks. "But don't worry, you'll become familiar with it. And by the end of the week, just when it won't do you any good whatsoever, you'll know it like the back of your hand."

More laughter. Hannah took advantage of the distraction to slip away from Renee Epstein, moving purposefully in the direction of one corner bar. She accepted a mimosa from a brown-eyed steward, flashed her best PR smile, and turned to find that the woman had followed her. "Have you done the reading?"

Hannah blinked. "I'm sorry?"

"The books they sent us. The background reading."

"Oh," she said. "No. I'm afraid I didn't get the chance."

"Well, that's a shame. To get the most out of a cruise like this, you should really do the reading. A little background helps so much. I personally don't think it's necessary to do the whole list—there are fifteen, you know, five 'essential' and ten 'highly recommended.' But a sampling, I think, is a good idea. And one of the books they gave us is truly excellent. *The Chronicles of the Crusades*, by Joinville and Villehardouin."

Hannah sipped at her mimosa. "Hm," she said.

"Some historical context gives the whole experience much more . . . resonance. Do you have a copy?"

"No, I'm afraid I don't. I must have left it at home."

"Then you'll need to borrow ours. We've both already read it—Steven finished in the hotel just last night."

"Oh, I could never—"

"Nonsense. *Resonance*," Renee Epstein said. "Come by our cabin after the orientation and I'll give you our copy. And you can meet

Steven, if he hasn't locked himself in the bathroom. He's not feeling well, I'm afraid. But then, he never does well on cruises. Oh, and look at him when you speak to him—he's losing his hearing."

"I wouldn't want to—"

"You must try to get the full experience," Renee said forcefully. "And that means putting a little something into it, doesn't it? You don't want to be lazy, dear. A chance like this doesn't come along every day."

Hannah kept smiling, although her cheeks were beginning to ache. The smile, she thought, must be turning neurasthenic. She should turn away without another word; let the woman think what she liked.

"I absolutely insist," Renee said. "You really must read it. It is excellent."

"That's very nice of you. But I do need to unpack. Maybe after—"

"It won't take a minute. Come on," Renee said, and took her hand. "They're finishing up here anyway."

Hannah looked at the hand on hers. Thin bluish veins riddled the back; the fingers were delicate and spindly.

She may have found herself doing things, as of late, of which she never would have thought herself capable. But could she do this—pull her hand from that arthritic grip, and hurt an old woman who was only trying to be friendly?

Of course you can, she thought. *And you will. Right now.*

So she was surprised to hear the words coming out of her own mouth:

"That's very nice of you," she said. "Just for one minute. Thank you."

3.

She could hear the husband—Steven Epstein, she remembered—vomiting from the bathroom.

Now Hannah's smile was apologetic. She felt very much the intruder, standing in this man's sickroom as his wife fluttered busily among their luggage, looking for the book and still talking a mile a minute.

"He's awful on cruises. Just awful. To tell the truth, after the last disaster I didn't think he'd ever agree to another one. Originally, I was planning on bringing my friend Martha on this trip. Martha and I have traveled together quite a bit lately. Two years ago we did Vietnam; the year before that, a cruise down the Nile. Next year we hope to do the Yangtze. But at the last second my Steven changed his mind, and decided to keep me company after all. There's a lesson there somewhere, dear." She raised her voice. "Did you take the Bonine? There was Bonine in the nightstand."

No answer from the bathroom.

"Here we go," Renee said. She turned from a suitcase and handed a paperback book to Hannah. On the cover, armored men with swords jousted, fired arrows, stormed castles, lay dying.

"Thank you," Hannah said, and backed toward the door. "So I'll see you at the welcome dinner . . ."

"Steven. Do you feel well enough to come meet our guest?"

Still no answer.

"I hope you feel better, Mr. Epstein," Hannah called. "No need to come out. I'll see you later."

"Dear, don't rush off! Wouldn't you like a glass of champagne? I have some pictures of Charlie around here someplace. I understand that you're taken, of course, but perhaps you've got a friend . . ."

"Thank you so much. But I do need to unpack. And thank you for the book. 'Bye, now!"

Hannah slipped outside and closed the door before the woman could argue.

She stood for a moment in the red-carpeted hallway by the Epsteins' cabin—47 was written on the door in gold-plated numbers—and then began to move back in the direction of her own stateroom. Her calves felt spongy and unreliable. She hadn't gotten her *sea legs* yet, she supposed. Or was *sea legs* another outdated term, like *portholes?*

She made the journey carefully, keeping one hand pressed against a wall for support, wondering if she had made yet another mistake in accompanying the woman to her room. The last thing she needed right now was to make new friends. So many mistakes, lately . . .

No harm done, she thought. *She's only being polite.*

Don't get paranoid.

Even if they *had* followed her onto the ship—which hardly seemed possible—it was unlikely that their agent would have been an elderly woman with a recent face-lift. No, it would be a man in a suit, probably with mirrored sunglasses. No tie, but mirrored sunglasses and an off-the-rack gray jacket. But that wasn't accurate either, was it? If they knew where she was, they wouldn't send a man on board the ship at all. They would wait for her to go ashore before they arrested her.

But she was getting ahead of herself. There was nobody following her. Of that, she was nearly certain.

Once inside her stateroom, she locked the door. She tossed the paperback onto the bed and went to look out the window. One corner of the Church of St. Mark was visible behind a dilapidated warehouse, with the Italian flag flapping in a breeze.

The funny little flicker of disappointment occurred again.

It should have been very romantic and dramatic: docked at Venice, about to embark on a cruise through the Greek Isles. And yet the boat was filled with senior citizens, and somehow she already had received her first homework assignment. *The Chronicles of the Crusades.*

She sighed.

She looked out the window for another moment, staring through her own wavering reflection.

Then she turned, and moved toward her luggage.

4.

She had overpacked.

As she transferred her clothes from suitcase to dresser, Hannah couldn't help but marvel at her own indulgence. The cruise would last only a single week. Yet she'd brought enough clothes to keep her occupied for a month, at least: blouses and halter tops and cashmere sweaters with sweetheart necklines, jeans and skirts and bikinis and Pashmina scarves. Her beauty regimen took up an entire small bag of its own. Judging from the contents of her luggage, she thought, one might almost assume that she never intended to go back home again.

But that would be untrue. She had come here only to clear her head. The opportunity had presented itself, she'd had the sick days to spare, and she'd been getting strange vibes from Frank. So she had packed—overpacked—and now here she was. But the situation, of course, was only temporary. When the cruise was finished, she would return to Chicago.

Where else did she have to go, after all?

After unpacking her clothes, she spread her papers on the bedspread and considered them. Two thousand dollars in traveler's checks, and another five hundred in cash. So of course she would go back. She couldn't live long on that money, not in the style to which she had grown accustomed.

A part of her mind spoke up: *Don't forget the joint account, Hannah.*

She hadn't forgotten. There were one hundred and twelve thousand additional dollars in the joint account back in the States. But if her feeling about Frank had been right, that account might soon be frozen. That money would be lost to her.

Next to the money was the brochure for the cruise, which Vicky had given to her during their meeting at the airport. Until now Hannah had only browsed through it. Her mind had been occupied with other things—unable to wrap itself around any of them, trying in vain to juggle all of them at once. Now she picked up the brochure and flipped through it cursorily.

Had the feeling about Frank been completely off base? Had it been only paranoia? Or had it been the opposite—too little, too late? Perhaps they would be waiting for her at the next port. And the following week her picture would be splashed across the front page of the *Tribune,* one of those grainy photos in which the criminal had a jacket draped over her head, trying to hide her face as men maneuvered her toward a waiting car. FUGITIVE IN MEDICARE FRAUD CASE APPREHENDED, the headline would read. *International manhunt ends in arrest.*

But no—there was no international manhunt. As far as the company knew, there wasn't even any fraud. She'd picked up a feeling from Frank, nothing more. Just a feeling. It was probably all in her mind.

Until Vicky had left the message on her answering machine, however, Hannah had believed completely that her life was finished. She'd been sitting on her couch, head in her hands, trying to block the sinking sensation that had been coming on ever since her latest conversation with Frank. Then the phone had chimed, the machine had clicked on, and Vicky's voice had come streaming into the room:

Hannah, pick up. The words tumbling over each other; Vicky bursting with pride and, below that, ripe self-satisfaction. *I know you're there. Pick up! Greg has received the most amazing honor. They're sending him to London to negotiate some multimillion-dollar contract. Maggie and I are going along. But it means we can't go on our vacation, and it's too late to get a refund—the flight leaves tomorrow. So how would you feel about a free trip to Venice? You've got some vacation days coming, don't you? And God knows you could stand to unwind a little. There's even an extra ticket, in case there's someone you want to bring along. Give me a call on my cell if you get this—*

Hannah had picked up.

Even then, she'd felt a trace of concern about the cruise. Run blindly to the other side of the planet? With almost no cash, with no prospects of anywhere to go after it was finished? Ridiculous. But the thought of just taking off, of leaving it all behind, had been too tempting to resist. Of course, it would be only temporary. Of course she intended to come back to her life . . .

So why are you traveling under Vicky's name? the niggling part of her mind asked. *Why did you put a fresh tape in the answering machine before you left, and destroy the one with Vicky's message?*

Only to keep her options open, she answered. Only in case of the very worst.

Within twenty-four hours of Vicky's call, they'd been meeting at the airport, exchanging tickets and brochures, thanks and farewells.

She fingered the brochure thoughtfully, then set it down.

Next to the brochure was her address book. Next to the address book was the forged passport. And next to the passport, the paperback book she had borrowed from Renee Epstein—which wasn't even really hers. Suddenly, the overpacking seemed very far from indulgent. What if Frank was arrested, during the coming week, and she could never go back? What if this was all she had for the rest of her life?

Some collection, she thought dimly. Some collection for a Yale graduate who had once been the brightest rising young star at Associated Health Care of Illinois.

She reached for the passport and opened it. Her own face stared back from the glossy photo inside: pale, dark-eyed, unsmiling beneath a halo of dirty-blond hair. A very pretty young woman who could have been beautiful, as her mother had often said, if only she didn't look so serious. Looking at the photograph now, Hannah supposed she could see her mother's point. Her eyes were like black diamonds, hard and piercing.

But was this the face of an international fugitive? It was difficult to believe.

Even more difficult to believe was the fact that the passport had passed inspection. To Hannah's eyes, her work looked patently faked. The blue-and-red pattern behind the personal information was pixelated, the best she'd been able to do on her color printer at home in a rush. The signature *Vicky Ludlow* looked too tight, too carefully calculated, as if she had never signed it before—probably because she hadn't. Worst of all, she had chosen a date of issuance of April 2002; this should have been one of the new passports, the post–September 11th passports, with a digital image and secret enhancements. It wasn't. But the customs agent had been too busy looking at her legs to pay very close attention.

She wondered if evidence of the forged passport remained on the computer in her apartment. She had reformatted the entire hard drive. As far as she understood, any data on the drive would be impossible to recall. Yet she had the nagging feeling that traces remained, somewhere, and that a trained technician would be able to find them.

If, that was, worse came to worst.

There was always her father, of course. If worse did come to worst, then her father could possibly get this . . . little problem . . . taken care of.

Except she would rather die than swallow her pride and go begging to her father.

She set down the passport and picked up the address book. For a moment she was tempted to open it, to find Frank's number and demand some answers. But perhaps his phone was tapped and the FBI was sitting by it, waiting for her call. Or would it be U.S. Marshals? Or the Postal Inspection Service, or some office of the Inspector General?

She put down the address book, found two Xanax, and swallowed them. Her hand moved, without her realizing it, to stroke at the pale scars that crossed the inside of her left wrist. In times of stress, her hand tended to move toward those old scars unconsciously, instinctively.

Suddenly, she felt queasy again. A realization took her with almost physical force: Why, she was nearly penniless. Not since the days fresh out of college, following her first falling-out with her father, had she been nearly penniless. Even in the worst of her debt, she'd had credit on which to fall back. Now, if she truly had been caught, her credit would be as frozen as the stateside account. Now she needed to face reality: the prospect of going hungry, going cold.

No. Frank would not turn on her.

This was a vacation. Nothing more.

She lay down on the bed, and closed her eyes.

Then she thought of her plants, and her eyes opened. She hadn't made any allowances for the plants. It would have been an easy matter to ask Craig, the doorman at her building, to go up and water the plants once in a while. Craig did nothing all day except sit behind his desk and stare at a tremendous pile of books that he never quite got around to reading. He could have taken care of the plants easily. Yet she hadn't thought to ask. Now it was too late. By now, the plants were probably dying.

By now, they might even be dead.

At that moment, Hannah Gray almost envied them.

TWO

Daisy smiled up from behind her desk, and held forth a small stack of message sheets.

Keyes glanced through them as he moved into his office. WHILE YOU WERE OUT, the sheets read. First was a message from Rachel. He crumpled it into a ball without reading any further. Let her talk to the goddamned lawyer, if she needed to talk to somebody. He was in no mood for her today.

The next few messages would demand his attention, but there was no great urgency. He set the sheets on the corner of his desk. The last, however, made him pause. It reported a phone call from Leonard. The time of the call was illegible. Below the time, Daisy had scrawled a single word: *Negative.*

Negative, Keyes thought.

His eyes, already swollen from fatigue, crinkled into thin slits.

He fell into the chair behind his desk, reached for the phone, and stabbed a button. Through the cracked-open door, he could hear the buzz from the next room. "Yes?" Daisy said, through the intercom.

"When did Leonard call? I can't read your handwriting."

He heard the edge in his own voice, and tried to press it down. A moment passed. Paper rustled. Everything at Applied Data Systems was done in old-fashioned triplicate. Until he had started on this goddamned diet, that had never seemed quite so irritating.

"Three-fifty," Daisy said. She had injected a hint of solemnity into her tone, sensing his mood. "He'll call back."

"What did he say, exactly?"

"Just *'negative.'*"

"When he calls, put it through. No matter what."

"All right," she said.

He pressed the button again, and the speaker went dead.

Negative.

What in hell was that supposed to mean?

He touched an index finger to either temple, made small circles for a few moments—tight circles, circles within circles—then knuckled at his eyes, reached for the messages, and went to work.

Dick Bierman had called from INFOSEC with a question about Applied Data Systems's network's "ping response time," whatever that was. Keyes scrawled an evasive answer on a Post-it note—Bierman was eternally digging, coming up with stupid questions in an effort to learn details about ADS's computer setup—then affixed it to the message sheet. The message sheet with the Post-it note attached went into the Out basket. Let Daisy handle Dick Bierman. Next was a message from Alex Petrov, in charge of the screen house at gamma site in Nevada. Petrov needed more water pumps, which meant he needed more money; yet the man was too impatient to go through the regular routine of paperwork. He would rather waste Keyes's valuable time. Keyes read the figure Petrov suggested, cut it in half, and slapped another Post-it with the new figure onto the sheet. Into the Out basket. Let Daisy handle all of it. He was too hungry to think straight. He was in no goddamned mood for any of it.

He stared at the next note for a full minute before his mind switched gears and he was able to comprehend it. The caterer's quote for his daughter's wedding—criminal, but they could get away with it, he supposed, thanks to their reputation. And they had cleverly waited until the last minute to provide the quote, leaving him in the lurch. Nothing but the best, he thought sourly, and crumpled the note into a ball.

Negative.

What the hell was that?

Perhaps he had made a mistake, in leaving Epstein up to Leonard. Perhaps he should have followed official channels . . .

No. This wasn't brain surgery. It was one elderly scientist who had run on the spur of the moment. According to Roger Ford, Leonard was more than capable of handling it.

Lunch would make him feel better.

"If Leonard calls," he told Daisy on his way out, "patch it through to my cell."

2.

There was a blackboard in the elevator.

In the goddamned *elevator*, Keyes thought; for Christ's sake. Did the eggheads truly need that? Was it really probable that inspiration would strike during the five or ten seconds they spent traveling between floors, and if they couldn't scrawl down some figures at that very moment they would lose the inspiration forever? Well, perhaps it was. The truth was that he didn't understand how their minds worked. Half of them couldn't drive a car, program a VCR, or do their own laundry—but those same men could recite *pi* to two hundred decimal places, right off the top of their heads.

The doors hissed open onto the compound's ground floor.

Through wide picture windows, the government-subsidized green of the lawn sloped off to distant chain-link fences. Guard posts were placed at regular intervals around the compound's fencing. To the naked eye, they looked fairly benign, like security checkpoints at any other major corporation. The local Vermonters could never know that each guard post contained three sentries armed with M134 machine guns—just as they could never know that Applied Data Systems's compound spread out underground for a half mile in every direction, buried a thousand yards beneath their houses, their woodsheds, and the graves they dug for their daughters' hamsters.

Keyes moved toward the cafeteria, nodding to various acquaintances, turning over possibilities for lunch in his mind. According to the diet, he was allowed only salad for lunch. But he had skipped breakfast, so perhaps he could cheat a little. And he had fit into his tuxedo just that morning, in preparation for the wedding; he felt as if he deserved some kind of reward. As long as he kept it to fifteen hundred calories a day—

The cell burred against his leg.

He immediately detoured in the direction of the nearest door and stepped out into a Japanese-style garden, where secretaries were sitting on benches and eating tuna-fish sandwiches under the midday sunshine. He moved past them, finding a quiet corner before bringing the phone to his ear.

"It's Leonard," Daisy said. "I'm putting him through."

Keyes listened to the hollow, underwater beeping of the long-distance connection being made; then to the hollow, underwater beeping of the encryption system kicking in. A gardener was doing something to a nearby fish pond, crouching and crab-walking around the perimeter. At last, something clicked. "Keyes?" piped a voice.

"Yes," Keyes said, and then took the phone away from his ear as Leonard launched into a string of epithets.

It was always strange to hear that squeaking, little-boy voice delivering obscenities. Leonard was nearly thirty years old, but thanks to his condition—hypopituitarism, he had explained, with what had struck Keyes as an admirable lack of self-pity—he looked and sounded no older than a boy of twelve or thirteen.

Or perhaps Leonard had no reason for self-pity. If he hadn't "suffered" from his condition, after all, he would not have excelled at his current profession. Before Roger Ford had found him, Leonard had been part of a freak show with a traveling circus. The CIA was a definite step up.

Presently he wound down. Keyes put the phone back to his ear. "What happened?" he asked.

"I had the wrong cocksucking room. That's what happened."

"The wrong room?"

"Right name. Wrong person."

Keyes closed his eyes.

Leonard was starting to swear again. The man could curse like a stevedore—a skill he had no doubt learned with the circus. Keyes opened his eyes and looked at the fish pond. A sliver of orange darted below the surface. The beauty and balance of nature, he thought. The fish moved in tiny circles—circles within circles. The entire garden was oriented to create natural, soothing flows of energy. *Relax.*

"The damned bellboy," Leonard was saying. "He gave me the wrong—"

"I'll take care of it," Keyes promised.

"Easy for you to say. You're not the one—"

"Relax," Keyes said, and then exhaled, trying to take his own advice. "I need you to hang on. Where are you?"

"I'll call back," Leonard said, and the connection went dead.

3.

He was missing lunch as well as breakfast.

He used the thought of the dinner awaiting him—a big dinner, a one-thousand-five-hundred-calorie dinner—to keep his spirits up as he prepared for Leonard's return call. He desperately needed *something* to keep his spirits up. All these resources and all these employees, he thought—all this feng shui and all the fish in their little Japanese gardens—and still events were spiraling out of his control.

Should have gone to the DIA, he thought.

The Defense Intelligence Agency was officially responsible for security concerning Applied Data Systems. But if it came out that Epstein had run, those higher-up might lose faith in Keyes's ability to direct this particular show. In reality, of course, the fault lay not with Keyes, but with chance. The damned Italian bellboy had given the wrong room, because there had been two Epsteins in the hotel. A stupid mistake; an unpredictable one.

Don't make it worse, he thought.

Go to the DIA.

No. Barbarians at the gate. As long as he had other options—such as Roger Ford and Ron Nichols—he would use them.

Roger Ford had been a friend since college. The friendship had deepened after graduation, when they'd both found themselves inside the Beltway, two ambitious young bachelors trying to make their careers. In the years since, they had gone their separate ways; Ford had ended up CIA, Keyes ADS. Yet the foundation had been laid, and the friendship remained.

Ron Nichols was an employee of ADS whose official position was "Crisis Management Counselor." Each year, Ron Nichols collected a paycheck of one hundred and eighty-six thousand dollars. But Ron Nichols did not exist. Keyes had created the identity sixteen months before, to maintain an emergency fund for special occasions just such as this. When Ford supplied a name as a personal favor, the expenses were paid out of Ron Nichols's pocket.

ADS, existing as it did in a shadow capacity, experienced both advantages and disadvantages compared to other government agencies. The advantages were primarily financial. Keyes's budget pinched a little here, a little there. The Defense Advanced Research Projects Agency, DARPA, had come up with the lion's share of the money. From LANL—Los Alamos National Labs—he had lifted some key personnel, in addition to a hefty chunk of funding. The rest had been appropriated from the NSA, whose funding was entirely black—not specifically accounted for in the general U.S. budget, resulting in the nickname "No Such Agency." The five-thousand-dollar ashtrays purchased by the White House helped, in reality, to finance the NSA.

But there was a flip side. So many chefs in the kitchen meant that everybody felt ADS should be accountable to them. There were dozens of people, scores of people, like Dick Bierman, just waiting for Keyes to fuck up. Then they would step in and make a grab for the reins themselves.

So he couldn't go to the DIA—not while there were other options available to him.

Daisy came into the office and set a file on his desk. He gave her a nod and turned his attention back to the phone in his hands. He was speaking with an Italian policeman who believed Keyes was a detective second grade of the New York City Police Department, tracking a murder suspect who, according to a tip from his ex-wife, had fled to Venice.

By the time Leonard called again, he was ready.

"Epstein boarded the ship this morning," Keyes said. "It means he doesn't think anyone's followed him. So you'll have no problem."

Leonard muttered something.

"Spilled milk," Keyes said. "No use in dwelling on it."

Leonard said nothing. Keyes quickly moved on, all business.

"They'll reach Methoni tomorrow, spend the day there, and pull out again after dinner. What I want you to do is get yourself to that is-land tonight—"

He consulted one of the several files open on his blotter.

"—and find a room. There are six hotels; any one will do. The near-est airport is Kalamata, about thirty miles away. Once you've got that taken care of, let Daisy know the details. I'm putting together some backup on this end. They'll meet you at the hotel, and lend a hand."

"Backup?" Leonard said.

"Mm. After you book the room—"

"I work alone," Leonard interrupted.

"Not this time, you don't. If it had gone right in the hotel . . ."

"That wasn't my fault."

"I realize that," Keyes said steadily. "But you'll need backup. Be-cause you're going to do it at the fortress of Sapienza, tomorrow morning. And while you're doing it, we'll need someone to go aboard the ship, to clean out the man's cabin."

In fact, Keyes thought, this was likely not necessary. Epstein may or may not have destroyed the paper Greenwich had glimpsed, which contained formulae that predicted the lifetime of microscopic black holes, according to Greenwich, so brilliantly. But whether or not the paper still existed hardly mattered. Greenwich had assured Keyes that Epstein's results could be repeated—by Greenwich himself.

All that mattered was that Epstein be silenced before he caused too much of a stir. Regaining the formula itself, however, would let Keyes rest easier over these coming days. Not only would he have it for himself, but he would also be assured that it hadn't fallen into other hands. And although he did not exactly doubt Greenwich's claim that he could reproduce the results, he would rather leave nothing to chance. So he would err on the side of caution.

"Fortress of what?" Leonard was saying.

"Sapienza. That's where the tour group's heading tomorrow. Find a spot where you'll be able to get it done. And leave no witnesses. Can you handle that?"

"I'll handle it," Leonard assured him.

"Let Daisy know the details," Keyes said, and hung up.

For a minute, he did nothing but stare blankly at his desk. Then he reached for the phone again, and dialed Roger Ford in Washington. Lately he had been calling in too many favors. Even the oldest friendships—perhaps especially the oldest friendships—could be taxed only so far. But he was willing to take the chance. He needed to finish this now, and that meant playing hardball.

When it came to playing hardball, nobody beat Roger Ford.

Ford sounded busy; they ran through pleasantries in record time. Then Ford asked if Leonard had been able to supply the services that Keyes had required. Keyes informed him that there had been a slight problem—no fault of Leonard's—and he was anxious to put together a team to set things right.

"A small team," Keyes said. "Just one or two. Men who can get the job done. And they have to be available now—today."

Ford sounded distracted; Keyes could hear fingers tapping on a keyboard. "What kind of job are we talking about?"

"He'll need to penetrate a secure area and conduct a search. And be able to handle himself if something goes wrong."

Ford paused. Keyes waited, unsure if the man was considering the problem or working on something else.

"I'm thinking of a name . . ."

Keyes reached for a pen.

"A man named Dietz. He retired a few years ago. But he still does us a favor from time to time, off the record."

"Background?"

"A decade at Langley in the seventies. In eighty-three he became part of a joint FBI-CIA operation called COURTSHIP. Working in New York City, recruiting KGB to spy for Uncle Sam. When the FSB—Federal'naya Sluzhba Bezopasnosti—came around, the game changed a bit. New blood. By spring of ninety-one Dietz burned out, and took early retirement. But once or twice a year, he comes out again—off the record, as I said. For the paycheck, I assume."

Keyes frowned. "I was hoping for field experience."

"Dietz qualifies. When he does a job for us now, it's not pushing papers."

"Got a number?"

Ford gave him a number. They ran through more cursory pleasantries, then Ford announced that he had a meeting and hung up.

Before making his next call, Keyes paused.

Could the two of them—Leonard and Dietz—get it done? If he went ahead with his own people now, instead of going to the DIA, he would be committing himself even more than he had already.

They could get it done, Keyes thought. They were professionals, and there wouldn't be anyone aboard the ship equipped to offer much trouble, even if he felt so inclined. The passengers were most likely elderly. The crew was doubtless underpaid. At worst there would be an overzealous security officer, who would quickly find himself in over his head if he tried to interfere. Yes, Epstein had made a fatal mistake in running to the ship.

At first, Keyes had assumed it was a feint—Epstein had let his wife make the reservations in order to throw ADS off his track. But the Italian police had seen him boarding the ship that morning, and so now he was trapped. A sitting duck.

Strange, that so brilliant a man could make such a stupid mistake.

But mistakes happened. Witness the hotel room fiasco, he thought. Mistakes happened all the time, and geniuses like Epstein were no less prone to them than others. In fact, Epstein was notoriously absent-minded, even among his own colleagues. The sort of brain that could juggle imaginary numbers like bowling pins was not the same sort of brain that paid the rent on time each month.

And Epstein had run almost on a whim, at the beck of some strange higher moral calling. After making his breakthrough, the week before, he had panicked. He had not thought things through.

But maybe Keyes should give the man more credit. Maybe Epstein's moral qualms were only a matter of Keyes's own projection. Maybe the man planned on selling his secrets to the highest bidder. Or perhaps he had run so blindly only because he had no intention of living long enough to be captured. If he had stumbled onto something that could make the atom bomb look like a child's toy, after all, he might have felt that suicide was the only way to keep his discovery safe . . .

. . . well, that would be just fine. Epstein's results would be repeated by Greenwich. On that, he had Greenwich's word.

The important thing was to silence the man. Within twenty-four hours, it would be done. Then things could get back to normal.

An explosion thundered, from far underground. The photograph of his son jittered on his desk. Keyes reached out and straightened it.

Back to normal, he thought again. Or as normal as things ever got, around ADS.

He reached for his phone and dialed the number Roger Ford had given him.

THREE

I.

"My first time on a cruise," Jill Murphy said, "I was puking the whole time."

She shoveled a forkful of bacon and eggs into her mouth—a diminutive woman of about sixty-five, with close-shorn platinum-blond hair and lively emerald eyes. *Spitfire* was the word that came to Hannah's mind to describe her. That was likely a more generous term than Jackie Burns, the cruise director, would have chosen. Jackie was watching the woman warily, no doubt concerned that Jill Murphy would throw a wet blanket over her carefully cultivated atmosphere of good cheer.

Jill Murphy chewed for a moment, swallowed, and then went on.

"That was on the *Illyria,* eight years ago. Right after my Harold passed away. I remember it clear as day. I was working on a letter to my daughter, and I'd be writing a sentence, then going into the bathroom for five minutes and throwing up, then coming back and writing another sentence—"

Hannah looked sullenly at her bowl of fruit and yogurt, and set down the spoon in her hand.

Four people sat around the aluminum table on the Boat Deck, in matching wooden chairs with floral-printed cushions on the armrests. To Hannah's left was Jackie Burns, with her auburn hair still damp from her morning shower. Then Jill Murphy, chattering on blithely about vomiting every five minutes. Across the table was a man who had been introduced only as Yildirim: a Turk in his mid-forties, raw-boned and handsome, with jug-handle ears and sleepy eyes that remained focused on his plate.

"I'm sorry," Jill said. "Is this gross? Vicky doesn't look as if she feels very well."

It took Hannah a moment to realize that the reference had been to her. Then she waved a hand. "I had a rough night," she said.

"Who didn't?" Jill asked. "I was up half the night watching them cart out that guy from twenty-one. If I was the superstitious type, I'd say it was a bad omen. And you know, now that I mention it, isn't *twenty-one* an unlucky number? Three times seven, or something like that?"

"Seven's lucky," Jackie corrected.

"Oh, probably I shouldn't say it too loud. Most of these people have one foot in the grave already."

Hannah felt as if she had come into a conversation already under way. "Someone . . . died?"

"Last night," Jill said. "It happens all the time on these things. Right, Jackie?"

Jackie only shrugged.

"The poor man." Jill scraped a thread of egg onto the edge of her fork. She raised it halfway to her mouth, and paused. "I was talking to him just yesterday. Bruce Greene, was his name. And his poor wife. I can't imagine."

"Anyway," Jackie said. "Is everybody looking forward to the . . ."

"First time I saw one die," Jill Murphy interrupted, "was on my third cruise. On the Italian Riviera. Helen Lowenthal was her name; I'll never forget it. They didn't know what to do with her, so they put her in the meat locker until we could reach a port. And do you know what happened? She froze stiff. By the time we docked, they couldn't get her around the corners in the corridors. We had to stay in port until she defrosted enough to bend. The funny part of it is, nobody thought just to stand her up and get her around the corners that way! Can you imagine?"

Hannah looked away. She felt quite ill enough without this kind of talk. The sea around them was calm; it did not seem right that she should have felt quite so ill. The water shaded from a dazzling turquoise near the ship to a deep, rich blue by the horizon. Foam-tipped waves marched steadily away from the swath cut by the *Aurora II*, leaving swirling whitecaps in the wake.

Renee Epstein was passing the table, shielding herself from the sun with a raised forearm. Jackie Burns turned in her chair. "Mrs. Epstein," she called. "Would you tell your husband that it won't be any problem to mail his package? If he just leaves it outside of the cabin door, I'll make sure it gets to a post office. The charge will show up on your incidentals."

Renee Epstein slowed. "Package?" she said.

"Yes—he asked me yesterday about mailing something."

"Oh." Renee seemed mildly perplexed. "Yes, I'll tell him. How is everyone doing this morning?"

"Better than Bruce Greene," Jill started. "I was up half the night—"

A loudspeaker above the deck crackled, cutting her off. Then the captain's voice came booming out, speaking English with a thick Greek accent.

"Attention, all passengers," he said. "We will be docking at the port of Methoni within the hour. Any passengers who would like to participate in today's tour of the fortress of Sapienza"—he pronounced the name crisply, with gusto—"please write your names on the sign-up sheet at the reception area. If you choose not to accompany us on the tour, you will have free time in the city of Methoni. Please remember that all-aboard time is five-thirty, and we sail at six. Thank you, and have a good day."

The loudspeaker clicked off with a series of beeps and whines.

2.

As the *Aurora II* drifted into port, a heavily built man stood at one end of the dock's parking lot, smoking cigarettes and watching.

An observer would have been hard-pressed to identify the man's origin. He was lighter complexioned than the locals, but dressed with a similar Mediterranean flair: a colorful shirt worn open at the collar, loose chinos, and faded Naot sandals. A gold chain glimmered in a mat of graying chest hair; a battered brown leather bag hung across one broad shoulder. If one noticed the man at all, one likely would have assumed that he worked as staff aboard one of the half dozen ships moored along the quay—some larger than the *Aurora II,* some smaller, each flying a flag of a different nationality.

The parking-lot area abutting the dock was modern and Americanized, if several years out of step with America. Near the man stood a tourist stand displaying T-shirts—the Backstreet Boys, 'NSync, and

Ricky Martin—above rows of distinctive Marlboro red-and-white packaging. Past the stand was a cluster of pay phones, a stall selling ice cream, and a sun-browned child hawking batteries and headphones.

Behind the parking lot was the town of Methoni, which was neither modern nor Americanized. The small houses were peach and yellow and light brown, soft pastel colors that set off the rich blue-green of the surrounding water. Many of the houses had flowerpots lining the sills. Many of the flowerpots had dozing cats sprawled among them. Stunted trees dotted the landscape, offering thin and threadbare patches of shade.

For a half hour after the *Aurora II* had docked, the man stayed where he was, lighting fresh cigarettes and watching. During this time, a ramp was affixed to the side of the ship, and a dilapidated tour bus pulled up. The passengers disembarked and clustered around the bus, buzzing.

Francis Dietz checked his wristwatch. He ran one hand through his curly, silvering hair. The cigarette in his other hand moved to his mouth and away with a slow, regular motion.

3.

"Vicky," Jackie called. "You coming?"

Hannah turned back. "Give me one minute."

"You've got five." Jackie's voice, as ever, contained a hard note of forced cheer. "But don't make it longer. If the bus goes without you, you'll get all day on the island to yourself—and unless you brought your Mace, I don't think you want that."

Hannah smiled vaguely, and turned away again.

As she covered the distance to the pay phone, she revolved that one over in her mind. *Unless you brought your Mace, I don't think you want that.* Because the Greeks were sexually aggressive? That must have been Jackie's meaning. A pretty young woman—if Hannah might allow herself the conceit, at age thirty-two, of still being relatively young—did not want to spend an entire day alone, unchaperoned, on a Greek island.

Or perhaps she was misunderstanding. Often she thought that people were coming on to her—she was a fine catch, after all, well-off and pretty and from a good family—and then was embarrassed to discover that it had all been in her imagination. Her mind tended to skew in naughty directions. The skin patch in the end table, for instance, which she had assumed was a condom; thank goodness she hadn't mentioned *that* to anyone. Further inspection had revealed that it was a seasickness medication, which would release scopolamine into the bloodstream when placed on the skin.

But in this case, she didn't think she was mistaken. Already she had seen the way the crew looked at her—not quite leeringly, but knowingly, and with an element of salacious interest. They thought that she was on the make. A quaint term, *on the make,* which she associated more with her parents' generation than her own. But that must have been the impression she gave: a married woman on a cruise without her husband, whose wedding band had mysteriously disappeared.

If that was their idea, she would let them have it. It was better, after all, than the truth.

She reached the pay phone and then removed the small address book from her pocketbook. *Not a good idea,* she thought, even as she spread it open to Frank's number on the gum-caked grille beneath the phone. The sun had liquefied the gum. *Not a good idea, Hannah. Don't do this.*

But if she didn't, she would never know for sure.

If she didn't, she might return to Chicago to find herself walking into a nightmare; she imagined a whirl of spinning headlines out of an old movie. So she needed to call Frank, to confirm that it really was safe to return to Chicago. She would be as careful as possible. She wouldn't use her credit card. She would call collect, and stay on the line for less than a minute. Was that how long it might take to trace a call? According to movies and television, if she remembered correctly, it was. But who knew if movies and television were accurate?

She got an operator, spoke English, was transferred, got another operator, was transferred again, and then found someone who understood her as she recited the number.

Then, as the connection began to hiss with static, she turned to look at the town spread before her. The sun was nearing its midday apex; the town was taking a siesta, and the locals had retreated indoors. A sleepy feeling of timelessness hung in the air.

Beautiful, she thought.

If only she had managed to lay her hands on more money, before running, she might have been content to spend the next few years traveling around islands such as these, absorbing the local color. If only—

The phone was ringing.

4.

The operator asked for her name. She nearly said *Vicky Ludlow;* then she nearly said *Hannah Gray.* Then she caught herself, thought quickly, and said: "Pooh Bear."

It had been Frank's pet name for her. It had been Frank's pet name for everyone, as it so happened. But how many of his exes would be placing a collect call under that particular alias? She could only hope he would catch on.

The phone rang twice; then the voice mail picked up. She could hear Frank's raspy, familiar voice, thinned by the miles of long-distance connection. The operator came back on: an American now, with a nasal southern twang. "It's an answering machine," she said. "Would you like—"

Hannah hung up.

She stood looking at the phone, wondering if she should try again.

Of course she shouldn't. She shouldn't have been trying in the first place. For she already knew the answer. Deep down, in a place of instinct and intuition, she knew. Frank had turned on her. He would plea-bargain her right into prison. In all likelihood, he was doing it at that very moment.

I tried to talk her out of it, he'd be saying, *but you know the type.*

By now he would have gotten the Feds on his side with some comment about a ball game, some shared joke at the expense of a woman. They would be nodding along with him, half smiling. The male fraternity. *You know the type. She gets an idea in her head and there's just no talking her out of it . . .*

But in reality, Hannah thought, she had been guilty of nothing except poor judgment.

When she'd stumbled onto the first case of fraud, she should have gone straight to Bill Scarborough and filed a report. It had been a case of DRG upcoding, and as she'd pored over the documents she had realized that only one person could be responsible—Frank Anderson himself.

Instead of going to Scarborough, however, she'd gone to Frank, looking for an explanation. And she'd fallen for his excuse, flimsy though it may have been. To be honest, she thought now, maybe it had been his Lake Shore Drive apartment for which she had fallen. His spectacular view, his high-thread-count silk sheets.

When she had caught him the second time, redistributing and re-

billing for prescription drugs after the original patient had died, she'd again considered going to Scarborough. Under the False Claims Act, a whistle-blower was entitled to a minimum of 15 percent of any judgment. If she had turned Frank in, she'd be sitting pretty right now. But of course, she hadn't. Instead she had tried to protect him. Daddy's little girl had learned some lessons early on about protecting the men in one's life.

By the time she had caught him the third time, it had been too late.

By then the sexual part of the relationship had been over. Hannah had gone to Frank feeling strong, determined to put an end to it. *Next time,* she'd announced, *I won't be there to cover for you. And if they come asking questions, I'll tell them everything I know.*

Frank had grinned—a disconcertingly easy grin. They'd been sitting in a TGIF, sipping pints of Brooklyn Lager along with the rest of the Chicagoland Friday happy hour crowd.

"Pooh Bear," he'd said, almost kindly. "You should remember—your hands aren't exactly clean."

Almost as if he'd been waiting for her to make her threat. Almost as if he had planned for this.

He had suggested the joint account, entwining her more tightly in his web, protecting himself at the same time. And after a bit of prevarication, she had agreed. The romantic part of their relationship had been finished by then, but the business part had been only beginning.

She'd let Frank convince her that they weren't taking any real risk. *This company is big,* he'd said. A dollop of foam from the beer on his upper lip as he'd said it; the easy smile winking on again. *This company is huge. They can afford it. They'll never even notice, Pooh Bear. I promise.*

She had believed him.

And now it was too late. In retrospect, the vibes she had picked up from Frank, during their last conversation, seemed undeniable. They were finished—busted. He hadn't come out and said it, but she knew it nevertheless. And in Frank's version, the original fraud would have been Hannah's. In Frank's version, she would be a Machiavellian force, a manipulative bitch, enticing him with her wiles.

Someone was coming up behind her. She guiltily jammed the address book into her pocketbook, and turned to face Jackie Burns.

"Come on," Jackie said. "We're going."

They crossed the dusty lot together, passing a man who stood smoking cigarettes and watching them. Jackie ushered Hannah aboard the waiting bus, where she was immediately waylaid by Renee Epstein.

"Here she is!" Renee said. "Darling, this is the young woman I was telling you about—Vicky Ludlow."

The man sitting beside Renee Epstein was older than Hannah had expected, somewhere north of eighty. He had a liver-spotted pate and deceptively quiet eyes that locked on her face. "This is the one?" he said. His accent was faint, with roots in Eastern Europe.

"Isn't she lovely? She's married, of course. But I think it's possible that she might have a friend who would be right for—"

"Do you have the book?"

His manner was direct, almost accusatory. Hannah felt slightly taken aback. Renee smiled wider, as if accustomed to covering for her husband's social faux pas.

"Dear," she said to Hannah. "I'm so sorry, but I seem to have made a mistake. Steven hadn't finished the book after all."

Hannah slipped into a seat across the aisle, and found a smile. "I haven't even started it yet," she said. "As soon as we get back to the ship, I'll be glad to bring it by your cabin."

Jackie Burns stepped into the bus, conferred briefly with the driver, and reached for a microphone.

"Good morning!" she chirped as they pulled away from the quay.

"We've got a special treat today, ladies and gentlemen. The world-famous fortress of Sapienza. Construction was begun by the Venetians in the thirteenth century . . ."

5.

Francis Dietz waited until the bus had gone, rattling away up the hill. Then he pitched away his cigarette and began to move toward the gangplank of the *Aurora II.*

Three men stood at the base of the gangplank, all wearing the white uniform of hired stewards. Two were Filipino; the third was Greek. As Dietz drew close, one hand dipped into his battered leather bag. The men rose to their full heights, and the Greek crossed his thick arms in front of his chest. "Can I help you?" he asked, with exaggerated cordiality.

Dietz smiled—he had a winning smile, which transformed his face from stolid and serious to open and appealing—and took his hand from the bag. "I need to take a look on board," he said. "Security issues. It won't take a minute."

"'Security issues,'" the man repeated. "What kind of security?"

"National security," Dietz said, and reached out for a sudden handshake.

Three pairs of eyes followed his hand. Inside the palm, barely visible through the crooked thumb, was a roll of bills.

The Greek reached out and shook the hand.

"Five minutes," he said.

The other two men exchanged a glance. Dietz bowed his head, stepped around the men, and trotted up the gangplank. As he stepped aboard, he could hear the beginnings of an argument behind him.

FOUR

I.

The handful of rose petals felt soft, and lighter than air.

Keyes held it by his side, looking at the church doors and waiting for his daughter to step out into the sunshine with her new husband. The idea that his daughter's college boyfriend was now his son-in-law seemed—like the rose petals in his palm—lighter than air, and barely real. Until today, Keyes had been able to imagine that the boy was merely an unfortunate detour on his daughter's trek through life. But he had just watched the vows being exchanged. He had just seen the rings being slipped onto fingers, and then the kiss . . .

The two rows of people around him, clutching similar handfuls of rose petals, also looked at the church door anxiously. Until now, the wedding had gone smoothly enough. But where were the bride and groom? Keyes saw Rachel trying to catch his eye. She wanted to blame him, somehow, for the fact that they hadn't yet made their appearance. He carefully avoided looking at her, and kept his eyes focused on the door.

The cell phone burred against his leg.

He ignored it. Now they were coming out—Margot grinning widely, looking happier than he had seen her looking for years; even sullen Joe Cifelli, Jr., looked happy for once—and Keyes raised the handful of petals. Whether or not he approved of the match, it was over now. Margot was an adult, capable of making her own choices. And as the proud father, his job now was to be gracious.

He flung the flowers heavenward, along with a dozen and a half other people, and for a few moments the air was filled with a shower of fluttering rose petals.

Then the bride and groom were slipping into a waiting limousine, to be whisked to the reception. Rachel was still trying to catch his eye. The phone was still burring against his leg. He turned away, reaching down and shutting it off. Today was his daughter's wedding. Today he wasn't available.

But Daisy knew what day it was. She wouldn't be calling unless it was an emergency . . .

Dick Faulk, Margot's godfather, was slapping his back. "Congratulations," he said. Dick, Keyes thought, seemed pained. He also could not believe that Margot had settled for Cifelli, and his backslapping was too strong to mask his pity. "Congratulations, Jim. What a day. What a day."

2.

Joe Cifelli, Sr., was talking in a smooth, never-ending flow.

Keyes stood, watching the mouth move and trying not to pay attention to the words. *Water off a duck's back,* he thought. *Water off a duck's back.*

"It's to the girl's credit that she's ready to try marriage," Cifelli said. "After what happened with you and the missus, I mean. But just because one generation gets it wrong doesn't mean the next can't get it right. Am I right, or am I right?"

Keyes nodded, stone-faced.

Behind Cifelli, the band was meandering through "Autumn Leaves." Keyes wished they'd get to the end and then skip the rest of the cocktail jazz, and move right to the toasts. Until the toasts had come and gone, this miserable night would never end.

A caterer moved past on his left, wheeling a tray piled with salmon and pork. His eyes followed of their own volition. He was starving.

"Now, if you ask me," Cifelli was saying, "it's not your fault, Jim, no matter what they say. Not everybody's as lucky as me and Rosalie. And besides, you had the accident, didn't you? You lose a child and the whole marriage crumbles. I hope I'm not overstepping my bounds, here. We're family now, aren't we? So we need to be straight with each other."

Margot appeared from nowhere, hugged Keyes, hugged Cifelli, hugged Keyes again—she was in a tizzy, in a whirl—and said, "Mom's crying behind the tent."

Keyes blinked.

"Go talk to her," Margot said. "Please?"

"Honey—I don't think she wants to talk to me."

"Don't ruin this for me, Dad. Please."

"Me?"

"Please. Just go talk to her."

He looked at his daughter—pale and overwrought, just like her mother—looked at Cifelli, then sighed, and nodded.

But he had no goddamned intention of talking to Rachel. He threaded his way between tables and stepped outside. Before him the inn—low, sprawling, and determinedly quaint—looked muted and quiet beside the glowing tent. "Autumn Leaves" segued into "Misty." So he had a few minutes, at least, before the toasts.

He made certain he was unobserved, then reached down and turned on his phone. It was ringing again; or perhaps it had been ringing the entire time. The LCD indicated that the call was coming from Daisy. He brought it to his ear and thumbed a button. "Yes," he said.

Daisy's voice, flickering in and out. ". . . bother you . . ."

He waited.

". . . gamma . . . critical."

His mouth tightened.

". . . fireworks," she said.

"How bad?"

The connection was getting worse. Waves of static rolled into his ear. Then, for one moment, it became crystal clear. "Isaac's gone to supervise. Greenwich is going crazy. The fireworks . . ."

Suddenly Keyes understood. *Fireworks*. Not an explosion; not a setback. An accomplishment. Critical Achievement Two—a fireworks display of electrons, photons, muons, and positrons. A burst of subatomic particles, symbolizing that they had done it.

They had done it.

Joy leaped inside of him; he quickly pressed it down. Time to celebrate later. But the joy remained there, percolating below the surface. All these months, all these years, and now they had Critical Achievement Two.

"What about Epstein?" he asked. His mind was already rolling ahead, greedily, to Critical Achievement Three. Greenwich had violated the moratorium on experiments imposed after Epstein's disappearance—until they had secured Epstein's formula, which could be used to predict precisely the lifetime of the black holes, work was to have stopped completely—but the man's instincts had been right. He had gone ahead, and gamma site still existed. So it was natural to look ahead to Three. Greenwich, no doubt, would be doing the same.

Only crackling. "Any word?" he pressed.

". . . yet," Daisy said, and then something that was swallowed by static.

"I can get away from here in an hour or two. You still at the office? I'll need transportation to gamma."

". . . weekend," she said.

"I appreciate it, Daisy. Thanks in advance."

". . . raise," she said.

He smiled, clicked off the phone, and slipped it back into his pocket.

Fireworks.

So they had done it. And now, as soon as the Epstein situation was brought to a conclusion, there would be nothing left in the way.

Something rustled behind him. He turned, and saw that it was Rachel.

Her mascara ran down her face in twin blue tear-streams—but she looked lovely in her black gown, with her hair piled atop her head and a slim silver necklace encircling her throat. In that first instant, he could almost see the girl who had once lived inside that woman's body, the girl with whom he had fallen in love.

In the beginning, he remembered, all their time together had been good. They had been just kids themselves. Then life had grown more complicated; the marriage had shaded into something more comfortable, more complex. For years they had walked a tightrope, through the good times and the bad.

Then had come the time in the hospital room, unlike any other. And when that time had ended, so had the marriage. Keyes had gone to a place deep inside himself. For a long while, he had stayed there. When he had resurfaced, Rachel was gone.

She took a step forward. "You don't return my calls," she said.

Keyes licked his lips, and didn't answer.

"You look tired," she said.

"I was just thinking how nice *you* look."

"And thin. Have you been losing weight?"

He shrugged, as if it was something that had happened accidentally.

"Too thin," she said. She took another step forward. Her hand brushed his. Then she was hugging him, pressing her face into his chest.

Her shoulders heaved. Keyes let her cry, his hands moving awkwardly, uncertain where to settle. Inside the tent, "Misty" came to an end; no other song began. In a moment, then, would come the toasts.

"Our little girl," Rachel said, her words muffled by his chest.

"She looks happy," Keyes said.

"I don't know. Does she? I can't tell."

He found one hand moving to stroke her hair. The hair felt dry, desiccated; she colored it too often these days. A surge of pity came to complement the other feelings inside him. Poor Rachel, he thought. She had lost everything, hadn't she? For an instant he almost found himself saying ridiculous things to her. Things about the Project, and how, once they reached Critical Achievement Three, everything might change. Things about how there were ways . . . how there might have been ways . . . to put everything back together again, to pretend none of it had ever happened . . .

. . . a malfunctioning turn signal; was that how God intended to take his boy? Impossible. Even chance could not be so finicky. The accident had been a mistake. And mistakes, with enough effort, could be corrected, no matter how large the scale.

But Rachel would think he had lost his mind, if he said something like that.

"The toasts are starting," he said instead.

She nodded, her chin rustling against his shirt. "We should go in there together. To show Margot we can do it."

"Your mascara is running. You look like a raccoon."

She sniffled, pulled back, produced a wad of Kleenex from somewhere—Rachel secreted Kleenex on her person like a con man concealing aces—and swiped at her cheeks.

Then she crooked out her arm, and managed to smile bravely.

They had tragedy to bind them, he thought as he took the arm. Tragedy had torn them apart, and yet the same tragedy bound them together. It didn't make any sense. Ever since the accident had taken Jeremy, nothing seemed to make sense.

Their arms locked. He put his other hand reassuringly on her elbow. Tomorrow, no doubt, they would be back to talking through lawyers. But for tonight, they could be civil with each other. It was a good night—Joe Cifelli, Jr., aside.

Fireworks.

They had done it.

He bowed his head, and returned the smile, and together they moved back into the tent.

FIVE

I.

Forty-foot stone walls topped with ragged battlements rose up against a turquoise sky.

Somehow the colors in this part of the world looked exaggerated, Hannah thought. The gray of the stone was layered and rich, the blue of the sky brilliantly vivid. Farther off, a strip of ochre rock led into the sea: reddish-yellow-gray against the green water, terminating in a small island that featured the prison tower of Sapienza.

The tour group strolled slowly among the ruins, inspecting the escarpments and the lions of Venice carved into the stone, making their gradual way in the direction of the tower.

"*Sapienza*," Jackie Burns said. "It means *wisdom*. This island was a strategic point in the route from the Ionian to the Aegean Sea—and more generally, in the route from Italy to the eastern Mediterranean. Notice, as we walk, evidence of the many different civilizations that had a hand in building parts of this fortress throughout the ages. The prison tower at which our tour will conclude was built by the Turks in the sixteenth century. Yet the fortress proper was begun three hundred years earlier—"

Hannah, despite herself, found herself enjoying the stroll. The view was idyllic, the wind soft and balmy. A constant nibble of apprehension threatened to spoil her pleasure, but for the moment she had it under control. For all she knew, after all, this was only a vacation. In a week she would return to her life with a clear head and a clean conscience, and start over again. And this time, she would get it right.

The subversive part of her mind, never content to let things rest, spoke up. *What about the plants?* the voice said. *Your poor plants. You could at least have made allowances for the plants . . .*

Hannah ignored the voice. There were enough other voices competing for her attention. On one side was Jackie Burns, still lecturing. On the other were the Epsteins, who were sticking to her like glue.

Mr. Epstein was asking her for the third time to make absolutely certain that she returned his book as soon as they arrived back at the ship. Hannah paid no attention. She had given him the assurance already, each time he had asked. There was something weird about his need to keep asking, she thought. Perhaps the man suffered from Alzheimer's.

"Okay," Jackie Burns said. She raised a hand, and the group piled to a stop around her. "Now we're going to head to the prison tower. Please try to stay together. There are other tour groups, as you can see, and they have a way of getting mixed up together. We'd like to avoid that. And be careful on the stones. They're slippery."

The sleepy-eyed Turk—Yildirim—was standing near the back of the group like a shepherd watching over a flock. Hannah looked at the man, looked away, and then looked back. He was really quite good-looking, in a rather exotic way. Tall, dark, and handsome. And he was much closer to her own age than the Epsteins.

As long as she was here, she might as well try to enjoy the experience to the fullest. Who knew the next time she would find herself in the Greek Isles?

She made her way toward Yildirim, conscious of the fact that Mr. and Mrs. Epstein were still following her, sticking close. But when she reached the spot where he had been, he was gone—having slipped around to the other side of the group, to share a word with Jackie Burns. She was left, once again, with the elderly couple. The woman's husband was looking away, off at the horizon; but in truth it seemed he was looking inside himself.

Alzheimer's, she thought again. That must be it.

"We'll enter the tower in groups of three," Jackie was saying. "Please find two buddies to accompany you. If you can't find a buddy, there's always me or Mr. Yildirim."

Mrs. Epstein gave Hannah a smile. "What do you say?" she asked. "Buddies?"

Hannah tried to keep her disappointment from showing. It could have been worse, she supposed. In a way—despite the age difference, the irritating homework assignments, and the crusty husband—she was growing to like this woman. Because she reminded Hannah of her grandmother, perhaps. Once, long ago, Hannah and her grandmother had been very close.

"Buddies," she said.

The group began moving again, with Hannah and the Epsteins bringing up the rear.

2.

The argument went back and forth in Steven Epstein's head: Procrastination, posing as rational consideration.

Already his procrastination had come back to haunt him. In the bathroom of the hotel in Venice, moments after watching the flame consume the last of the paper, he had scribbled the equations inside the back cover of the book. Immediately after making what had seemed like an irreversible decision, he had changed his mind. And now Renee had given the book away.

Part of him would be pleased, to have the formula slip through his fingers and continue to survive. For the work, of course, was the ultimate achievement of Epstein's career. It took Greenwich's efforts and leapfrogged years, if not decades, ahead. But those in control would take his discovery as license to press the Project at ever-increasing speed, despite the fact that a misstep would make the Phoenix reaction, which had been feared during the Manhattan Project, look like just a spill on an existential carpet.

And still this did not confront Epstein's greatest fear: that the Project would be a success. That the fruits of his genius would result, somewhere down the line, in the creation of a weapon unparalleled in the existence of man.

So his achievement had to vanish. Without it, even Keyes would not be able to force the Project ahead.

But was it really necessary that it vanish forever?

Procrastination, he thought. *Foolishness.*

The entire past decade, it seemed in retrospect, had been an exercise in procrastination. When he had first accepted the post at ADS, he'd had his doubts. But he had put the doubts off, and bent himself to his task. There always would be time, he had thought, to change his mind. Now his time had run out.

The book must be destroyed.

Yet the scientist in him obstinately refused to accept this fact. There were places that knowledge could be kept safe. In the right hands—cautious, learned, philosophical hands—the knowledge could be kept safe.

For the hundredth time, he reached a decision. He would remove himself from the equation, frustrating ADS. But he would connive to let his work fall into the right hands, so that his discovery would not vanish forever. A compromise.

When they returned to the ship, he would retrieve the book from the woman, put it in an envelope, and have the cruise director mail it to his colleague in Princeton. Then he would lock himself in the bathroom and swallow the entire vial of propoxyphene. He would claim seasickness; Renee would not bother him. Within five minutes, he would be dead, and as far as ADS knew the formula would be lost. They would be forced to slow down, for a decade, or a century . . . to let the slumbering beast of progress remain asleep, until they were better prepared to deal with it.

It was the only way.

So that was it. He had reached his decision. And this time he would stick to it.

Why, this is my last day on earth, Epstein thought.

It seemed that it should be a profound day, a special day. The sunlight should look remarkably golden; the conversation surrounding him should be gravid and insightful. Yet the sun was a bleached-out white, and the conversation was prosaic. A couple ahead of them was concerned that the batteries in their camera would die before the end of the tour. A man to their left was complaining about drinking warm bottled water.

His wife and the young woman—Vicky Ludlow—were walking just behind him, talking. Epstein listened with half an ear. Did this woman realize what she had, back in her cabin? Of course not. She was an innocent. She had stumbled into this entirely by mistake.

He cast his eyes around at the other tour groups dotting the fortress grounds. Had someone from ADS followed him? It seemed possible. Yet he didn't see anything to justify his concern. Nobody was paying any attention to him, except for a young boy who seemed to have become separated from his own group—a lad of twelve or thirteen, looking at him with bright eyes from under the brim of a baseball cap.

Their eyes met, and the boy turned away.

Foolishness, Epstein thought again. The boy is just a boy. It was natural to feel concern, considering his situation. But in just a few more hours, it would be finished for good.

Or would it? He had reached this decision before, and then balked. But this time was different. This time, he would go ahead.

Renee was calling his name. The tour group was venturing out across the spit of rock that led to the tower. He shot one more glance at the boy in the baseball cap. The boy was moving away now, heading in the opposite direction.

For a moment, Epstein looked after him.

Then he turned back to his wife, and went to join her.

3.

"I want you to close your eyes," Jackie Burns said dramatically, "and try to imagine this place as it looked nearly eight centuries ago."

To Hannah's surprise, everyone in the tour group immediately obeyed. The elderly were like children, she thought. They left this world as they had come into it, with their food cut up for them, their hands held, and their activities structured by others. And sure enough, like children, a few of them promptly began cheating— surreptitiously lifting eyelids, and stealing peeks.

"Five centuries ago," Jackie intoned, "a naval assault on the fortress of Sapienza would have reached this prison tower first. Now: I want you to imagine that you are a Greek soldier who has been captured on an earlier expedition. You know something that your Venetian captors don't—another expedition is following close behind. You expect to be rescued. But now, as the day on which you expect your saviors approaches, something is happening. You're being moved out to this tower. As we explore inside, think of what must be going through your mind. When the next ship comes, they'll reach this tower first. And will they recognize you as their brothers? No. They'll be in the grip of a blood lust—primed and raring to go, after so long on the open seas. When they throw their ladders against the tower walls, they'll climb them with swords drawn."

The group was assembling outside a rusted iron gate. Past the gate, inside the confines of the tower, were crumbling stone steps half lost in shadow. Nearby, the sea pounded against the shoals of the island and dissolved into droplets of spray.

"And as you're chained to these walls, the irony of your situation slowly begins to impress itself upon you. Hour after hour, day after day, you're forced to live with the knowledge that when your brothers arrive, the first to fall beneath their swords will be you and your brethren. The thought tortures you—chained in your own filth, starving, desperate. Eventually, perhaps, you'll call to your captors. You'll tell them everything you know about the coming expedition in exchange for a drink of water. But the best mercy you'll receive is a quick death . . ."

Eyes were opening all around now. Even Renee Epstein, who had been listening with rigid concentration, was peering out from below a heavily made-up ridge of eyelashes.

"All right!" Jackie said sunnily. "Please be very careful on the steps inside, which are as slippery as the rock bridge. And make sure to stay with your buddies. We'd hate to lose any of you. And if you see any ghosts in there, don't stare too long! We don't want them following us back to the ship."

Lukewarm laughter. Then the crowd was reassembling, shifting into groups of three. Somehow, Hannah and the Epsteins had moved up to the front of the pack. Hannah glanced across the bridge that led back to the fortress. A young boy was moving across the rocks in their direction, evidently unable to wait for his own group.

"We're next," Renee Epstein said. One hand took her husband's; the other moved for Hannah's.

4.

As they stepped into the prison tower, Hannah could hear Jackie Burns, from outside, continuing her lecture in loud, insistent tones.

"This fortress occupies a key position—the watchtower of the eastern Mediterranean. The essence of its fortification comes by virtue of the location. Shoals on one side, a bay on the other. It's always easier to defend a bay, of course; you just block off the mouth. And the Venetians, whenever possible, preferred to conduct their military business on the sea."

The first floor of the tower smelled of lichen and centuries. The space in which Hannah stood with the Epsteins was circular, almost twenty feet in diameter, made of rough gray stone with nooks carved into the walls. Beside each nook was a set of iron clamps. A spiral stairway of rock, leading up, was illuminated by weak sunlight trickling through higher windows.

Renee Epstein stood beside her in the gloom, examining the stairway. "That doesn't look safe," she said timidly.

"It'll be fine," Hannah assured her, although secretly she found herself thinking the same. The stone of the steps looked weathered and treacherous.

A moment passed. Then they began to climb, Hannah in the lead, the Epsteins close behind. Outside, Jackie was still talking.

"When you reach the second story, you'll notice a wooden ladder leading to the third. Whether or not you choose to climb the ladder is up to you—but if you do, please be very careful. The ladder, of course, has not been a part of the tower since the thirteenth century. It's a recent addition, for the benefit of tours like ours. In reality, the tower consisted of only two stories. Why, then, does the ladder lead up to a stone platform on the third? Look closely and you'll notice the remains of a gallows up there. Imagine the psychological effect of having your fellow soldiers dangling beside you, as you're locked in one of these stone nooks, too small even to turn around in . . . and think twice about that before you complain about your cabins on board being too claustrophobic."

Mild laughter; but only mild. Already the passengers had become weary of Jackie's ceaseless attempts at wit.

Hannah was coming off onto the second floor now. The ladder leading higher looked none too sturdy. She waited until the Epsteins had joined her, and then said, "What do you think?"

"I think," Renee said, "we'll wait here, dear."

The woman's husband hardly seemed to have heard the question. He was peering back toward the first floor, frowning.

Hannah reached for the ladder. It creaked, but held. Once she had reached the third story, the interior of the tower looked even smaller.

She could see the top of the Epsteins' heads, and the metallic shine of the manacles set into the wall.

She turned to look out through the window at the sea. The view was stunning: sweeping water, craggy rocks, a tremendous azure sky. It really *was* unchanged, she thought. Through all those civilizations, all those centuries. How could there not be such a thing as second chances, with so much time in the world?

A sound came from below.

She looked down from the window. Another figure was coming onto the second story. It was the boy she had seen following them across the bridge, she thought. How had he gotten past Jackie Burns? Perhaps he had come around the back of the tower, and slipped through one of the crevasses in the rock.

The boy reached into a pocket—or something like it—and raised a small silver object. There was a puff, almost a sigh. Then Steven Epstein was choking.

Hannah stared.

The boy circled around behind Renee Epstein as she reached for her husband. Now Steven Epstein was sinking to his knees, still choking. And the boy was not a boy at all, Hannah thought. His carriage was that of an adult; his face, in the gloom, was oddly ageless.

As Hannah watched, the man-child stabbed Renee Epstein in the side. She saw it very clearly—the blade moving in and then out, three times in quick succession.

Mrs. Epstein crumpled onto the floor beside her husband.

The boy looked up. His gaze fell on Hannah. He reached for the ladder, and began to climb.

Hannah's eyes slid to the top of the ladder. The wood was old, mossy and half rotted. She took a step toward it and raised a foot. She watched, almost curiously, as her foot hammered down onto the top rung. It splintered, buckling.

The boy pulled himself up again. The world had slowed; time drew out in a thin blade.

Thank God I'm wearing flats, Hannah thought distantly, as she kicked again at the rung.

Then the ladder was groaning, separating from the wall. The boy was retreating, scaling down, dropping to the second floor and covering his head as the ladder came free.

He looked up at her with baleful eyes. In the next instant, he had turned, and vanished down the stairs.

Hannah stared after him.

The Epsteins lay still, their bodies touching, a pool of blood spreading slowly between them.

SIX

I.

The loudspeaker behind the bed crackled.

Hannah pushed her head into the pillow, trying to block it out. The speaker gave a series of rising tones and then the voice of Jackie Burns, sounding oddly subdued:

"Good evening, ladies and gentlemen." Jackie's tone was solemn and formal. "In light of today's tragic occurrence at the fortress of Sapienza, the captain has asked me to brief all passengers on a change in our itinerary . . ."

There had been ammonia on the doctor's hands when he'd given Hannah the shot. She could still smell it, faint and lingering.

"—we will not be docking at the port of Malta. Instead the *Aurora* will now take several days at sea, and sail directly to Istanbul. Once we arrive, the question of refunds will be taken up with all appropriate dispatch. We regret this change in plans. Please allow me to offer the sincere apologies of both myself and all personnel affiliated with Adventure Dynamics and the *Aurora II*."

Dark waves leaped high outside the cabin's window. A trio of seagulls whirled, dipping and swirling. Hannah's eyes followed them mechanically.

She had seen Renee Epstein stabbed to death.

She had grown fond of the woman, after a fashion. Her fondness had manifested itself as irritation, much as it had with Hannah's own grandmother. It was always the way. Only when it was too late did she learn to express her feelings. Her grandmother; Renee Epstein; loved only in absentia.

Her mind was floating, skipping like a stone across a pond.

She had witnessed a murder.

She would never sleep again.

She moaned, and dug her face deeper into the pillow.

2.

"Vicky?"

Her eyes opened. Jackie Burns was sitting by the side of the bed.

"How do you feel?"

Hannah struggled up onto one elbow. "Thirsty," she managed.

Jackie moved to the refrigerette. The window had been shuttered, Hannah saw; the standing lamp was on, emitting a soft glow.

After finding a liter of Evian, Jackie came back to the bedside. Hannah returned her head to the pillow without opening the bottle. Her eyes moved to the digital clock. It was twenty minutes past eight. But did that mean morning or night?

Jackie was looking at her pityingly. She reached out and smoothed a strand of hair off Hannah's forehead. "Did you manage to sleep at all?"

Hannah didn't answer. The hand on her brow felt cool, soothing, almost matronly.

"We're all a little shook up," Jackie said. "You more than anyone, I bet . . ."

It was an understatement.

In reality, Hannah hadn't let herself shut down until the moment that the doctor had given her the shot. Until then she'd kept herself superficially together—all through the long wait on the tower platform, and all through the conversation with Jackie and the sleepy-eyed Turk, as she had described the incident to the best of her ability. Yet on the inside, where it counted, she had shut down right there on the third-story landing.

Witnessing the murders had been enough trauma. Having the man-child come after her had been even worse. The three hours spent trapped on the platform, as they'd tried to figure out how to jury-rig a ladder to bring Hannah back down to earth, had been only the icing on the cake. She'd watched as the Epsteins' bodies were covered with blankets and then laboriously removed from the prison tower. She'd kept watching, trapped, as the shakes had come and gone.

". . . but you'll be glad to know," Jackie was saying, "everything's been worked out now. I don't know if you heard the announcement—but we've decided to skip the rest of our islands. We're going straight to Istanbul."

"'Istanbul,'" Hannah repeated dully.

"The FBI spent the afternoon conducting a preliminary investigation on the island, and they've decided to let us go on ahead. In a case like this, jurisdiction is determined by the first port at which we dock following the incident. Of course, the incident took place *at* a port.

But we put in a call to the head office, and they spoke with the State Department, and now everybody's on the same page—the company, the FBI, the Greeks, and the Turks. We'll go straight to Istanbul." She paused. "Once we get there, Vicky, the FBI is going to want to interview you. Since you're a witness."

Hannah kept her face blank. "Why not now?" she asked.

Jackie picked an invisible speck of lint off her tan slacks.

"Well," she said. "It's not clear just what's happened. But evidently the Bureau is satisfied that there aren't any more answers to be found on Methoni. And the Greeks would be just as happy not to have an incident like this, now, on their soil. They've put a lot of effort into breaking up this terrorist group, November 17, recently, and aren't eager to have their international relationships complicated. We're already in bed with the Turks, of course, so they've got to welcome us regardless. It's a tragedy, what's happened with the Epsteins. There's no getting around that. But now we need to look ahead, and make things as easy as possible on the rest of us."

Hannah nodded.

"I've discussed the situation with Chief Security Officer Yildirim. We both agree that the important thing now is for you to get some rest. So that once we do reach port, you'll be ready to help as much as possible."

Hannah nodded again.

"It seems that Mr. Epstein was sort of an important person," Jackie said. "Did you just meet him on the boat?"

"Yes—just on the boat."

Jackie gave Hannah a searching look. Then her face, once again, turned kindly and professionally blank.

"Well. I just thought you ought to know the whole situation. Are you waking up now?"

". . . Still logy."

"That's the sedative the doctor gave you. It should be wearing off soon. Are you hungry?"

Hannah thought about it. She shook her head.

"Well," Jackie said again. "I need to show my face at dinner, to keep up appearances. But if you decide you can handle some food, just pick up the phone. Call the purser. He'll bring you anything you want."

"Thank you."

"And if you want to talk about anything, or want anything at all . . ."

"I think I'll just sleep for a while."

"All right," Jackie said. She stood. "Sleep well."

"Thank you."

"Sleep well," Jackie said again. She gave Hannah a final empty smile, and left.

3.

That doesn't look safe, Renee Epstein had said.

It'll be fine, Hannah had assured her.

Yet it hadn't, of course. It had been very far from fine.

Had it all been a dream? That face, oddly ageless. The Epsteins, touching each other in death.

All a fever dream, she decided. She was sick. The weather seemed to be worsening, which didn't help. The sea had turned choppy; the boat pitched and yawed relentlessly. She kept her eyes tightly closed.

She was finished.

When they reached Istanbul, they would be met by the FBI. Every person on board the ship would be put under a microscope. They would look at her passport, and see that it had been forged. And she would be finished.

She was as bad as Jackie Burns, in her way. She had witnessed two murders. And yet already her mind was turning to her own concerns. *Now we need to look ahead, and make things as easy as possible on the rest of us.*

Perhaps it was just part of life, Hannah thought. Perhaps life meant moving ahead, when death showed its face.

In her case, however, the only place to move ahead to was prison.

When the niggling voice spoke, her eyes opened halfway.

Remember: there's no record of your presence here.

Suddenly she felt overly warm. She shoved the blanket aside and then lay on her back, limbs splayed, aspirating shallowly.

It was true. There was no proof that she had ever been on the ship. Vicky was the one who had been on board, according to the passenger roster. So if she could somehow find a way to slip away undetected, then she might still have a chance. If she could get herself home, to her father . . .

How would he react now, if she appeared on his doorstep with a warrant out for her arrest? There had been bad blood between them. But would he turn on his own daughter? No. Instead he would help her broker a deal, an exchange. He was a criminal lawyer in Baltimore; he would get her the best possible terms. She would turn over Frank, and in return the company would forgive her mistakes and wipe her record clean. A fresh start.

Wishful thinking.

But was there any other option?

She bit her lip, trying to think of one, and came up empty. Her mistakes over the past few months had whittled her options down to nothing.

Slowly, her mind turned to Yildirim.

He was chief security officer aboard the boat. If the chief of security couldn't find a way around his own rules—a way to help her slip unnoticed through customs at Istanbul—then who could?

For another ten minutes, she stayed where she was, her brow creased. Then she got out of bed. The feeling of sickness had passed. Only shock, after all. She looked at herself in the mirror above the dresser. Her hair wound crazily in a half-dozen directions. The skin beneath her eyes was purplish and bruised-looking. She wouldn't get far with Yildirim, not looking like this.

Which was, of course, why God had created makeup.

She went into the bathroom, took a long shower, and then considered herself again in the mirror. Better. There was something to work with, at least. Something was better than nothing.

Anything was better than nothing.

She reached for her makeup, and went to work.

4.

Francis Dietz stood on the hotel balcony, considering.

Before him, night had fallen. The town of Methoni was waking up. Tablecloths were unrolled in outdoor cafés as pretty hostesses took up spots on winding sidewalks to waylay tourists. Behind him, Leonard was grabbing some sleep on the room's couch. Dietz could hear the sounds of his breathing, labored and stertorous in the heavy air.

He returned to his thoughts. The Epsteins' cabin had been empty. Leonard had taken care of the couple—yet they still did not have the formula. Perhaps this meant that there had been no physical copy. Perhaps this game was already finished, before it had truly begun.

Leonard, however, had reported a young woman in the Epsteins' company on the tour. If she was involved somehow, perhaps she could lead them to the formula.

He would have to report back to Keyes, though. Keyes couldn't be cut out of the loop just yet. That would create more troubles than it would solve.

He moved into the room quietly, to avoid waking Leonard. He found the telephone near the front door and placed his call. Keyes was not in the office. Dietz left a message, then hung up, returned to the balcony, and took out his pack of cigarettes.

Who would he approach? Yurchenko, he thought. Yurchenko had been a member of the FSB back when it had been the KGB. Yurchenko knew both the old guard and the new guard. In all likelihood, Yurchenko would put him in touch with Ismayalov. Vladimir Ismayalov, the agent's cagey, self-promoting ex-boss, known as the vulture. The vulture's network of contacts was international. He'd be able to find an interested buyer, Dietz was sure of it.

But he was getting ahead of himself. When the moment arrived, he would make his move. Until then, he needed to be patient.

He lit a cigarette. *Patience,* he thought.

SEVEN

I.

Hannah Gray accepted a vodka tonic from a waiter, signed for the drink, and then turned her eyes to the lounge before her.

At minutes before midnight, the space was nearly deserted. The ship's piano player was navigating a desultory version of "Summertime." An elderly couple sat before the piano, singing along in soft, cracked voices. Except for two waiters and Hannah herself, there was nobody else in sight. The rough seas, combined with the shock of the afternoon, had driven most of the passengers on board to retire early. In a way, Hannah was surprised to see anybody at all here in the lounge. Death had intruded on this tranquil voyage; and in its face, the passengers had retreated to solitude.

Then Yildirim was coming out of the rest room on her left, heading for the corner table where he had left a whiskey and a pack of English Ovals. Hannah counted to three before stepping into his path. When they collided, her carefully positioned drink spilled down the front of her blouse. She grimaced.

"My fault," she said, as he said, "Forgive me—"

He found a pile of cocktail napkins on a nearby bar, realized that he could not start mopping at Hannah's blouse, and handed one to her awkwardly.

"I'm sorry," he said. "Please, forgive me."

"My fault. I'm still rattled, I guess."

"Let me get you another."

"Oh, you don't need to do that. I'll just—"

"Please," he said, and gestured toward his corner table. "Please. I insist."

2.

"If you ask me," she said, "it's a question of legality, not morality."

Yildirim was listening, his head cocked to one side. Before he had a chance to comment, she rushed on:

"Frank and I fell out of love a long time ago. We've only stayed together for the children. But that's a mistake, I'm coming to realize. It's better for the children to have divorced parents than parents stuck in an unhappy marriage. Don't you think?"

He made a loose, careless gesture with the hand holding his cigarette.

"So I agreed to come on this cruise with Lucas. Maybe I shouldn't have done that. But we're in love. You know how that is, don't you? It's such a good feeling. What can be wrong with something that feels so good? But oh, it was a mistake. I see that now. Lucas couldn't make it, at the last second, so I came alone—but now I'm going to get caught in a lie. Because my husband thinks I'm at a symposium in San Francisco. And now there's going to be an investigation and my husband will find out I lied to him and we're not even legally separated yet and he's going to get custody of the kids and it's going to be all my fault, because I was stupid enough to try to take a cruise with Lucas when I should have waited. I guess it's just . . . Oh, God," she said. "I'm rambling, aren't I?"

Yildirim shrugged.

"I'm sorry. I'm a little tipsy. And to be honest, I think I'm in shock."

"That's not surprising," he said. "Considering what you've been through today. I think we're all a little . . . out of sorts."

"I'm sorry. I shouldn't have said anything. It's just . . . well, you're a good listener."

He shrugged again.

"Let's talk about you," Hannah said. She straightened in her seat. "You have a very interesting accent."

Yildirim smiled. He had the kind of smile that very serious men have when they occasionally loosen up: tight and reluctant, somehow boyish. "Do you think so?"

"Mm. Definitely. Is it Turkish?"

"By way of Ohio. I was born in Istanbul, but my parents moved to America when I was fourteen."

"So you grew up there?"

"For four years, yes. Then back to Istanbul. And you come from Chicago, is that right?"

"Born in Washington, D.C.; raised in the windy city. But I'm going to move out west, I think, once the divorce comes through. The City of Angels. That's where Lucas lives. Have you ever been?"

He shook his head, and raised his drink.

"Chicago is the Midwest," she said, "technically. But it feels more like the East than Ohio. People walk fast, and they look at their feet. In California, things are different. No baggage. People look up; they look ahead. A person can reinvent herself in California."

He chased the drink with a drag from his cigarette, and nodded.

"One thing I never thought I'd do is get divorced. Once you get married, you stay married; that's what I thought. But I couldn't see how life would work out. People grow apart, you know. It's a cliché, but it's true. Many clichés are true, I find as I get older."

As she spoke, she paid attention to Yildirim's body language, trying to gauge his interest in her. Would the path to pursue now be seduction or a dig for sympathy? Judging from the cant of his body, the latter approach seemed more promising. He faced away from her in the chair, his feet pointing toward the piano player.

She reached for tears. There were none waiting. She dug deeper. There—a trickle, in the corner of one eye. She wiped at it. "Oh, God damn it."

"It's all right."

"No, it's not. It's . . ." Her voice caught. She drew a shuddering breath, bravely controlling herself. "It was stupid and selfish of me. And now the kids will pay the price. It doesn't seem fair for them to have to pay the price, just because there's been some bad luck. I'm very sorry for the Epsteins, of course, but . . . who would have expected . . . it just all seems so . . ."

"I know."

"What happened to them, do you think?"

Yildirim shook his head. "It's out of our hands now," he said.

"I don't mean to sound selfish. I don't think I'll ever get over . . . that. But now I need to think of myself, and my children. If only there was some way for me to get off the ship, before we reach Istanbul—I might still be able to dodge this bullet."

Yildirim stabbed out his cigarette. "Your presence on board," he said, "is a matter of record."

"No, it's not. I'm using an alias. It was Lucas's idea, just to be safe. If I could get off now, then I could still fix things. You don't know my husband, Mr. Yildirim. He drinks, and when he drinks, he loses his temper. Do you think . . ."

She trailed off. He waited, watching her.

"Do you think there's any way you might be able to . . . Oh, God." She laughed shakily. "I don't even know what I'm saying."

"Able to what?"

"Help me . . . you know . . ."

His smile was gone.

". . . disappear."

He looked at her stonily.

"I'll make it worth your while," she said. "I've got money. And it's for a good cause, you know. My children."

A moment passed.

"I'm afraid you're not thinking straight," he said then. "After what you've been through, it's no surprise. But Mrs. Ludlow . . ."

"That's not my name."

He stopped.

"My husband broke Teddy's arm once, after he'd been drinking. Oh, I know I shouldn't have come on the cruise in the first place. It was stupid and selfish. But I fell in love, Mr. Yildirim. Haven't you ever fallen in love?"

He lit another cigarette, and didn't answer.

"How much would it take?" she said. "Two thousand dollars?"

His lips pressed together.

"Three thousand?" she said. "I could go higher—if that's what it would take. I don't have it on me, of course. But I could call my accountant. I could arrange something."

"Mrs. . . . Even if . . ."

It was her turn to wait.

"Supposing it *was* for a good cause . . ."

"It is. Believe me."

"It still wouldn't be possible. I'm sorry about your children, of course. But——"

"Four thousand," she said. "I'm not sure you understand how much this means to me. And the fact is, Mr. Yildirim, that you might lose your job over this. Right? A little extra cash might come in handy, over the next few months."

He said nothing. His eyes flickered.

"Five thousand dollars," she said, and then added: "Please. Mr. Yildirim, I swear to God, I don't know where else to turn."

3.

He promised to sleep on it.

This, Hannah suspected, meant he would do it. Had it been the tears or the money? Some combination, probably. And who really cared what it had been? As long as he helped her, two days hence, when they pulled into Istanbul . . .

Back in her cabin, she took another shower. But no matter how hard she scrubbed, a tickle of self-disgust remained. Some nice sob story she had come up with—that helping her get off the ship would help fictional children avoid an abusive father. Some nice person she had turned out to be.

Nobody's nice, she thought, and then immediately: *Besides, he'll only really do it for the money.*

And was it her fault that the Epsteins had been murdered? Not at all. It was a shame—a tragedy, as Jackie Burns had said—but it had nothing to do with her. Bad luck had put her in this position, and nothing else. So a little white lie was permissible.

After the shower, she collapsed naked across her bed. The effect of the single drink she'd had was fading, leaving her wanting another. Her right hand moved to the pale scars inside her left wrist. The scars were eight months old, but they still itched. The itching was in her mind, she realized—a variation on the itching of a phantom limb. She scratched them for a moment, idly, then took her hand back.

The scars belonged to the past. She would never be that person again. She had not even been that person at the time; that was why the attempt had been so halfhearted. *A cry for help*, they called it. What it really had been was an embarrassment.

She tried to turn the thoughts off. In the future, she would do better. If God would only see fit to help her get off the ship, undetected, at Istanbul . . .

Some nice person she had turned out to be.

She stood, found a Xanax, and threw a Valium on top. She collapsed across the bed again and then turned off the lamp and lay still, facedown, as the ship rocked her gently toward sleep.

Once she had been good. Hadn't she? As a child. Or maybe not. Maybe she had never been good.

But that wasn't true. Before Frank had gotten his claws into her, she had not been a criminal. Why, she had never so much as stolen a pack of gum from the corner store. She was not a thief.

Maybe a library book, once. But who hadn't stolen a library book?

You can do better than that, the voice spoke up. *What about your mother's purse?*

Okay. So she had taken some money, once or twice, from her mother's purse. Everybody did that, she thought. That did not make her a thief.

But now that she thought about it in these terms, she couldn't get off the hook quite so easily. She had written off entire vacations as business expenses, using the thinnest rationalizations. She had bought carpets in London and arranged to charge half the price on her credit card and half C.O.D., thereby avoiding customs. A steady progression, she saw now, toward her larger crimes. And then a leap off the deep end, with Frank to show her the way . . . and one night the half-assed suicide attempt, sobbing at her own sorry reflection in the bathroom mirror.

God, she thought. *Help me out here and I swear I'll do better. I swear I'll make it up to You.*

The prayer—if that was what it was—only deepened the feeling of self-disgust. Here was Hannah Gray, facile to the end. Promising God that she would reform if only He would deign to help her one more time. She hadn't changed, after all.

But she meant it. She was not evil. At worst, she'd been a bit . . . spoiled.

She rolled over, sleepy. It was not too late for her, she thought. If things worked out, then it would not be too late.

She hoped it wasn't too late.

The rocking of the boat felt comforting; her body had adjusted to the rhythm of the waves. When she fell asleep, she slept surprisingly well—very nearly the sleep of the innocent.

EIGHT

I.

They turned off the road, onto gravel, and the tires began to crunch.

In the backseat of the Town Car, Keyes stirred. He yawned, stretched, and peered out through his window. The reactor wasn't on line yet, which meant that the only visible man-made light came from the guard towers and the four wooden houses that existed above-ground. In comparison to the brilliant Nevada night sky, gamma site seemed positively inconsequential.

Despite the summer, the desert air was cold; he shivered as he was searched. Then he accepted his credentials back from the guard and entered the largest of the four buildings. He stepped into a game room that featured a pool table, a pinball machine, two low couches, and a darkened TV. Set into the center of the wall opposite the front door was an empty bookshelf. He placed his right eye against the retinal scanner disguised as a knot in the wood. He could hear the mechanisms of the lock tumbling; then the bookshelf split open.

Behind the bookshelf was an elevator. Inside the elevator was a blackboard. As the elevator hummed down, Keyes eyed the blackboard darkly.

Ed Greenwich was waiting for him.

Greenwich was an eccentric Frankenstein of a man, six feet four inches tall, with febrile green eyes and a prominent Adam's apple beneath sagging dewlaps. He began to speak as soon as Keyes stepped off the elevator, as if they'd been in the midst of a conversation that had been only momentarily interrupted. Greenwich, Keyes thought, was in a manic phase. His hands were in constant motion: rotating incessantly at the wrists, the fingers twiddling against nothing.

"Seventeen TeV isn't necessary after all," Greenwich said. He immediately turned and began to lead Keyes down a polished steel corridor, heels rapping. "Oh, I knew it already. I think I've always known it. But yesterday—beautiful; beautiful; beautiful. But of course, Three is an entirely different ball game."

Keyes nodded. He was noticing the vast amount of electricity being consumed around them. Noticing this made him feel like a parent who scolded his children for leaving on too many lights; yet he couldn't help himself. There was nobody else here to keep an eye on the bottom line. Until the reactor came on, they were siphoning their power from the main grid. If they got too greedy, it could create problems.

Greenwich kept talking, eager to demonstrate that even he was not willing to move farther without Epstein's results to guide him. It was a preemptive strike, Keyes thought, against any possible official reproof for what he had done.

"—subnanometer realm displays exactly the predicted values. That means, thanks to the inverse cube law, that it's possible. And possible, in this case, means inevitable. Yes, yes, yes. In fact it *was* done—yesterday—on the smallest possible scale."

Now they were stepping into the detector room on the main particle ring. The superconducting magnets, kept by liquid nitrogen at a temperature of two hundred degrees below zero, let off billowing icy clouds of condensation. Cranes moved three-ton equipment with the offhanded casualness of a man picking up a Styrofoam cup. Cables as thick as elephant legs snaked under the feet of men who stepped over them to consult computer monitors, yell to each other over the din, and make notations on clipboards.

"... as of yesterday, we're ahead of everyone else. There's no doubt of that anymore. Hadron won't be on line until two thousand and six; and we have every reason to expect success within three months, if my computer time isn't diminished. Yes. Every reason."

It took Keyes a moment to realize that Greenwich had stopped talking. He looked up from the floor and saw the man watching him expectantly. "Good," Keyes said simply.

"But I need that computer time. If we have to stop now, we'll lose all the momentum we've built up."

"Don't worry. You'll have it."

"Once the ball gets rolling, on something like this, you can't stop it. No, no. You just can't."

"Don't worry about the computers," Keyes said. "Worry about your end, Ed. Let me worry about mine."

2.

Twenty minutes later, they were back in the game room with the stuttering lights of the pinball machine, drinking coffee that burned straight through Keyes's stomach.

Greenwich was talking again. As the man spoke, Keyes noticed, he was picking his nose.

". . . above the board, at some point down the line. Of course, I realize the need for security. These days more than ever. That goes without saying. But in five years, or ten, I'm not sure I see the harm . . ."

Keyes could read between the lines. Greenwich, between picks, was thinking about the Nobel again. "Ed," he said. "First things first. Okay?"

"Sure," Greenwich said. "First things first. I'm just thinking aloud."

"Think all you want. No harm in thinking."

The reprimand was implied: *As long as you don't do what you did yesterday. As long as you keep it in the realm of thought.*

Personally, Keyes was pleased that Greenwich had gone ahead. But officially, he had responsibilities—no matter how eager he might have been to bring the Project to quick fruition.

He could sense the man's frustration at his response. Greenwich thought that Keyes was a bureaucrat, interested only in the nuts-and-bolts results of the Project—the liberated vacuum energy, the defensive applications, the research potential. Greenwich thought he couldn't see the deeper philosophical implications of what they were trying to accomplish here. But if that had been the case, would Keyes have taken the chance he was taking by providing cover for Greenwich now? Would he have taken the chance of hitching his cart to this particular horse, after Greenwich had gone ahead the previous day without authorization? No. He understood the importance of the Project, all right. He understood it on every level. And Greenwich's refusal to recognize this struck him as patronizing.

Greenwich wasn't going to let go of the topic, Keyes realized, despite the implied reprimand. The man wanted some guarantee of credit.

"Without these machines," Greenwich said loftily, "we would be incapable of reaching so far. But without *this* machine"—he tapped an index finger against one bony temple—"we would never have known to reach in the first place."

This was undeniably true. Greenwich had been the one who had developed the model of space-time with compactified extra dimensions, thereby opening the door for the Project to proceed.

Keyes remembered the very first time the man had explained the Project to him—putting it in such simple terms that everything had clicked together, even for an admittedly literal-minded man like Keyes. *Space-time is finite yet unbounded,* Greenwich had said. *Picture a globe representing the earth. You can travel in any one direction on the globe and never hit a boundary. Yet the surface area is finite. That's how space-time is, Jim. And all we're going to do is poke a little hole—make a tunnel from one side of the globe to the other. Cut right through the middle. But you've got to remember, it's time as well as space we'll be crossing . . .*

Later had come other metaphors. They would bend space-time into the shape of a saddle and leap from one horn to another. None of the metaphors were strictly accurate, since three-dimensional beings were by definition incapable of picturing four-dimensional space-time. But it was the first metaphor, of the globe, to which Keyes had clung. That picture, he could understand. *Finite, yet unbounded.*

Greenwich had even managed to provide Keyes with some sense of context—a thumbnail sketch of physics and relativity. Relativity, Greenwich had explained, was not nearly as difficult a subject as was widely believed. The secret, he said, was simple.

The secret was light.

They'd been sitting in Keyes's Vermont office, discussing the nature of the universe calmly and quietly, drinking ice water from a cut-glass decanter.

We've known for centuries that light does not travel infinitely fast. A

Dutch astronomer figured this out way back in 1676—by observing that the eclipses of Jupiter's moons occur later in the night when Jupiter is farther away from earth. That means that the light has traveled to us at a less-than-infinite speed. He even took a shot at naming that speed; and he got pretty close, considering what he had to work with. He suggested that light travels at 140,000 miles per second. We now know that the figure is closer to 186,000 miles per second. Are you with me so far?

Keyes had assured the man that he was.

But when you measure something's speed, you need to measure that speed relative to something. A young patent clerk named Albert Einstein answered the question "What is light moving relative to?" thus: Light is the speed limit of the universe, and everybody measures it the same no matter how fast they are moving through space. Time stretches to make this possible. Distance, of course, is simply rate multiplied by time. If distances vary, and yet the rate of light always stays the same, something in the equation has to give—in this case, time.

He'd seen the frown appearing on Keyes's brow. *It's not so hard,* he'd said quickly. *Say a pulse of light is coming toward us. I'm standing still; you're walking forward. You're moving at four miles per hour. By conventional thinking, the light would seem that much slower to you. Yet we both see the light traveling at 186,000 miles per second. Time stretches to make this possible.*

The frown had diminished, but remained.

You just need to give up the idea of absolute time, Greenwich had said. *You need to accept that space and time are two sides of the same coin—space-time—both existing without absolutes, and both relative to one's motion.*

It was a difficult idea for humans, he admitted, because humans saw time as moving forward, unchanging. But that was wrong. To understand the Project, Keyes would need to accept this fact.

He had accepted it gladly. Time was only an illusion? Yes, he could happily embrace that idea. The philosophical implications were not only staggering, but rather pleasing.

Yes, yes. So. A few years after publishing his "special" theory of relativity, Einstein published a "general" theory of relativity. Gravity is not like other forces, he said, but is a result of the fact that space-time is warped by the distribution of mass and energy in it. Planets don't circle around the sun; they follow the nearest thing to a straight path in curved space-time. Observation of the orbits of our own planets, you know, confirms this theory. Einstein's equations predict them more accurately than Newton's.

We as a species, Greenwich was saying, are too small to see the universe the way it is. The simple fact is that we are three-dimensional beings living in a four-dimensional world, and the fourth dimension is time. And if one could travel a great enough distance through space-time, one might come out not only somewhere else, but some-*when* else.

Greenwich had given him a moment to absorb this, and then continued:

Black holes, Jim, are holes in space-time, created when the terrific gravity and energy-density of a collapsing star puncture the fabric of our universe. If we could create a black hole in a laboratory . . .

. . . which would most likely be accomplished by smashing together matter at high speeds, he had explained, in a particle accelerator like the one that formed the core of gamma site . . .

. . . perhaps we could break out from the restrictions of being three-dimensional, of experiencing time in a simple linear fashion.

But it would not be a risk-free proposition. For if the black hole manufactured in the laboratory proved beyond their ability to control, the consequences could be devastating.

Yet Epstein's formula would enable them to accurately predict the lifetime of the black holes they would be making in the lab, to avoid such an event. This was a very good thing, Greenwich had explained; for they faced competition, and time was of the essence. The Large Hadron Collider under construction at CERN, the European laboratory for particle physics near Geneva, was scheduled to start smashing together protons and antiprotons in 2006.

By the time Greenwich had finished talking, Keyes had been convinced. Not to take the risk would be foolish. If one wanted to play in the big leagues, one had to take the big chances. In this case, the *very* big chances. But the potential benefits made it worth the risk—more than worth the risk.

"Ed," he said gravely. "You won't be forgotten."

"It's not about credit," Greenwich said, unconvincingly.

"I know. I just want to assure you—you won't be forgotten."

Greenwich pursed his lips. He sipped his coffee; his Adam's apple jumped.

"You might get a call from Chen," he said then. "Chen's getting cold feet."

Keyes nodded.

"Don't listen to him. All men have doubts. It's only human to have doubts."

"I understand." Keyes refrained from adding, *I'm on your side, here. Can't you see that?*

"Remember the moon landing," Greenwich said. "'For one priceless moment, in the history of man, all the people of this earth are truly one.' That's what we're aiming for, Jim."

"You don't have to tell me, Ed. I'm with you on this."

"When Chen calls, hear him out. Otherwise he might try to go over your head."

"All right."

"And don't forget who stayed on your side."

That seemed a fine note on which to end. Keyes nodded again, stood, and offered his hand. They shook. He moved outside, into the waiting Town Car.

Greenwich wouldn't be forgotten, he thought as they rumbled back down the gravel road; that was true. The man was all too concerned with getting due credit. Science for the sake of science sounded good on paper, but when it came down to it, Greenwich would insist that his contribution be recognized. Like Epstein, he didn't have his feet on the ground. He had no appreciation for matters of security. And if he felt that his reward was not adequate for the services he had rendered, how would he react?

Would he run, like Epstein? Would he try to find another sponsor besides the U.S. government?

In time, Greenwich would be dealt with. In time, all the loose ends would be tied up. But first they needed to move on to Critical Achievement Three. And to do that, he needed Greenwich to repeat Epstein's results.

Soon, Keyes thought.

Two minutes passed. The gravel turned to pavement; Keyes began to feel drowsy. The desert around them was uninterrupted, and lulling in its vastness.

Once the ball gets rolling, on something like this, you can't stop it.

And they had picked up a fair amount of momentum, hadn't they? He could envision the ball rolling—a ball of snow thundering down a hill, accreting more snow as it went, becoming heavier and unstoppable.

Jeremy, he thought then, had possessed some dizzying momentum of his own.

Jeremy had been forever in motion. When he had pedaled his bicycle into the driveway, he had managed a trick—dismounting without losing even an iota of his remarkable momentum. No matter how many times he had been chastised, he had kept on. In his mind's eye, Keyes could see the trick as clearly as if he had seen it just yesterday. Jeremy slipping off the banana seat, barging toward the front door as the bicycle continued to roll into the carport, finally coming to rest against one wall. The bicycle never fell down. Why *should* Jeremy have stopped doing the trick, despite the scolding? The bicycle never fell down. It rolled neatly over the gravel and came gently to rest, propping itself against a wall as if by magic, and by then Jeremy was inside the house, finding a snack, moving toward the television or the computer, having maintained that remarkable momentum that had carried him through life at such high speeds . . .

He was dozing.

No, he was awake. He shifted in the seat. Up front, the driver was listening to quiet talk radio.

He yawned. He wasn't dozing. He wasn't even sleepy.

The radio droned.

He slept.

3.

There was a message from Dietz.

Keyes sat in his darkened office, dialing. *Let it be good news,* he thought. If it was good news—if they had found Epstein, and finally taken care of the man—then he would reward himself with a morning off. A heavy breakfast, followed by a nap. If it was good news, the diet could go to blazes. But if not . . .

"Dietz," a voice said.

"It's Jim Keyes," Keyes said.

Dietz hesitated—and Keyes knew immediately that it was not good news.

They had taken care of Epstein, Dietz reported. But there had been complications.

The man's cabin and luggage had been searched, to no result. So it seemed as if Epstein had left no record of his work. But there was a possible problem. Leonard had seen the man and his wife talking with a young woman, at the fortress of Sapienza, in a way that Leonard had judged to be all too intense. There had been something between them—something of considerable importance to Epstein. And so it was possible, Dietz admitted, that in fact Epstein *had* kept a record of his work. It was even possible that he had been in league with the young woman, in some capacity. Perhaps she represented a foreign interest . . .

Keyes put his head in one hand as his other held the telephone. His fingers moved: small circles, circles within circles. So Epstein had sold out, after all. After so much progress, they would be stopped by this—an old-fashioned security leak. Not only would they lose the formula, but it might also fall into enemy hands. And the prospect of the formula in the wrong hands was utterly terrifying.

But Keyes himself wouldn't be around long enough to suffer the consequences. When the Project came tumbling down, whose shoulders would the ruins come to rest on? On his shoulders, of course. He had not gone to the DIA, when it had become necessary, looking for help. He had run cover for Greenwich. And now he would be the one to pay the price.

It was all finished.

"Who is she?" he asked, still rubbing at his temple.

"That's a good question." Dietz sounded faintly amused. The man's voice, Keyes thought, possessed a rather disturbing ironic distance. "Perhaps I could ask her myself. Somehow they cut a deal with the local authorities; the ship's heading straight to Istanbul. We could meet it there and take her off."

"Istanbul," Keyes repeated.

"Right. Day after tomorrow . . ."

"What hotel?" Keyes asked. "I'm coming out."

NINE

I.

Henri Jansen reached across Madeleine's body, found his pack of Gauloises on the nightstand, and lit two.

"I need to go," Madeleine said.

But she accepted a cigarette anyway. She smoked with her eyes shut, a faint smile playing around her lips.

"I've got a big day tomorrow," she went on. "My husband has organized a hiking trip from les Cabassols. Tony Blair's best friend from childhood is going to be there. And a Saudi prince. And a famous American, a white-collar criminal. Why is it that Americans get famous for being criminals?"

Henri looked off into the gloom, and didn't answer.

"Oh, I guess it's not just Americans," Madeleine said airily. She was an attractive woman in her mid-thirties—careless and flirty, on the surface, although from time to time Henri had seen something sweetly sad beneath the careless veneer. "Anyway. Can you imagination how the conversation will go? All about horse racing, I bet. They all own thoroughbreds, you know. They race them, like boys with toy cars."

Henri smoked, and made no comment.

"Well," she said, and handed the Gauloise back to him. "I've really got to go."

As she showered, he stayed in bed, alternating drags from each cigarette. Depression was nipping at him, stealthy and insistent. But there was no need to feel depressed, Henri thought. Why, this was what he had always dreamed of. Look how far he had come from the days when he hadn't been able to afford even a single cigarette—the days when, as a child in Paris, he had been forced to forage butts off the street.

But now: a cigarette for each hand. A different woman for each part of the day. A beautiful house, rent-free. Who could have asked for more?

When the shower was finished, he watched Madeleine dress. Then he left the bed, kissed the back of her neck, and walked her to her car, naked. He kissed her again and watched as the Audi rolled away down the long driveway.

He stood alone in the cool twilight, trying to keep the nipping depression at bay.

The mistral, he noticed, was gaining force.

This surprised him. During summers, the cool north wind was usually manageable. It was during the winters that it escorted ice-cold air down from the Rhône, blasting across southern France with a vengeance. But in the winters, of course, Henri was not here to see it. In the winters he went to Aspen, or the Ivory Coast, or South Beach. He had never owned a house in his life—but he had many friends who owned houses in the best locations, who were always eager to offer them for Henri Jansen's use.

Patrons, he thought. By making their fancy houses available to him, the friends were supporting his career as a photographer . . . although nearly a full year had passed since he had last put film in his camera, let alone snapped a picture. Yes; in the old days, they would have been called patrons.

The depression stirred again.

Before going back inside, he took a short stroll around the grounds. The sun was purpling, sinking toward the horizon. The vineyards were never more lovely than at sunset, Henri thought. He took his time on the walk, waiting for his mood to lighten. At one point the neighbor's dog—a terrier mutt named Sylvie—fell into step beside him. For about ten minutes, they walked together. Then Sylvie caught sight of a butterfly and charged off into the fields, leaving Henri alone.

By the time he returned to the house, full dark was falling.

He showered. Madeleine's scent was still on him, in his hair and on his fingers, giving him a pleasurable tingle. They had been getting along well lately, he and Madeleine. Perhaps they had been getting along a bit too well.

Madeleine's husband, Vladimir, was a high-ranking Russian politician who once had been intimately involved with the KGB and now was intimately involved with the ongoing reform of the Russian court system. The Russian court system, Madeleine reported, was rife with corruption. And her husband, she reported, was growing filthy rich off said corruption. Lately, they spent more and more time here in Provence, squandering his ever-increasing fortune with the elite club that populated southern France during the dog days of summer: wealthy industrialists, movie stars, royalty, politicians, and socialites.

Henri was glad to have Madeleine around more often. They enjoyed each other; they had fun together. And yet her husband would not be a good man to have as an enemy. He was known in certain circles as the vulture—only in part because of his hawklike mien. The nickname also came from the man's predatory habits, and his lack of hesitancy in pursuing them. If Henri and Madeleine grew too close, Ismayalov might take notice. And that could become a problem.

But no: It was just a fling. A summer thing. Henri knew it, and he was fairly sure that Madeleine knew it, too.

After the shower, he made a quick circuit through the house, shuttering windows in case a storm came while he was out for dinner. In the sunken living room, he knelt before the fireplace to make certain the flue was closed. When he stood, he found himself looking at the room's tremendous picture windows. A lot of good shuttering the small panes all through the house would do, with these sheets of glass still open to the elements. Yet he was only following orders.

Officially, Henri was here as a house-sitter. It was his responsibility to make sure the pipes didn't burst, the scorpions didn't run wild, the refrigerator and the wine cellar didn't become empty. In reality, of course, he was here to be available to the lady of the house—an American whom he jokingly called Princess—whenever the mood took her. But Princess was in Rome, at least through the end of the month, with her husband.

At some point in the near future, Princess had hinted, she might even make a gift of this house to Henri. That would have been a blessing. Two rambling stories near Aix-en-Provence, with ten acres and three guest bungalows and a swimming pool and proximity to all the best summering celebrities, would have been a very nice blessing indeed. If he owned this house, he wouldn't need to worry so much about the constant upkeep of his body and his tan. He could allow himself to age gracefully. Perhaps he could even find the time to concentrate again on his photography.

But he didn't own the house, not for the time being. And he did not believe that Princess really intended to make a gift of it, ever. It was simply a lure that she dangled in front of him, to keep him interested.

So it was time to go to work.

Work, tonight, involved an Italian named Isabella DiMeglio, whose husband spent too much time in the office and not enough time focusing on his wife. The husband owned a house in the Bahamas. Henri had his eye on that house.

He finished his check of the windows, returned to the bedroom, splashed on cologne, and checked himself in the mirror. He flashed a grin, fixed his cuffs, and then went to keep his dinner date.

PART TWO

TEN

I.

Keyes closed the suitcase and then glanced at the clock radio by the bedside. In twenty minutes, the car would arrive. He went through a final mental checklist—toothbrush, laptop, latest Grisham paperback, cell phone. All in order.

He tried to think of other things, things he would inevitably remember as soon as he was on his way. Visit the bathroom before leaving, of course, as his mother had drilled into him before every trip they had ever taken as a family. He stepped into the bathroom and unzipped. Grab a fresh battery for the cell, he thought. And—

The doorbell rang.

He zipped up quickly, left the bathroom, and trotted down the stairs, his footsteps echoing tremendously. The thought that they had once been concerned about having enough room, in this cavernous house, now seemed laughable. Back then there had been Rachel and Jeremy and Margot, in addition to Keyes himself, to fill the empty space. What would they do when grandchildren came? They had seriously considered building an addition. Now Jeremy was gone, Margot was gone, and Rachel was gone—moved in with her mother in Belmont. Even Keyes himself felt half gone. Once four people had lived in this house. Now, he thought, there was but a half a person, half a man.

Ah, but he knew that maudlin voice. His shrink had warned him about listening to that voice. He moved to the front door, forcing his mind back to the present. One thing he had learned never to expect was an early car—but life was full of surprises.

He opened the door and found himself facing Henry Chen.

2.

They carried diet lemonade to the patio around back.

Chen was on the short side, with a prematurely graying beard, wire-rimmed spectacles, and narrow shoulders shaped like a coat hanger. Unlike many of the scientists with whom Keyes dealt, Chen took the trouble to groom himself. This morning he was wearing a blue oxford shirt open at the collar, khakis, and loafers. Yet he was eccentric, as all the geniuses of the world seemed to be. A perpetual grin was plastered on his face, as if he understood the importance of this social convention; but the grin bore no relation to anything. Chen wore it as a mask, and the disconnect between his words and his expression was sometimes eerie.

After they had stepped onto the patio, Chen spent a moment looking out at the back lawn, grinning. The lawn was stippled with red, white, and blue pinwheels left over from the Fourth of July. Keyes noted this with mild surprise. The holiday was nearly a month in the past. If Rachel had still lived here, she would have cleared away the pinwheels long ago.

Presently, Chen turned from the yard. "I'm sorry to stop by so early," he said. "I hoped to catch you before you hit the office."

Keyes waved a dismissive hand, as if he was accustomed to having employees drop by at all hours unannounced. He took a seat in a gingham-pillowed lawn chair, as if time was of no matter and he was not expecting a car at any minute. If he could get rid of Chen before the car arrived, he would be spared making any explanations. He sipped at the lemonade—cool and clean, cutting through the humidity like a blade through water.

Chen moved to a second piece of lawn furniture, and seemed on the verge of sitting. Then he turned to look at the unlit floodlights hanging in the backyard. "Put those in recently?" he asked.

Keyes tried and failed to recall when Chen had been at his house before. "About a year ago," he said. "You should see it in the winter— the way the light hits the snow."

"Oh, I bet. Must be beautiful."

An awkward silence ensued. Chen tilted his head back farther, to drink in the buttery dawn.

"Do you know," he asked conversationally, "that Eratosthenes was able to figure out the approximate circumference of the earth, using only the sun to guide him? He compared the angles the sun made at Syene and Alexandria. He wasn't exactly right, but he was fairly close—considering."

"Smart guy," Keyes said.

"Amazing accomplishment," Chen agreed. "But you've got some guys working for you that are nearly as impressive, you know. Ed Greenwich, for instance. The man's a flat-out genius. And Steve Epstein . . . wow. I'll tell you something, Jim. These guys are way out of my league."

Keyes waited to see where the false modesty was leading. He thought he had a pretty good idea of where that might be.

"Speaking of Steve," Chen said casually. "I've been wondering . . ."

He looked away from the sky. His eyes, in the faint light, looked large and exceptionally soft.

"Where *is* Steve?"

Keyes said nothing; a quiet wind stirred the pinwheels into motion.

For a few moments, they looked at each other in silence. Then—amazingly—for the first time in Keyes's experience—Chen's grin slipped away.

"He disappeared last week," Chen said. "No good-byes, nothing. So I did a little poking around. All records of his work are gone. But you know that already, don't you?"

Keyes nodded soberly.

"Where is he?"

"On vacation. With his wife."

"Just like that?"

Keyes shrugged.

"And his work?"

"Evidently he felt the need to erase it."

"Because he'd found something. Something that scared him."

Again, Keyes said nothing.

"How are you going to handle this?" Chen asked.

"I'm not sure I know what . . ."

"His results concerned him—enough for him to take them away. Because he didn't think you'd listen, I guess, if he tried to put the brakes on. You, or those above you. Are you going to respect his decision?"

Keyes pretended the question had been rhetorical.

"I'd like to think he was wrong," Chen continued after a moment. "I'd like to think that you are willing to listen to reason. That's why I'm here, Jim. To try to talk some sense into you."

Keyes felt a flash of anger at Chen's condescension. He pushed it down. "Talk away," he said. "I'm listening."

"There's always a danger, when concerns of science get wrapped up with industry or politics. That's why we're lucky to have men like you at the top. Men who understand the possible repercussions of what we do. Your own background in differential geometry may not be strong, Jim, but you're smart enough to trust the opinions of those who do know."

Flattery now, Keyes thought. Just another form of condescension. He felt the flash of anger again, and drowned it in some diet lemonade.

"Between nanotechnology and genetic engineering, nuclear waste and stem cells, projects like ours . . . humanity is going to need to navigate some new moral terrain in the very near future. I'm a scientist, Jim. I know better than anyone that progress is inevitable. But we must progress carefully—and we must do what we do for the right reasons. If we allow political or industrial pressures to dictate—"

"Henry," Keyes interrupted. "I'm sorry, but I've got an early meeting. Could we cut to the chase?"

Chen paused, choosing his next words carefully.

"Put on the brakes. Until we see what Steve saw, that concerned him so much—we need to shut her down."

"That sounds excessive."

"Ed has told you he can repeat the results. Hasn't he? That's why you're not more concerned about this."

"Do I not seem concerned?"

"Ed's wrong," Chen said decisively. "He's a genius, sure. But he doesn't know his own limitations. I believe Steve is one of only a handful of men and women on earth capable of coming up with . . . whatever it was he found. A formula to precisely predict the lifetime of the singularities, wasn't it?"

Keyes raised his lemonade, just to do something, and sipped. Was that the car, pulling up around front? No, only the wind.

"What do you see as the goal of the Project?" Chen asked suddenly.

It was a trick question, Keyes sensed. He gave the textbook answer, straight from Greenwich's initial proposal. "Creating under controlled conditions a gravitational singularity that can be sustained and manipulated . . ."

"Not the textbook answer," Chen said. "The *real* goal."

"Liberated vacuum energy. Cheap, clean, safe power . . . possible defensive applications . . ."

"All bottom line. That's just my point. You've got no respect for nature. And if you don't respect Mother Nature, Jim, you're asking for serious trouble."

Keyes made a tight line out of his mouth.

"I don't mean to make threats," Chen said softly. "But if you won't listen to reason, I intend on going over your head. I respect Steve, and his opinion—more than you do, I'm afraid."

Keyes ran a hand over his face. For a few moments, both men were quiet.

"Christ," Keyes said then.

"I'm sorry to pull this on you, Jim."

"If I had any doubts, I wouldn't even consider . . ."

"You *should* have doubts. Any sane man would. That's what I'm trying to do, is raise doubts in your mind."

"I wouldn't dream of moving ahead without all possible precautions being taken."

"That's not good enough."

"What would be good enough?"

"Convince Steve that it's safe for him to share his results with us. I'll tell you how to do that. Convene a panel of outsiders to analyze the data. Outsiders with no agenda."

"By doing that, we take the chance of someone else taking the lead."

"God willing," Chen said, "they'll be careful too."

Keyes didn't answer. He rubbed at his face again. Suddenly he felt weary—weary, ancient, and somewhere near furious.

Chen was accusing him of something, he thought. At best, of hubris; at worst, of stupidity. It was all well and good for Chen to lecture him about not respecting Mother Nature. But if he turned it around and lectured Chen, about not understanding the realities of management and competition in today's world, would it get him anywhere? No. The man was an egotist, in his way. He would give advice without hesitating, but he wouldn't take it in return.

What Keyes would have liked to say was simple: that perhaps Chen respected Mother Nature too much. His respect would make him overly cautious, and they would lose the spectacular chance that faced them. As long as man was willing to accept this sad lot with which God had presented him, how could they ever truly evolve?

The universe, Keyes knew from Greenwich, was a mere fourteen billion years old. It was scientists like Chen who had arrived at this figure; yet those same scientists failed to see the dark humor of their discovery. Fourteen billion. It struck Keyes as a tiny number. For the universe to produce awe, it should have been a billion billion years old, at the very least; something incomprehensible. Not *fourteen* billion. At merely fourteen billion years old, the universe was not that impressive at all. It was like a cheap trinket one might find in a box of Cracker Jacks. Why *should* they respect this universe, and accept their lot without question? It would be cowardly, and weak.

But Chen had never needed to bury a child, he reminded himself. To Chen, the universe did not seem nearly as disrespectable as it seemed to Keyes. And so saying these things would have been a waste of breath. Worse, they would have convinced Chen that he was right—and then Chen would indeed go over his head.

Instead, he decided to placate the man.

He made a show of reluctance. He made a show of agonizing. Then he said, "You've got a point."

"I'm glad to hear you say that."

"You're right. Epstein did run. Probably because he doesn't trust me. And Greenwich has promised that he can repeat the results."

"I knew it already."

"I'll convene your panel," Keyes said. "But beyond that, I don't promise a thing. If they report that it's safe to proceed . . ."

"That's all I ask."

"Henry—thanks for coming to me. Instead of simply going up the ladder."

Chen looked taken aback, almost touched. "You're a good man," he said. "I know that."

"Trying my best."

"You've made the right decision, Jim."

"I hope so."

"I know so," Chen said.

Abruptly, Keyes stood. Chen picked up on the signal, and moved toward the screen door leading back into the house. They dropped off their glasses in the kitchen; then Keyes escorted Chen to the front door. "How's Beth?" he asked.

"Good—thank you."

"The kids?"

"Great. Amazing."

"Give them my best."

"I will," Chen said. He hesitated. "Jim," he said. "It's the right way. The only way."

A moment passed. "Drive safely," Keyes said then.

Chen grinned at him. He turned and crossed the gravel driveway, passing the carport where Jeremy had once done his trick with the bicycle, getting into his Subaru. As he left the driveway, he beeped the horn, once.

Keyes raised a hand, and watched him go.

Twenty seconds later, another car was pulling into the driveway. Keyes held up an index finger: *One second*. He went back inside, climbed the stairs, and found his suitcase.

Before leaving the bedroom, he moved to the telephone sitting by the clock radio. He picked it up and then thought for a moment, scowling. He sat down on the edge of the bed and dialed a number from memory.

Someone would need to handle Chen, and quickly, before he realized that Keyes had lied. He listened as the phone rang.

"Yello," said a voice. In the background was a television set— *Good Morning America,* Keyes thought—and a woman, talking loudly from another room.

"Roger," Keyes said. "Sorry to bother you at home . . ."

ELEVEN

I.

Yildirim seemed nervous.

Of course he did. If he was caught, he would lose his job. But it was nothing compared to what Hannah would face if they were caught, and so she had a hard time finding much sympathy for the man.

They stood together on the Sun Deck, watching as the *Aurora II* slid into port in Istanbul. From this vantage point she could make out the local wharf rats, standing with ropes in hand, waiting. She could also make out a group of men standing farther back on the dock, wearing business suits and gold watches that glistened in the twilight. Those would be the authorities, she supposed. Those would be the ones to avoid.

Yildirim used the remains of one cigarette to light another. He pitched the butt overboard, then pointed with the second cigarette at the men in suits and watches. "See there?"

Hannah nodded.

As Yildirim spoke, his eyes scanned the dock restlessly. "One more time," he said. "Once you get to Victor's home—"

Meaning Victor Bascara, the husband of a maid who worked aboard the ship. Hannah had memorized the man's address in the Western suburbs. If she was able to slip through the net, she was to get in a taxi and repeat the address to the driver. Yildirim would meet her there as soon as possible, at which point they would work out the remaining fine points: getting her on a plane at Atatürk Airport and, more important from his point of view, placing a call to her accountant, to arrange the wiring of the money.

"—be patient," he said. "It may take some time for me to get away from here. Especially once they realize you're gone."

"All right."

"But I *will* get there. Just be patient."

"All right."

Yildirim stifled a cough with his fist. "I must be losing my mind," he murmured.

As if she was to believe that he was doing this from the goodness of his heart. As if the money wasn't even part of the equation.

Hannah said nothing.

Beyond the dock lay the city of Istanbul at dusk. If it had been earlier in the night, she thought—if there had been more light in the sky—then perhaps Istanbul would have looked more exotic. As it was, she could hardly make out the ancient mosques, looming over the city behind veils of smog. The old city, which had been a world power for sixteen long centuries—first as Byzantium, then as Constantinople, and now as Istanbul—was nowhere to be seen. In its stead were congested traffic, fast-food restaurants, and distant buildings almost tall enough to be called skyscrapers.

Now the wharf rats were coming forward, catching lines thrown from the ship and throwing lines back in exchange. Yildirim drew on his cigarette so hard that the tobacco crackled. "Ready?" he asked.

Hannah hesitated for a moment before answering. The night was warm, but once she was in the water it would be cold. She had never been fond of water. But beggars couldn't be choosers.

She nodded again. "As I'll ever be," she said.

2.

Keyes overate on the flight—accepting everything offered to him, and then taking seconds.

To hell with the diet, he thought. He popped a jumbo shrimp into his mouth and chewed greedily. When this was finished, he would go back on the straight and narrow. Until then he needed to be at his most alert, which could hardly be done on fifteen hundred calories a day.

After gorging himself, he leaned back, trying to clear his mind. Around him the Gulfstream IV-SP whispered soft white noise. This was a chance for rest. He closed his eyes, hoping to doze.

Upon landing, he checked his cell phone. He had forgotten a fresh battery but it hardly mattered; his network evidently didn't have a server in Turkey. The phone was useless.

He was pleased to find that Dietz had come to pick him up personally.

They drove into the city—heading directly for the quay, Dietz explained, because the ship had already docked and the passengers would be disembarking within the hour. Everything was under control. By the end of the day, they would have the woman, whoever she was, safely in custody. From the passenger roster he had gotten a name—Victoria Ludlow—but that was almost certainly an alias.

Dietz hardly lived up to the picture Keyes had assembled of the man in his mind. He was tall and barrel-chested, in his late fifties, with a wide jaw and squarish head that reminded Keyes of the actor James Caan. His most striking feature was his gray eyes, which were mild and drifting, with a buzz underneath. Except for that buzz, Dietz didn't strike Keyes as a particularly forceful type. He seemed more like an aging hippie, a gentle soul who had somehow gone adrift—a Jimmy Caan who had learned a few hard life lessons, who had gotten his fill of bar brawls and was now looking elsewhere for answers.

Keyes remembered the man's tone over the telephone, the hint of ironic distance that he had found disturbing. Perhaps there had been a personal betrayal in his past, Keyes thought. Perhaps that was why the man seemed so gentle, on the surface, with a hint of something curdled underneath. Some vital part of him had given up.

But a dark side had been there once. Otherwise he would not have been in Roger Ford's Rolodex. And must still be there somewhere, Keyes guessed, buried beneath the deceptively calm façade.

Leonard was at the dock, Dietz explained in his laid-back way, in case the woman tried to disembark early. As the passengers came off the ship, their papers would be checked. Then, if Dietz had read things correctly, they would be escorted by the local authorities to the Istanbul Hyatt. There they would be interviewed by the FBI, who had taken a pair of suites on the top floor. The time to take the woman into custody would be before the FBI became involved—before she was brought to the hotel. With the Turks, a few dollars greasing the right palm would do the trick.

Keyes listened. The FBI could become a problem, he thought. To have the Bureau sniffing around ADS was all he needed. He would need to call in a favor to stop the investigation before it went too far. But he would worry about that later. After they had the woman; after they had their answers.

They were approaching the twilit city. Soon, now, he thought.

Somehow, despite his overeating on the flight, he was hungry again already.

3.

The crane on the *Aurora II*'s port side—located directly opposite the disembarkation ramp on the starboard—was used to raise and lower Zodiacs, tenders, or lifeboats, depending on the ship's location and circumstances. But this, Hannah thought, was surely the first time it had been used on human cargo.

She watched apprehensively as Yildirim lowered the steel cable, letting it out a few jerky feet at a time so that the sound of the gears would not attract undue attention. Her suspicion that someone would come on deck and catch them was near certainty. Yildirim had assured her that there was no cause for concern. Double-checking the ship's equipment, as the crew prepared to disembark at the end of a cruise, fell well within his purview. Hannah supposed that made sense. If she hadn't felt so wound up, she supposed, then she wouldn't have been worrying so much.

But she *was* wound up. Her blood was pumping through her veins, making her insides feel loose and shaky. Her face felt hot. For the first time in longer than she could remember, she had a craving for a cigarette.

Yildirim leaned over the side of the ship, checked the cable's progress, let out another foot for good measure, and then straightened. He nodded. Hannah stepped forward cautiously. Farther out on the water, ferries and ocean liners slipped stealthily through the night.

As she looked over the railing, her spirit quailed. The drop was not far—even if she lost her grip on the cable, she would tumble only a dozen and a half feet—but the water looked brackish and chilly. As a matter of course she had always avoided chlorinated swimming pools. And now she was going to immerse herself in this polluted water . . .

She swallowed, with a click.

Then put her hands on the cable—it was oily; her hands would be filthy from touching that cable—and let him help her put one leg over the side.

She was wearing a pair of shorts and a tank top. Her purse, doubly wrapped in a plastic laundry bag from her cabin's closet, was slung across her chest like a knapsack. Would the plastic bag keep the water out? Her money and traveler's checks and passport and jewelry and a change of clothes were all inside that purse, along with a few miscellaneous items that had been in there already: the *Chronicles* book, her pills, her makeup. Without the purse, she had nothing.

Before raising her other leg, she shot a glance over her shoulder. The quay was filling with people. Once she had reached the water, she would need to take a deep breath and swim underwater for at least fifty feet, or the people would see her. Her eyes moved to the end of the dock—past the assembling crowd and the crane jibs and the white fingers of light coming from the customs office. If she could get that far, she would be safe. But she would not be able to do it with a single breath. At some point, she would need to rise to the surface to take a second breath, and hope that nobody was looking at that particular spot of water at that particular instant.

No, no, no, she thought petulantly. *I don't want to. You can't make me.*

A few seconds passed. She remained frozen, one leg hiked over the railing, both hands clutching the steel line.

Then Yildirim was urging her other leg up.

She took a deep breath and threw her weight forward, onto the cable.

4.

Keyes and Dietz stood inside the customs station, looking out at the ship as the passengers disembarked. A pair of customs agents checked the passengers' papers as they came off the gangplank, then steered them into a different section of the building. Behind the *Aurora II*, the Bosporus glittered dully.

After a few moments of watching, Keyes looked back into the rear of the station. Leonard was there, jangling car keys in one hand. When the woman came off the ship, she would be ushered into this room by one of the customs officers. Then Keyes and Dietz would take over, following Leonard out a rear exit, into a waiting car. The local authorities would not interfere. Two hundred dollars had taken care of that. Somehow, this suddenly struck Keyes as funny. The budget for the Project was astronomical; and yet a mere two hundred dollars, for this most crucial part of things, had been more than sufficient. A minute smile tugged at his lips.

In a moment, they would have the woman. Then he could go home, and get back to the business of business.

He looked out the window again, at the passengers filing slowly forward, and the smile slipped away.

Something was wrong.

No. Everything had been set up just so.

But the feeling remained. The woman was no amateur, after all. She had not gotten this far by chance. And she would not walk right into their clutches, now—not without putting up a fight. But how? There was nowhere for her to go.

Suddenly he wished he could see the other side of the ship, the side facing away from the dock.

For another moment, he stood, fighting the impulse to leave the customs station. Then he turned to Dietz.

"Wait here," he said, and headed for the door.

5.

Docks were like snowflakes, Keyes thought as he stepped outside: all the same, yet all different.

This one was light on the fish smell, for which he was grateful. During his childhood he had spent enough time on fishy-smelling docks in New England to last him for the rest of his lifetime. It was heavy on bustle and chill (somehow a dock could be chilly even on the warmest evenings) and slippery concrete.

He took a few steps toward the *Aurora*'s stern. He would not be able to see around to the ship's port side, no matter how far down the dock he walked. But he would be able to see where the woman went *after* she had come off the port side, if she came in this direction.

Where had this idea come from? He didn't know. Logic was hardly involved. In all likelihood, he was just tired. But there was nothing to be lost by strolling a few dozen feet down the quay, by checking things out, to be on the safe side.

Someone in the city was singing: a high, ululating trill that set his nerves on edge.

When he had gone perhaps forty feet, he turned to look back. Beyond the tangled cranes, the passengers were still filing slowly off the ship. The ship itself looked remarkably diminutive, from this small remove. To his right was the Bosporus, chopping in the evening breeze; to his left, beyond the fringe of buildings, the sprawling city.

It wouldn't do to get too far away. When they took the woman into custody, things would happen fast. He would not want to be left behind.

But he turned and strolled a little farther anyway.

Here, at the end of the dock, was a low chain-link fence. By the fence were people. There were two or three—men, he thought; just sitting, smoking and drinking. Vagrants, or dockworkers taking a break. Either way, he didn't feel comfortable walking into their midst. He had come far enough.

He stopped walking again, then raised a hand to rub at his eyes. His instincts had been wrong. There was nothing down this way except the men and the fence.

When he took his hand from his eyes, he saw the woman.

She had appeared very near the fence. She looked like a wet rat—staying low to the ground, dripping and sleek. A shimmering trail led from her feet to the water's edge.

He blinked. Yes, it was a woman. She was moving directly toward the vagrants, or whatever they were. She was saying something. They answered with muted laughter. Then she was bending down—still very near to the ground, so near that she might have been only a shadow—and slipping through a tear in the fence.

Had he imagined it? His eyes were tired; his brain was tired.

No. He saw her again, through the fence now, straightening up on the other side. She was holding something. Epstein's formula?

For a moment, he hesitated. Then he moved forward.

TWELVE

I.

Hannah was freezing.

As she'd gone through the fence, she had scraped her arm. Now, half jogging across an empty lot beside the dock—heading toward an alley that seemed to feed into the city proper—she cradled the arm into her body. The scraped, chilly flesh was stippled with goose bumps. There would be fresh scars, she thought, right beside the old pale ones. Her body would become a canvas, telling the story of her various hardships in a rainbow of welts and blemishes. Thirty years of salons, seaweed wraps, and massages had left her flesh too tender for the real world. Now her body was receiving a wake-up call.

Once she had reached the alley, she drew herself to her full height. Her hands scrabbled at the plastic bag around the purse, tearing it off.

Her hands were shaking, but she tried to ignore that. She would change out of the wet clothes right here, in this relative privacy—pedestrians passed by the mouth of the alley, but didn't seem to be glancing into the darkness. Her hair would still be damp when she got into a cab, but there was nothing to be done about that.

The water of the Bosporus had been oily. She could smell it clinging to her skin. Upon opening the purse, she spied a vial of perfume, seized it with her shaky hands, and splashed a drop into her palm. The palm moved behind her ears, under her neck, touched the inside of her wrist. The perfume went back into the purse. She reached for the change of clothes—

—and then some overpowering intuition made her glance back over her shoulder.

A man was hurrying across the lot. Moving in her direction.

Fear took her in a strong, crushing bear hug; suddenly she was no longer cold.

2.

Keyes had the cell phone to his ear before he remembered that it was useless.

He jammed it back into his pocket with a curse. All the preparation in the world—all the resources and the employees and the feng shui and the 900 MHz cell phones using spread-spectrum technology—all a waste of time.

For a moment, he was torn by indecision. He was unable to contact his men. Should he follow the woman himself, on foot, or head back and let Dietz know what had happened?

There was no time. Already she was moving away again. She had seen him.

He gave chase.

By the time he reached the alley, the woman was gone. A wet trail showed her path toward the sidewalk. Keyes moved past a pile of garbage that reeked of rotten spices. Mingled with the stench was the incongruous odor of perfume. Would the woman really have paused, at that crucial moment, to apply perfume? He couldn't believe it.

His first impression upon reaching the street was that the city looked far more modern than he had expected.

Reckless drivers, horns blaring, wove in and out of throngs of jay-walkers. The sun had gone down, but women walked on the street with not only their faces and shoulders uncovered, but also their arms, legs, and a fair amount of thigh—thoroughly liberated Muslims. Hot-pretzel vendors kicked pigeons out of their way as they wheeled their carts backward through cramped streets. To his right was a Pizza Hut; to his left, a McDonald's.

His second impression was that the woman had already disappeared.

Not possible. His eyes moved down to the trail of water, snaking away into the crowd. He followed it, bulling his way forward.

There—a yellow taxicab, half a block away. The back of the woman's head was visible through the rear windshield. The cab was idling in the heavy traffic.

Then the traffic opened up, and the cab pulled away.

Keyes turned, looking for a cab of his own. Since arriving, he had not changed any money. He had only American dollars. But a taxi was there, one of a large fleet of taxis, so he hailed it anyway. He slipped into the backseat and then delivered a line that made him feel suddenly absurd: "Follow that cab."

The driver looked at him blankly. He pointed, gesturing. "Follow," he said. "Please."

The driver nodded, and the cab jerked forward.

He had left the meter untouched, meaning that he would try to gouge Keyes when the ride was finished. Keyes leaned back in the seat, holding his breath without realizing it.

At the next light, the woman's cab turned right. They followed. The street narrowed as pavement gave way to cobblestones; fast-food joints were replaced by European-style cafés and boutiques. They turned again, and suddenly clotheslines crossed from one overhead window to another. A man in a three-piece suit blocked their way. Beside the man was a donkey cart—a shocking juxtaposition. The driver leaned on his horn. The man in the suit and the donkey cart got out of the way; the driver goosed the accelerator and slipped between them.

For almost a full minute, they drove at a good clip. Now there were fewer cars, more carts; the streets narrowed further, and the architecture turned antiquated. Then the woman's cab was slowing again, blocked by a stream of Japanese tourists coming out of a recessed doorway. They had reached the famed Kapali Çarşi: the Old Bazaar.

In the next moment the woman was leaving her cab, ducking past the Japanese, losing herself in the crowd.

Keyes threw open his own door, ignoring the driver who called after him. One good cheat, he thought fleetingly, deserved another.

3.

Stepping into the covered main passage of the Old Bazaar was like stepping back in time.

The air filled with the odors of brass polish, incense, sweat, roasting lamb, and oil; the smells of exhaust and hot pretzels fell away. The local Turks wore turbans and veils, as compared to the modern clothing that Hannah had seen on the streets outside. There were Kurds,

Jews, Greeks, Armenians, Japanese, Americans, Germans, French. The wood-floored hall was crowded with silver and gold, amber, leather, carpets, platinum, silks, samovars, stuffed cobras, antique firearms, and everywhere the lilt of vendors hawking their wares:

"Genuine weapons from the Ottoman Empire! Swords and daggers, mother-of-pearl on the sheaths! Replicas of fine revolvers!"

"Handcrafted silver serving trays! Fine silks and cloths, pillows and gowns, robes and veils, souvenirs, bargain prices!"

"Copper and brass! Hand-beaten pots! Ceramics! Sterling silver! Kilims, Sumaks!"

Hannah plunged into the crowd, casting a glance back to see if the man was following. What was he? FBI? A U.S. Marshal? Or just an overeager local customs authority? The doorway leading to the street already was lost behind the crush of people. But she thought that she caught a glimpse of the man, plowing into the sea of humanity, still on her trail.

She faced forward again.

The bazaar was divided into a series of halls, with each hall focusing on a specific type of merchandise. As she moved down the main concourse—swept along by the tide of tourists and locals, hardly in control of her direction—she caught glimpses of corridors lined with silver, corridors lined with turquoise, corridors lined with hanging carpets. A crucial question came to mind: Did the corridors open onto separate exits, or did they terminate in dead ends? There was one way to find out, of course. But if the man followed her and it turned out to be a dead end . . .

. . . at least it was a chance.

She ducked to her right, nearly toppled a boy carrying a tray of sweet apple tea, then dodged a man balancing a pile of carpets on his head. For an instant, she considered entering a hallway lined with musical instruments: the narrow fiddle called *Kemençe,* the cylindrical *Zurna.* But the corridor was popular, and crowded. She chose a slightly less crowded hallway across the way, and took off.

The hallway featured brass: brass chessboards with pieces modeled on characters from *Lord of the Rings,* brass hookahs with aromatic incense burning in clay trays. For a crazy moment, some old part of her, the shopping part, wanted to pause and buy something. She could stop and haggle with one of these vendors, and perhaps she would blend in so naturally that the man behind her would simply pass her by. Shopping, after all, was her natural state.

Then she was approaching a stall that broke ranks from its neighbors by featuring silks, and the idea began to seem less crazy. She saw veils, hanging in rows beside gowns, robes, and a neon sign advertising *Coca-Cola/Budweiser/Marlboro.* Once donned, a veil would cover everything but her eyes.

The shopkeeper stepped forward to intercept her. *"Française?"* he said.

Hannah managed a smile. *"Non, américaine."*

"Mais vous parlez bien le français."

It was a prearranged speech, which no doubt flattered Middle American housewives to no end. She kept the smile on her face, reaching out to finger one of the silk scarves. "How much?" she asked.

"Kaç lira? Or American dollars?"

"Dollars, please."

Tourists streamed past, elbowing her rudely. She held her purse tighter and kept her eyes locked on the shopkeeper. If the man had seen her turn down the corridor, if he had followed, then he would be drawing near. "For you—twenty dollars."

"And with the—" She waved at one of the robes. What were they called in this part of the world? "How much with this?"

"That is my finest product. One hundred dollars. But for you? Eighty dollars with the yashmak. Because I like your face."

"Can I try them on?"

He showed a mouthful of blackened teeth, and took the yashmak and robe from their rack.

Hannah let the man help her slip into the silks, transferring her purse from her right hand to her left in the process. He must have felt the wet on her clothes. But he already would have seen that her hair was damp. Would he make a comment?

He did not. No doubt he had seen even stranger things, from American tourists on vacation in Istanbul.

"Very nice," he said, as he draped the yashmak over her hair. "A natural fit. As if it was made for you."

"Really?"

Someone passed by again, jostling the arm with the purse; she ignored it.

"So natural that I will lower the price: seventy-five dollars."

"Have you got a mirror?"

He swept an arm into the booth, cordially. She took a step forward and saw a glass mounted on the stall's back wall. She moved closer, wrapping the yashmak more tightly over her face. As she pretended to study her reflection, she stared at the corridor behind her.

The man who was following her was there.

4.

Had he been mistaken?

He could have sworn he had caught a glimpse of the woman slipping down this hallway. But he was within sight of the end—the corridor terminated abruptly in a grate before a wall of what looked like limestone. And he had not seen the woman.

He turned around again, frustrated. The hallways were a labyrinth; he found himself disoriented. Perhaps he should go back to the mouth of the Old Bazaar, and wait for her to make a reappearance. Or perhaps she had found some other exit, and he would just be wasting his time. If only the goddamned cell phone had been working, he could have called for backup. But no; he was on his own.

Around him, the Turks hawked their merchandise. An overweight American was arguing with one. "But I don't have anyplace to *put* a lamp," he was saying doubtfully. In the next stall, a woman was admiring her reflection in a mirror as she tried on the local uniform. Hardly an inch of her skin was exposed.

Keyes raised a hand to his temple. If only he'd slept more on the flight, and was thinking more clearly . . .

"At these prices," the American was being told, "what does it matter?"

Then Keyes began to move back toward the main corridor. She had not come down this hallway after all, he decided. This was a fool's errand. He was looking for a needle in a haystack.

But a feeling was with him: eyes burning into his back.

He was missing something, wasn't he? Yes. But what? The woman *had* come down this corridor. He had not imagined it. And then she had—

—stopped to buy a disguise.

He turned again.

The woman before the mirror was there, a dozen feet away, reaching into her pocketbook.

5.

"Seventy-five dollars," Hannah repeated.

It was highway robbery. No doubt the man had expected her to bargain him down to half that price—but she didn't have the time. She reached into her purse.

And found that her wallet was missing.

Her tongue came out and slipped over her lips. The book was there; her passport was there; her change of clothes was there. But the wallet was gone. When she had been jostled, she thought. That was when the pickpocket had struck.

She looked back up at the vendor and smiled weakly. "Oh dear," she started. "I'm afraid—"

Then a hand closed around her wrist, hard.

It was the man from customs—digging his fingers into her flesh with enough force to bruise. But he seemed at a loss for what to do next. If he dragged her away physically, how would the vendor react? Instead he wavered, holding on to her wrist with his right hand, his left coming up and then pausing.

Hannah had time to gather a hasty impression of the man. Late forties, slightly paunchy, with an intense cast to his features. He wore dark slacks and a white dress shirt with heavy sweat stains under the arms. He was not like any government agent she had imagined. He was an office worker, she thought—a bureaucrat. Who was this man, and what was he doing here, harassing her?

The vendor was watching nervously. Hannah reached out and grabbed the arm of her harasser, even as he held on to hers. They held each other and she turned to the vendor and said, very calmly, "This man has stolen my wallet."

The vendor looked away.

But now another man was coming forward—the overweight American who had been bargaining over the lamp. "Why don't you take your hand off the lady?" he asked.

Still the bureaucrat hesitated. "This man took my wallet," Hannah said again, louder.

"Pal," the tourist said. "Take your hands off her. All right?"

Now another group was moving in their direction—Europeans, on the young side, hardly more than teenagers. "Is problem?" one asked.

"It's under control," the American said. "If this gentleman would just let the lady go . . ."

The man let go of Hannah's arm; but she kept holding on to his. "He took my wallet. And he's been following me."

The teenagers were surrounding them in a loose circle. The man shook his head, and finally found his voice. "This woman is a fugitive. There's—"

"You got her wallet, buddy?"

"No, no. I represent a—"

"You wouldn't mind emptying your pockets, would you?"

Hannah let go and took a step away. The vendor's eyes followed her—she was still wearing the silks. When she realized the source of his concern, she immediately pulled off the yashmak and handed it back, then went to work on unwrapping the robe.

Now the bureaucrat was looking defensive. His eyes darted from the American to the teenagers, then fell on Hannah. For an instant, she saw something smoldering beneath the defensiveness—hot anger.

She finished peeling off the robe, and handed it to the vendor.

"Don't look at her," the American instructed. "Look at me. Let's see what's in your pockets."

"Sir. You don't—"

"I'm not going to ask again."

Suddenly, the bureaucrat's face turned agreeable, conciliatory. "Sir," he repeated. "I understand how this might look to you. But believe me, you don't have all the—"

Hannah slipped away.

She felt the bureaucrat lunging after her; and she felt the teenagers moving to restrain him. A final glance over her shoulder revealed that the American had his hand on the bureaucrat's shoulder now. She hurried off.

"—asked twice already. I warned you—"

Back past the *Lord of the Rings* chessboard, the incense-burning brass hookahs; then back into the main hall. A trio of blue-suited policemen was moving past her, the designation *emniyet* sewn onto their uniforms. They turned down the hall from which she had come, running toward voices still gaining in volume.

Then the crowd picked her up like so much driftwood, sweeping her back toward the main entrance.

THIRTEEN

I.

For as long as he could remember, Francis Dietz's eyes had drawn comment.

His mother, rest her soul, had praised their acuity and exceptional clarity. His schoolmates had praised their unique grayish hue. The agents he had run in New York had commented first on their quickness, and, as time had passed, on their unnatural depth—his eyes, more than one person had said, seemed to go on forever.

In the years since New York, his eyes had continued to change.

Now they no longer went on forever. Now they closed off after one penetrated any distance into them, driving the invader in a different direction, like a hall of mirrors. Behind the hall of mirrors, Dietz supposed, his eyes still went on forever. That was why he could see so much that others missed. But over the years he had learned to cover this look—to keep the interlopers out and keep his secrets for himself.

Dietz had many secrets.

Now, as his eyes flicked across the quay, Dietz saw many things.

He saw that something had gone wrong. Keyes had been gone for only six minutes, but intuition told Dietz that the man was not coming back any time soon. Somehow the woman had pulled something, and somehow Keyes had gotten pulled along with her. Because she was not working alone, Dietz thought. A single woman couldn't have pulled Keyes away without some kind of help.

And he saw something else. He saw it in the face of the chief security officer of the *Aurora II*, a Turk named Yildirim. Yildirim's eyes were sleepy, but beneath the lassitude was something else, something guilty and cagey.

Just intuition. But intuition had served Dietz well over the years. He had learned to trust it.

He stood in the customs office, betraying none of his suspicions, coolly watching the man named Yildirim through the frosted-glass window.

2.

The disembarkation went on for two and a half hours.

At last, the final passenger had been put into a car and sent to the hotel. The customs officials mused over clipboards, perhaps discussing the whereabouts of a single missing passenger, a young woman named Victoria Ludlow. Leonard milled around the outskirts of the cluster of men, trying to overhear snatches of conversation while looking as if he belonged there.

Chief Security Officer Yildirim was talking with the customs officers. He was shrugging. He looked angry and tired and frustrated. But his eyes and his body language betrayed something else: hidden secrets, and impatience to get away.

Dietz watched, taking it all in.

Presently, Leonard came back into the office. He moved to Dietz and said in a low voice, "Where the fuck is Keyes?"

Dietz glanced down, at the top of the little man's head. He was fond of Leonard. God had played a terrible joke on the man, but Dietz had not seen him manifest a trace of self-pity. Leonard reminded Dietz of the type of man he had been surrounded by when he had been a part of the agency. Men of purpose; men with backbone. Lately, he had not been surrounded by men like this. Lately, he had spent most of his time by himself: hiding on his farm, soaking in self-pity.

"This is fucked up," Leonard went on. "What are we supposed to do now?"

Dietz considered. "You'll wait here," he said. "In case Keyes shows up."

"What about you?"

"I'll be back. Keep an eye out. She may have found a hiding place on board, and plans to slip off in the middle of the night."

Leonard looked at him for a moment more, and seemed on the verge of asking something else. But he held his tongue. A good man, Dietz thought, who knew when to ask questions and when to keep his mouth shut. In this case, although Leonard didn't know it, he was very possibly saving his own life by keeping his mouth shut. If Leonard got in his way, despite any affection Dietz may have felt for the man, then he would pay the price.

Yildirim was still conferring with the customs officials—but things looked as if they were wrapping up. Dietz reached into the leather bag that never left his shoulder. His fingers slipped past the hidden compartment, which contained passports and driver's licenses for several false identities, both male and female. By touch, he checked his wallet, the gun, the suppressor. His eyes never left Yildirim.

Then Yildirim was coming into the station, not looking anywhere but at the floor. He moved past them, toward the exit in the back.

3.

The distance between Old and New Istanbul is considerably greater than the width of the slender strait that separates them.

On the European side of the Bosporus lies the Old City, steeped in tradition and history. The Asian side, paradoxically, features modernized, Western-style suburbs. Fast-food restaurants, gourmet shops, and trendy clubs flashed past the taxi's windows. Dietz noted a car dealership, then a shopping mall. Then the houses shrank, crowding closer together, growing poorer-looking, and there were no more car dealerships or shopping malls to be seen.

As they cruised past ramshackle wooden houses, Dietz's impenetrable eyes remained fixed on the little yellow car in front of them. The little car was slowing down. It was turning into a narrow alley between two of the humble wooden houses. Dietz grappled for the words he wanted—too many years had passed since he'd last spoken the language—then found them. *"Yavaş gidin,"* he murmured to the driver.

They drifted slowly past the alley; he saw Yildirim leaving the car.

After another hundred yards, Dietz instructed the cabby to pull over. He paid his fare in dollars, left the cab, and then stood for a moment, thinking.

It was a stroke of luck—if his instincts about Yildirim proved right, if indeed the man was about to lead him to the woman. It meant he would not need to risk harming Leonard or Keyes when he took her. Harming these men might have opened a rather messy can of worms, which he would much prefer to leave closed.

Nor was it the first stroke of luck, in the past few days. If Keyes had not tapped Dietz for this particular assignment, he would not have found this unexpected chance. He might have been forced to spend another year, or five, or ten, sitting on his farm and waiting for an opportunity to make a fortune large enough to impress Elizabeth Webster. Perhaps he would have needed to wait forever.

Yet Keyes *had* tapped him. And he had done it, for whatever reason, beneath the radar, outside of official channels. So when Dietz made his move, he would face no opposition except the rest of this rag-tag band Keyes had assembled . . . which seemed, as far as he could tell, to consist entirely of Leonard. To a man with Dietz's experience, Leonard offered little reason for concern.

The night was warm, stirred by a balmy breeze. Despite the modesty of the neighborhood, there was something pleasant in the air: a sense of community, of honest hard work. No matter where in the world he went, it was always the same. The poorer neighborhoods, despite everything, often emanated more contentment than the wealthier ones. Or perhaps it was only an illusion. Perhaps the contentment, if one actually lived here, would be revealed as resignation.

In the direction from which he had come, two children were taking turns with a single skateboard. Otherwise the street was deserted. Supper time, of course. The locals were settling down for the evening. Back in the city, the nightlife would be just gearing up; but out here, the day was already finished.

Dietz moved toward the children and then past, giving them a wide berth. Upon reaching the alley that held Yildirim's car, he cast his eyes around again. The children were moving away, laughing. An emaciated gray alley cat sat near the car's fender, looking at Dietz with one ear flicking.

For a moment, he looked back at the cat. Then he moved to the car and tried the door. Unlocked. A quick search revealed an empty pack of English Ovals, a dog-eared map of the city, an ashtray filled with butts, and little else.

He straightened, closing the door softly. The house on his right was dark and quiet—deserted; abandoned. The house on the left had a light twinkling behind white curtains. That was where the man had gone.

From his shoulder bag, Dietz withdrew the modified S&W Model 39 and the suppresser. The suppresser was nearly as large as the 9mm gun itself; the combination of the two, once he had screwed them together, felt unwieldy. But Dietz was accustomed to handling the silenced gun, unwieldy or not. The S&W Model 39—known as the Hush Puppy, thanks to its handiness in silencing guard dogs—was the regulation firearm used by U.S. Special Forces and Navy SEALs. It was also the weapon with which he had kept himself in training, during the long stretches of inactivity on the farm.

A car was moving down the street. He pressed himself back into the shadows, holding the gun by his side, watching.

It was another taxicab. As he watched, a woman came out of the back of the taxi. She stood for a second, half bent, exchanging a word with the driver. Then the taxi was pulling away. The woman took a moment and then moved up the walk of the house. She was a youngish woman, pretty if bedraggled, who looked exhausted.

So his instincts had been right, after all.

He kept watching as she looped a strand of hair behind one ear and knocked on the door. He strained to hear the exchange, but the wind took the voices, dashing them.

Then the woman was moving into the house. The door closed behind her.

Dietz licked his lips. He began to slow-breathe, six seconds in and six seconds out, preparing himself for what he was about to do.

FOURTEEN

I.

The driver hit the meter and then turned to look at Hannah.

She didn't meet his eyes. She reached into her purse, dug around, and found her watch. The Cosmograph Daytona had been a gift from Frank; at one point, it had been worth a pretty penny. But it was possible that the dunk in the water had ruined it. She handed it forward. "Okay?" she said.

The man took the watch, inspected it, held it to his ear. Hannah opened her door and stepped outside, clutching her purse against her chest. *Take it or leave it,* she thought.

A moment later, the cab was pulling away. So he had taken it.

Her eyes moved to the number on the shabby mailbox before the house. It was the address Yildirim had given her to memorize. But would he still help her, now that she didn't even have a wallet? Would he still believe that she could deliver the money she had promised?

It would have been nice to present a more authoritative façade. But she was in poor shape—the wet had traveled from her clothes and through her skin, into her bones. The scratches on her arm had turned an ugly red. In all likelihood she looked the way she felt: like a beaten, abandoned stray.

She closed her eyes, held them shut, then opened them and moved up the front walk of the little house. She hooked a lock of hair back behind one ear and knocked on the door. A moment passed.

"Evet?" a voice said.

Hannah licked her lips. "Hello?" she answered.

She heard locks being opened. The man who had answered the door was slim, Filipino, with wary eyes. He stepped aside, and Hannah entered.

The front room featured a kitchen and dim living area, with a television set playing music videos, a sagging couch, and a small dining table. Two children knelt on a carpet in front of the set. To Hannah's left, a woman was standing over a stove. Framed examples of calligraphy hung on the walls between white-curtained windows. There was another room past a cracked-open door; she caught a glimpse of bunk beds. Four people lived here, she thought, in this space that was roughly the size of her walk-in closet back in Chicago.

Yildirim was nowhere to be seen. The children were looking at her curiously. The woman by the stove hadn't turned.

The man waved negligently at the couch. Hannah went and sat, holding her purse tightly in her lap.

After a few moments, the children began to speak in quiet Turkish. The man disappeared into the back room. The woman set one pot aside, and put another on the burner.

For two minutes, Hannah sat motionless. The smells from the

stove were spicy and exotic; her stomach turned over lazily. She wondered if there was a bathroom where she could wash up. She didn't see one. Perhaps in the back room. She could ask. But she was loath to cause trouble, or draw attention to herself. She could wait.

How long would it take Yildirim to get here? She wanted to be on a plane, back to the States. Come what may, she was ready to go home.

When the two minutes had passed, she opened her purse. She removed a compact and looked at herself. Not surprisingly, she looked frightful—her hair a greasy tangle, her face smudged and puffy. She found a fresh Kleenex and wiped at herself, then found a tube of lipstick and began to apply it.

Suddenly, the children were kneeling in front of her. They were both girls, she realized with a small jolt, whose hair had been cropped short. They stared at her with huge, dark eyes. Hannah looked back stiffly. In the next moment, one girl was reaching for the compact. Hannah glanced at the woman to see if she would curb her child. But the woman was focused on the stove. There was no help there. Hannah let the girl take the compact; then the other girl reached for the lipstick.

The woman turned from the stove and looked at her daughters. She said nothing. She returned her attention to her pots.

Hannah leaned back into the couch, watching the girls play. Now that she was sitting still, exhaustion was catching up with her. She could almost steal a nap right here . . .

She shook her head, and straightened. Yildirim would arrive soon. Then she would move on.

The girls were laughing. They had traded treasures, and now the first daughter was putting on lipstick. Hannah smiled at them faintly. She reached into the purse, brushed past the book, and found a pair of nail scissors.

She waited, snipping absently around her cuticles.

2.

Leonard had made friends with one of the maids: a chubby, sunny-faced woman who seemed only too happy to linger around the dock speaking with him, although it was now well past sundown and everybody else from the *Aurora* had gone.

Keyes, watching again from the customs station, wondered if the woman believed that Leonard was a child. Perhaps that was why she was so willing to answer his questions. Then he wondered if *he* would have believed that Leonard was a child, had he not known the truth. It was hard to say. Once one knew a truth, he thought, it was nearly impossible to forget.

He heaved a sigh. Everything had gone wrong—so spectacularly, unexpectedly wrong—and time was leaking away. Nearly two precious hours had been lost at the police station before Keyes had found the person to whom he was meant to pay his bribe. Upon returning to the dock, he had discovered that both the woman and Dietz had vanished.

But Leonard and the maid kept chatting leisurely, as if there was no hurry whatsoever.

Keyes checked his watch, and kept waiting.

At last, Leonard separated himself from the woman, all smiles. As he walked over to Keyes, his good humor fell away. He came close and spoke in a low voice:

"His name is Yildirim. The chief security officer on board."

The man Dietz had followed away from the dock, he meant. Keyes grunted encouragingly.

"Cathy says—"

"Who?"

"Cathy. The maid."

"Yes."

"She says that Yildirim was friendly with another maid on board the ship, named Bascara. Usually, when they come into port, he goes to the woman's house for a meal with her family. According to Cathy, it's a custom."

"'The woman's house,'" Keyes repeated.

Leonard's smile winked back. "I've got an address," he said.

3.

Later, when she thought back on it, Hannah could reconstruct what had happened in the small house in the Western suburbs; but at the time, none of it seemed to make sense.

One second, she was sitting on the couch, holding the cuticle scissors and watching Yildirim. Yildirim had just come from the back room—he had been there, it seemed, since before her own arrival— but he had paid no attention to her beyond a single tight nod. He was busy flattering the woman by the stove, who giggled at his attention. It was odd to see this side of Yildirim, she remembered thinking. It was odd that such a taciturn man would be so open and friendly to the Filipino woman, when he had been so chilly with Hannah herself.

In the instant before everything stopped making sense, that was how it had been: Yildirim and the woman by the stove, Hannah on the couch, the children back in front of the TV with their treasures in hand, the husband still in the back room, out of sight.

Then the knock had come at the door.

Yildirim had stopped joking with the woman. Hannah had sat up on the couch, catching his eye. He'd held her gaze for a moment, then turned and said something under his breath. The woman abruptly swept up her children, scolding them into the back room.

And then Yildirim was checking a pistol, which had materialized seemingly from nowhere.

Hannah started to come off the couch. He waved her back and moved to the door, the pistol held by his thigh, straight-armed. Then things took a turn toward absurdity, toward surrealism—or so it seemed at the time.

Yildirim, by the door, swayed on his feet. A tiny hole had appeared in his back. Hannah saw it, but didn't believe it, for it made no sense. The door was still closed. How had the hole appeared? Her mind clamored for an explanation. Perhaps there had been a mouse in his pocket, she thought ridiculously. And perhaps the mouse had chewed its way out, very suddenly, through his back.

Yildirim sat down, hard. He made a sound like *oomph*. There was also a hole in the door, Hannah saw. Another mouse?

Then the door was no longer there.

Now she was coming off the couch in a panic. But as soon as she had gained her feet, she froze. A man had stepped into the house. He held something bright and shiny in one hand, trained on her. He was a large man—a *huge* man, she thought in that first shocked moment, as wide as he was tall, and moving with an eerie, confident grace.

He drifted across the dim room, the thing in his hand still trained on her, and stepped into the back of the house. Then he whispered something. It was an intimate whisper. He knew this family, Hannah thought. He had made a deal with them, hadn't he? She and Yildirim had been betrayed. This man, whoever he was, had been one step ahead of them. He whispered to the family in the back room—

—except he didn't whisper with his mouth; he whispered with the shiny object, which had moved from one hand to the other—

—and his whispers evidently convinced the family to keep to themselves. When he turned back to face Hannah, she knew that they would not be interfering. It took days for her mind to admit what she had actually witnessed during those five seconds.

The man approached her. The thing in his hand whipsawed toward her face, and she spilled back onto the couch. A slow fire began to burn on her right temple. Her eye filled with blood; she blinked rapidly. Then the man's hands were on her. He was patting her down, his fingers digging through the flimsy material of her tank top. A moment later, he was turning away, reaching for her purse. He began to search through it, spilling out the contents haphazardly.

Her eyes moved to the door—to the spot where the door had been. Beyond it was the street, and night.

Before she could move, he had done something, again, knocking her onto the floor. Then the man was straddling her. His knees were on her forearms. She opened her mouth to scream—

—and he backhanded her.

Fucker, she thought as her head rocked.

She was not afraid. Instead, she was filled with righteous fury. How *dare* he put his hands on her?

Her mouth was making words. The words did not reflect her anger. The words, she thought, were designed only to make the man get off of her. "It was Frank's idea," she heard herself saying. "It was all Frank's idea, but I went along with it, and it was a mistake, and please, please don't hit me again—"

Or perhaps the words were designed to distract him. For now the scissors in her hand were rising, in a whistling arc, and burying themselves in the man's shoulder.

His eyes flashed. The silver thing in his hand drew back again. And for a time after that, she remembered nothing.

4.

Leonard had something in his lap.

Keyes noticed this as the cab slowed. He leaned forward, peering curiously through the gloom. It was a weapon of some kind—a short tube. It was a good thing, he supposed, that Leonard was armed. Lord only knew what they would face inside the house. If the woman, whoever she was, had been skilled enough to delay Dietz . . .

. . . *delay,* he thought. What were the chances that Dietz had only been delayed?

In some deep part of himself, Keyes was very afraid. Yet he found himself able to isolate the fear, to marginalize it. There was a sense of predestination to all this, he thought. What would be, would be. He would do his best, until he couldn't. And that was that.

The cab had pulled over. The driver was looking at him expectantly in the rearview mirror. Keyes reached into his wallet, found a twenty-dollar bill, and held it forward. A moment later, they were outside, watching the taxi speed away.

Leonard was doing something with the weapon, withdrawing some kind of implement. Keyes averted his eyes self-consciously. He did not want to see this: the actual weapons that caused actual death. For years he had managed to avoid exposing himself to this reality. Behind his desk, it was all a puzzle, an intellectual game. Behind his desk, it was simply business.

Past Leonard, beside the house, was an alley. Light came from the alley, and the growl of an engine. There was a car idling there, he realized.

Then the car was pulling out, blinding him with headlights. The engine was opening up. Keyes understood, very clearly, that the car meant to run them down.

He began to move to his left. There seemed to be nowhere he could go that would provide cover. There was not enough time; the engine was screaming, filling the world, and the headlights were everywhere. He kept moving anyway. What would be, would be. He would do his best until he couldn't. And that was that.

The fender took him on his right hip, spinning him around. He heard the crisp, distinct sound of bone cracking. Then his face was scraping against the pavement. He tasted blood. He rolled onto his back, to see if the car would come around and finish the job.

But the car was moving away, still gaining speed. Leonard was rushing over, leaning down, his mouth moving.

Keyes closed his eyes. His breath was coming in shallow, hungry gulps. There was a terrific pressure on his hip. An elephant was kneeling on his hip. *Goddamned elephant,* he thought.

Yet there was a bright side. For the first time in longer than he could remember, he wasn't hungry in the least.

FIFTEEN

I.

Another call was coming in. "Mom," Daisy said. "I've got to put you on hold."

She punched the hold button, found the incoming call—line two—and hit it. "Jim Keyes's office."

"Hold for Dick Bierman," a voice said.

Daisy held for Dick Bierman. "Jim," the man said.

"This is Daisy Gilbert, Mr. Bierman. I'm afraid that Mr. Keyes is out of the office."

"Where is he?"

"I can't say, exactly. But I'll let him know that you—"

"Do you expect him this afternoon?"

"I can't say. But I'll make sure your call comes to his—"

"Well, give me a hint, Daisy, for Christ's sake." Bierman spoke with a chipper southern accent. "Out to lunch? On the golf course?"

"I'm not exactly sure. As soon as—"

"I'd like to fly up there this afternoon. Will he be there?"

"I couldn't promise that. It would probably be better to wait and speak with him yourself."

"I'll try his cell. What's the number?"

Line three was blinking. Daisy felt herself beginning to panic—they'd had the new phone system for nearly four months, but she still hadn't mastered it. "Mr. Bierman; please hold." She hit the button without waiting for an answer. On to line three. "Jim Keyes's office," she said.

"Daisy."

It was Keyes. He sounded horrible. She leaned forward in her chair. "What's the matter?" she asked.

A wheezy breath. "I'm okay," he said then. "There's been a little accident. But I'm okay. I need you do something. Call Roger Ford and ask him to send over a complete file on Francis Dietz. Tell him there's been a problem. We're not sure if Dietz is the problem or not."

Daisy scribbled a note. "I've got Dick Bierman on the other line," she said.

"Bierman?"

"He wants to come visit."

"Tell him you can't reach me."

"I did. But he's pushing. He wants to come up this afternoon. And he wants your cell number."

A long pause. "Tell him . . . tell him there's been a family emergency and I'm out of the office until . . . but God damn it, he'll come anyway, won't he?"

"He does sound eager," Daisy said.

"Dinner tomorrow. He can come up or I'll go down, whichever he likes."

"Got it."

"And don't forget the Dietz file. I need it yesterday."

"Got it."

"One more thing. Ask Casper to run down a name: Victoria Ludlow. From Chicago. Everything he can get."

The pen scratched across the pad. "Got it."

"Thanks a million, Daisy."

She hung up, and went back to Bierman.

"Mr. Bierman? I'm sorry about the—"

"It's me," her mother said.

"Mom. Sorry. Hold on."

She tried again. "Mr. Bierman?"

"Ms. Gilbert."

"I'm sorry about that, Mr. Bierman. I'm looking at his calendar right now. Would you be available for dinner tomorrow night?"

"I suppose I could be."

"Very good. I'm penciling you in for—"

"After dinner I'd like to have a tour of the grounds. Check my investment, you know."

"Of course," she said smoothly. "Shall we say eight o'clock? Would you like me to make a reservation at a local hotel? There's a beautiful little bed-and-breakfast . . ."

"I'll have my girl take care of it." The line went dead.

Daisy puckered her lips. She looked back at line one, which was blinking steadily. She hit it. "Mom?"

"Daisy. I don't appreciate—"

"I'll have to call you back," she said, and killed the connection.

2.

As Hannah came awake, she felt her neck twinge.

Perfect, she thought darkly. This was all she needed. She had enough on her mind, these days, without a stiff neck. Things at work were going badly. Things with Frank were going badly. And it was not only her neck that hurt. Her temple throbbed; her eye burned. Her head felt heavy, as if it had been emptied out and refilled with sand. This was the last time she would sleep . . . where?

In a car, she realized. Outside, it was raining. When she opened her eyes, she saw gray sky beyond the gray windshield. Wind tossed the raindrops into teasing, puckish whorls. The car wasn't moving. Only the rain was moving.

A man was sitting beside her with her purse in his lap. The man was around sixty, maybe a few years younger. He had a blocky head and a seamed face and a thick chest and sharp gray eyes. As she struggled up in the seat, he looked over at her.

He smiled.

It was an odd smile: knowing and a bit sad. He raised an object from the purse. The book she had borrowed from the Epstein woman, *The Chronicles of the Crusades*. The events of the past few days returned in a rush; she let out a soft moan. It was too much. Too much. Not real . . .

The man opened the book, revealing chicken-scratch handwriting inside the rear cover. Hannah saw a bit of text and a few scrawled equations. After satisfying himself that she had seen the chicken-scratch, the man returned the book to the purse. The purse stayed in his lap. This was the man, she was realizing, who had assaulted her, who had whispered the family into silence. And now that she looked for it, she saw the wound: a spot of blood on his left shoulder, where she had buried the cuticle scissors.

Her eyes moved to the door. The door appeared to be unlocked. But for some reason, the man didn't seem concerned that she would slip away.

"Let's talk," he said.

Hannah said nothing. The drizzle gained force, slapping a sheet of rain against the windshield. Past the sound of the rain was a long, slow drone. An airport, she thought. They were parked not far outside an airport.

"You're free to walk away, if you like. I won't stop you. I've got what I need."

He seemed to expect an answer. Yet she didn't even know what the question was. The man was FBI, she thought. Wasn't he? He had followed her halfway across the world, because of her crime back in Chicago. But why, then, was she free to walk away? It made no sense.

"But you may want to think about who you've thrown your lot in with, here. You may want to consider who could do the most for you now."

Seconds passed. Hannah stayed silent, motionless. He kept looking at her. "All right," he said at length. "Let's try it this way. I'll talk. You listen."

His left hand came up; she saw her passport. He opened it. "Victoria Ludlow," he read. "But that's not your name. Your real name is nowhere in this purse. Probably it's nowhere else, either."

Thunder rolled, far away.

Her eyes wanted to move back to the door. If she jumped out of the car and ran, would he follow? Suppose he did, and she managed to escape. He had her purse. She had no wallet, and no passport. She could find the American embassy, she supposed. Beg, borrow, or steal a ride, and find the embassy. They would take her in. But then she would be caught. It would all come out into the open.

Better than sitting here, she thought, stuck in this car with this madman.

Her hand began to inch toward the door.

"I'm going to make you an offer," he said.

One cautious inch at a time, so he wouldn't notice. She would hit the handle and roll out of the car in one motion, into the rain.

"In exchange for an explanation of what the formula means, in language I can use to drive up the price . . ."

She would go to jail, if she showed her face at the embassy. But at the moment, the thought of jail was almost appealing. In a cell she would be able to rest for a few minutes.

". . . fifty-fifty," he said. "I don't know what kind of offer Frank made you. But I can top it. I know several parties who would be interested in this. I'm thinking of a number . . ."

One more inch, and her hand would hit the latch.

". . . conservatively," he said, "and without knowing exactly what we've got here . . . but taking into account what I know about Keyes and his budget . . ."

Her fingers touched cool metal. She steeled herself to make the dash.

". . . ten million," he said. "And as I said: That's conservative."

Her hand paused.

"I expect I could drive it closer to fifteen. Who knows? It all depends. But the more information I can offer, the higher the figure."

He returned the passport to the purse. He reached into his breast pocket, took out a pack of cigarettes, shook one into his mouth, and punched the lighter in the dashboard.

"Or you can hit that handle and walk away."

Lightning flashed. A second passed; thunder rumbled again.

Hannah put her hand back into her lap.

"I think it's some kind of bomb," the man said conversationally. "That's what I think."

The lighter popped out. He lit his cigarette.

Pooh Bear, Hannah thought. *Don't get any crazy ideas, now.*

She would go to the embassy, and she would turn herself in. She would face the music. She would pay the piper. What other choice did she have? Getting herself into *this,* whatever this was, even deeper. But no—she had learned her lesson. She had done wrong, and there was no point in trying to avoid that truth. Two wrongs didn't make a right.

But the real crime had been Frank's. She had been guilty of nothing but poor judgment. Why should she rot in a cell, all because of Frank?

Ten million, she thought. *Fifty-fifty.*

And that's conservative.

How far would five million dollars take her? Far enough to make none of this matter. Far enough to buy a second chance, for real.

Yet she had nothing to sell. Until a few moments before, she hadn't even seen the chicken-scratch in the back of the book. If she tried to play the role that this man had assigned her, whatever it was, she would surely be caught in a lie.

No, she thought. *He doesn't know what it is, either.*

But he thinks I *know.*

The man exhaled a feather of smoke. He reached for his window, cracked it open, and then looked back at her.

"A shower," she said. "Fresh clothes. And a drink. Then we'll talk."

3.

Keyes opened the folder on his blotter, then lifted his glass of scotch as he considered it.

According to the clock on his desk, it was not quite five o'clock. Usually he wouldn't be drinking so early. But his sense of time was utterly skewed—the flight out, the flight back, chasing the sun and running from it; hell, it was past midnight on his internal clock. And his hip, beneath the bandages, was throbbing. In three hours, he would need to meet Dick Bierman, to fend the man off, to bargain for more time. Lord knew he could use a little self-medication.

He took a sip, set the glass down, rubbed at his eyes, and focused on the file.

The file concerned a woman named Victoria Ludlow. It was in her name that passage had been booked aboard the ship by the mysterious woman who had been in league with Epstein. Someone would need to enter the woman's apartment in Chicago, he thought—assuming that the address under which she was listed did indeed exist. The agent would pick up prints to be sent to IAFIS, the Integrated Automated Fingerprint Identification System, in Clarksburg. At the same time, a lock-in trace would be put on the apartment's telephone. The device would plug extra voltage into the phone line; once a trace on an incoming call had started, severing the connection would not derail it. Listening devices would be planted, computer surveillance software installed.

Yet he didn't *have* an agent to send to Chicago. His resources at ADS already were stretched to the breaking point. And he was reluctant to call in yet another favor from Roger Ford. Instead of chasing down every lead separately, he needed to achieve some sort of synthesis—some understanding of what had really happened, and who had been involved, and why.

He closed the first file, moved it aside, and reached for the second. This dossier concerned Francis Dietz. Keyes did not know who had been responsible for the massacre they had found in the Western suburbs of Istanbul. It could have been the woman, or Dietz, or both. Perhaps they were working together. Perhaps this was much larger than he had assumed, and Epstein had been countless steps ahead . . .

. . . no. At worst, there were a few people involved. A few bad apples in the barrel. He would figure it out, and handle it, and put a stop to it. And that would be that.

His hip pulsed. He took more scotch into his mouth, rolled it around, and swallowed.

From the file, it was hard to know what to make of the man.

Six years in New York City, working with the Russians as part of COURTSHIP. Had he turned over, there? It seemed possible. Yet in the years since, he'd hardly lived an extravagant lifestyle. An unexceptional farm in Pennsylvania, biannual jobs for Roger Ford, and—according to the file—an ongoing affair with a married woman named Elizabeth Webster. If Dietz had turned over, he had not made a very profitable time of it.

Keyes took another sip of whiskey, and read the page again.

Perhaps there was no conspiracy, he thought. Perhaps Dietz had simply sensed an opportunity, when he'd found himself alone with the mysterious woman. This was the chance, he may have thought, to make his fortune. And then he would whisk away Elizabeth Webster—a lovely woman in her early forties, nice smile, dirty-blond hair, photographed here with her husband at a charity event in Washington—and they would start somewhere fresh. Fresh, and rich. Dietz probably already had cover identities done up for the both of them, ready to go at a moment's notice.

It was a possibility. Dietz had run an entire network in New York, engaging in a years-long dance with agents and double agents, diplomats and ambassadors. He had contacts there who might have been able to find a buyer for Epstein's calculations.

But where did the woman fit in?

He flipped to the next page: Dietz's psychological profile. Here were more possible clues, and no hard answers. Dietz was what the author of the report described as a "remote personality." He had trouble creating and sustaining strong interpersonal relationships. Yet he had refused to seek treatment for this condition, because in Dietz's mind, his problems were not problems at all . . .

The intercom buzzed. Keyes reached out and found the button without raising his eyes. "Yes."

"Dick Bierman is here."

He looked up sharply. Bierman. Stopping by early. The man was playing games, he thought. God damn him. His timing couldn't have been worse.

Before answering, he raised his glass and took a long draft. His stomach was empty; the whiskey went straight to his head. Better.

"Send him in," he said.

4.

Five hours later, Keyes came back into the darkened office.

He set down a stack of message sheets, leaned his cane against the wall, fell into the chair behind the desk, and poured himself another drink. Then he stared into space without lifting the glass. Whiskey couldn't do the trick anymore, he feared. To take off this edge, he would need something stronger. Angel dust. Heroin.

Bierman was playing for keeps.

Did the man know something about Epstein? Was that why he was making his move now—he had sensed vulnerability? Or was it just dumb luck?

Keyes had found himself making promises that he knew very well he couldn't keep. Bierman's timing, he'd lied, couldn't have been better. In one week a test would be staged at gamma site, and any fears about ADS's effectiveness—and, by extension, about Keyes—would be put to rest. Representatives from INFOSEC, DARPA, and LANL all would be included. And they would be pleased by what they saw, Keyes had promised. It would exceed their grandest expectations. For what they would see would be nothing less than Critical Achievement Three.

Bierman had looked disappointed at the news. Here he'd thought he was within days of ousting Keyes, of grabbing the reins for himself. On the surface, of course, he had not betrayed his disappointment. He had expressed his genuine pleasure at the good news. Maybe he had realized that Keyes was making promises he couldn't keep. Maybe the pleasure had not been entirely feigned.

Acronyms swirled through his head. ADS, DIA, DARPA. IAFIS, INFOSEC. LANL.

FUBAR.

He raised the glass, drained it, and reached for the bottle.

One week, he thought. What were the chances that Greenwich and his banks of computers would reproduce the formula before then? Slim to none.

He was fucked.

The fault was Epstein's. And Dietz's. And the woman's—Victoria Ludlow's. It could not have been chance, he thought. They were all in it together, somehow. A conspiracy was allied against him. All these forces arrayed against one man—really, against half a man. He was far out of his league.

He could envision the forces that threatened him: entwined, impenetrably knotted. All at once, he found himself remembering a report Jeremy had done for his biology class perhaps a year before his death. The report had horrified Rachel to no end. But Jeremy had been pleased by it—by the clear plastic binder, by the fancy cover page, and most of all by the grisly subject matter. And so Keyes had been pleased by it as well. For he and Jeremy had understood each other, always, in a way that Rachel could never quite get.

The report had concerned a natural phenomenon called a rat king.

Keyes remembered reading it in his living room chair, with Jeremy squirming in his lap. Jeremy had been too big to sit in his lap by then, but on that evening he had done it, so that he could appreciate the report along with his father. Since the fourteenth century, according to the report, sixty rat kings had been reported across Europe and America, most recently in 1963. Science was unable to provide an explanation for the occurrence, which involved groups of rats—in one authenticated case, as many as thirty-two—becoming tangled up together. The rats' tails were not only knotted together but actually *grew* together, because the rats broke the bones in their tails before entwining themselves. When the bones healed, the rats had become subsumed by a organism larger than themselves. The rat king.

Was that what he faced now? Something so foul, so formidable?

The rat king, Jeremy had concluded, *is as much a mystery to modern scientists as it was to medieval alchemists.*

Of course it was. Science could go only so far. There were deeper truths than those honored by science.

But Keyes hadn't the heart to follow that thought to its conclusion. He had been fooling himself, that he could keep on top of all of this. The truth was, he was fucked. The game was over.

Simplify, he thought. *Make it manageable.*

Assume that there was no conspiracy. Push aside the panic; push aside the anxiety; focus. Assume that his earlier idea had been correct, and Dietz was only seizing a chance that had suddenly, unexpectedly, presented itself. If that theory was right, it might mean that Epstein had provided the woman—whoever she was—with a material copy of his work. That would be what had tempted Dietz; something concrete, substantial.

He seized on this thought. Something concrete would be just what the doctor ordered.

Keyes needed it for himself. And he needed it now.

Presently he reached for the message sheets and browsed through them. Rachel had called again. His lawyer had called. And there was a bit of sad news, scrawled in Daisy's semilegible handwriting. Henry Chen, it seemed, had suffered an unfortunate accident. His brakes had failed and his Subaru had gone off an embankment, not thirty miles from the spot where Keyes sat right now. Chen was in critical condition at a local hospital. His prognosis was not good.

He moved the sheets aside.

One week, he thought.

In the back of his mind was the beginning of an idea.

As he turned the idea over, he brightened a bit. It was not a bad idea at all. In fact, it might have been the best idea he'd had in some time.

Dietz had stolen the equations for himself—working with or without the woman. And so perhaps Keyes could find a reason to call in the DIA, even at this late stage in the game. If not for Dietz's betrayal, he would suggest, there would be no problem. But Dietz had gone bad, and now DIA needed to help him clean up the mess. In all likelihood Dietz would go to New York, trying to sell his secrets to an old associate. And Keyes had, in the file sitting on the desk, information concerning all the contacts Dietz had made during his days with COURTSHIP. What he didn't have was the manpower to follow through, to place them all under surveillance.

So he would go to the DIA, after all. And the DIA would help him press the investigation. He would not ask too much; he would not attract undue attention. A small handful of agents, to keep Dietz's contacts under watch. For the rest of it, Keyes would make do with himself and Leonard. Leonard would remain stationed in Istanbul, ready to follow the man's trail if they caught it. Keyes himself would visit the woman's apartment in Chicago and conduct an inspection.

You'll snap, something inside him warned.

If you try to juggle all this, you'll snap. Throw in the towel. Go to Bierman. Tell the truth.

No. They would find Dietz's trail; they would retrieve Epstein's work. And the experiment would go ahead, in one week's time. The barbarians at the gate would be silenced once and for all.

It was too bad about Chen. The man had a wife, a family. But he had not been a team player.

Epstein didn't think you'd listen, Chen had said, *if he tried to put the brakes on.*

He'd been right about that. Because Keyes had vision. Keyes was a risk taker. *The rat king is as much a mystery to modern scientists as it was to medieval alchemists.* Science, of course, could only take them so far.

In one week, they would move ahead to Critical Achievement Three. Then Keyes would be vindicated, if nothing went wrong.

And if something *did* go wrong, he supposed he wouldn't be around for very long to see it. If Epstein's fears turned out to be justified, then the gravitational singularity would sink through the floor of the lab, fall to the center of the earth, and commence absorbing matter. Before it was finished, the orbit now followed by earth would be occupied by only a black hole.

But there would be a bright side, he thought sourly. There would be an end to pain.

His eyes moved to the photograph of Jeremy on the desk. An end to pain, he thought again.

He lifted the glass, then lowered it. He needed to get himself to Chicago. Before doing that, he would visit Casper and outfit himself with the necessary equipment. Despite everything, he could handle it. He would not snap.

He pushed the glass aside and reached for the intercom.

SIXTEEN

I.

When Hannah came out of the bathroom, the man was nowhere to be seen.

Her mouth made a funny little shape. She turned in a slow circle, standing in the center of the well-appointed suite and holding the towel closed at her breasts with one hand. There was no sign of the man, no note—and nothing on the door or the window that would prevent her from getting out of there.

But her purse, she noticed, also was gone.

For a few seconds, she considered leaving anyway. It would be an easy matter to find the American embassy, turn herself in, and give up on second chances. But the suite was fifteen stories up; the window offered no help. And if she was to take the elevator, she might run into the man in the hallway or the lobby.

Besides, the suite was comfortable: part of the Four Seasons of Istanbul, an Ottoman building located in the shadow of the Blue Mosque. The décor was vaguely Asian, with tasteful prints on the walls, fluted vases on nearly every open surface, and pristine light-gray carpeting. The suite felt clean, quiet, and, after her recent adventures, almost decadently luxurious.

Instead of leaving, Hannah moved to the minibar. She fixed herself a vodka tonic and carried it to one of the beds. She lay down, closing her eyes, enjoying the whisper of the air-conditioning and the smell of fresh-cut flowers. It beat prison, she thought.

Yet it was crazy.

The man was dangerous. And she would never be able to get away with . . . whatever it was she was getting away with. Playing the role the man had assigned to her, when she didn't even know what the role was.

In a moment, she would find her courage. Then she would stand up. She would take her chances. In a moment . . .

The door opened.

The man came into the room. He set down the packages in his arms, raised his eyebrows at her, and said nothing. He went to the bathroom, with the leather bag still looped around his shoulder—her purse, she figured, was in that bag—and shut the door.

A few seconds passed; she heard the shower beginning to run.

She looked at the packages. Then she looked at the door of the suite. This was her chance.

She looked back at the packages. Her mouth made the funny shape again, and she reached for them.

2.

"You do the honors," she said.

Judging from the man's facility with the ordering, he had spent time in this part of the world before. He asked to see the fish before it was cooked, as if this was a natural request, and the waiter's reaction—despite the fact that the hotel's restaurant was decidedly upscale—was sanguine.

"In another week," he told her, after the waiter had gone, "we'd be out of luck. It's illegal to catch fish during the spawning season. But if it's fresh, we're in for a treat."

Besides making sure his turbot was fresh, the man seemed not to have a care in the world. When the waiter brought out the raw fish on a plate, he inspected the eyes and the gills and pronounced it acceptable. He ordered a bottle of wine and another vodka tonic for Hannah and then leaned back in his seat, sipping at complimentary tea. One hand rested protectively on his leather bag, sitting on the empty seat between them.

"The dress fits you well," he remarked.

She dimpled charmingly, from habit, as her mother had taught her a lady should when she receives a compliment.

The man continued to make small talk. A gentleman spy, Hannah thought; she hadn't known that such a thing actually existed. He pointed out the bouquet of the wine, then the baklava on a passing dessert cart. The tactic, she thought, was designed to put her at ease. And it was working, up to a point.

This man, it seemed, had many talents. He could order fish in Istanbul and he could assault a helpless woman, with equal finesse. She had not forgotten the assault. She would never forget it. And when the time came . . .

But the time was not now.

She wondered what his name was.

She wondered what he would do if he caught her in a lie.

She wondered what she thought she was doing.

"Until you've had Turkish Delight in Turkey," the man was saying, "you haven't had Turkish Delight. They call it *rahat lokum*— 'comfortable morsel.'"

He had experience in the Middle East, clearly. To Hannah's mind, that suggested CIA. Yet this assumption, like most of her assumptions about intelligence, was based on Hollywood and Tom Clancy novels. In this sphere, she could not trust what she thought she knew.

Hannah, the voice said. *What are we hoping to accomplish here, exactly?*

Their food arrived; and as she dug into it, she turned the question over in her mind.

She was not hoping to get rich. Despite her first, greedy reaction to the figure the man had mentioned—*five million dollars!*—reality already was setting in. Even if she could come up with some convincing bluff about the chicken-scratch in the book, she would never be able to carry the pretense through to its conclusion.

Yet perhaps the man could help her anyway. If he could get her to America, allowing her to avoid an embassy or official channels, then she could still reach her father. She could still plea-bargain herself into a new life.

So she needed a good-enough bluff that she could stick with it for the foreseeable future. She wondered what the man thought she was. A spy, it seemed. Had the Epsteins been spies as well? It made sense, as much as any of this made sense. She had stumbled into something big—yet nobody seemed to have all the answers.

The man thought it was a bomb. She tried to think of *Scientific American* articles she had read, *60 Minutes* features she had seen, anything that might give her a platform for a convincing lie. There had been a spate of pieces on terrorism, of course. Dirty bombs, suitcase nukes, smallpox genetically engineered in high-school-level laboratories. But these technologies were disturbingly available to the masses already. They would not be worth such a large figure as the man had stated. It had to be something bigger, and something technical enough that the man would accept her lack of a detailed explanation.

She remembered paging through an article in a doctor's office she had been visiting with Frank. The subject of the article had been something called a Hypersonic Scramjet; much of the language was still in her mind. The Australians had recently tested this new type of engine, which used a rush of air to ignite hydrogen fuel. According to the article, the test had been only partially successful. Yet once this technology was perfected, the repercussions would be wide—for a working Hypersonic Scramjet engine would propel aircraft and rockets at Mach 8, eight times the speed of sound.

The article had gone on to provide background for the technology. An American program, NASA's Hyper-X Project, had been initiated by President Reagan less than a week after the *Challenger* disaster of '86. For almost twenty years, NASA had been striving to perfect the technology. The article had speculated that perhaps now the Australians had passed the Americans. It had theorized that similar work was being repeated in Russia, Japan, China, and India. For a working Hypersonic Scramjet would result not only in exceptionally fast manned flight; it would also produce hypersonic cruise missiles, and bombers too swift to be shot down.

This would be a fine secret, she thought. The Hypersonic Scramjet.

"By the way . . ." the man said.

Hannah looked up from her plate. He was holding a hand forward. "James," he said.

She reached for the hand, and shook it. "Amy," she said.

"Amy. A pleasure."

"Mm."

"Let me know when you feel ready to talk particulars . . ."

She dabbed at the corner of her mouth with a napkin. "I could use a good night's sleep first."

"Understandable."

She turned her attention back to her plate.

"I wasn't planning on leaving until morning anyway. Then I thought we'd catch a train at Haydarpasa. Make some distance to the east before we double back—in case Keyes has Atatürk under watch."

She could feel the man's eyes on her, watching for a reaction to the name. She made a noncommittal sound.

"If you have reason to believe someone might be watching the trains, now might be a good time to mention it."

She shook her head.

He watched for another second, his gray eyes flickering.

"In any case," he said then, "there's an interesting story, behind Turkish Delight. In the late eighteenth century, they say, a man named Ali Muhiddin came to Istanbul from the mountain town of Kastamonu . . ."

3.

They pretended to sleep.

Hannah lay on one of the twin beds, trying not to look across the moonlit room at her roommate. She listened to the sound of his breathing, which seemed easy and unconcerned. But this, she thought, was an act. He was no more asleep than Hannah, and she knew it.

For a pillow, the man was using his leather bag; and inside the bag was the book.

She stared at the ceiling. There was a small network of cracks there, even in a hotel as fine as this. As she looked at the cracks, they blurred, forming Rorschach pictures. Her eyes were tired. All of her was tired. Yet she couldn't sleep.

She looked at the cracks, but what she saw was the Epstein couple, touching each other as blood spread slowly between them. She saw the man-child, climbing the ladder with his eyes burning cold in that macabre, unlined face.

Outside, the wind rustled. Distant music on an exotic scale swelled and dropped away. She heard a siren, so faint that it might have been only her imagination.

The cracks shifted, changing. Now they looked like bars. These would be the bars on her cell, she supposed. After she'd turned herself in. When it came time to face the music.

Why hadn't she done it yet?

She was biding her time, of course. Because in the morning, after she'd delivered her bluff, the man would contact his *interested parties*. Then they would arrange a meeting. With luck, it would be in America. So the man would bring her home; and then she would emancipate herself, get to Baltimore, and get to her father. He would work his magic. He was a fine criminal lawyer. She would turn on Frank; she would not go to prison at all. Perhaps she would even be rewarded.

It didn't hold together.

What if the meeting was not in America? Then she would be in trouble, even worse trouble than now. And what were the chances that her father could really make everything all better? It was the spoiled part of her that expected that—the little-girl part, the part that always believed Daddy could fix everything. The truth was, her situation now was out of her father's league.

She would be better off leaving the room at this very moment, as the man pretended to sleep, and heading straight for the embassy. Then, at least, she would have demonstrated good faith.

Yet she didn't move.

You want that book for yourself, the niggling voice said.

He had not let go of the book from the moment he first had laid hands on it. He kept it in that damned leather bag, and the damned leather bag stayed in his lap, or around his shoulder, or by his hand, or—as at this moment—under his head.

Was that it? Possession of the book might help ease things when it came time to make the plea bargain, that was true. But then, it might not.

Perhaps, the voice suggested tentatively, she wanted the book for a different reason.

It was valuable. Valuable enough that everybody wanted it. Valuable enough that men would kill for it.

For that was what had happened, in the suburbs outside of Istanbul. There was no percentage in trying to avoid that fact any longer. "James" had executed the entire family—the two little girls wearing Hannah's own makeup at the moment of death. And he had put his hands on Hannah herself. Despite his gentle manner, despite his politeness and his suavity and his ability to order the right kind of wine, he was a violent man. And what would a man such as that do, if he had the secret inside the book? Nothing good.

America had enemies these days. They would be eager to get their hands on a secret that could sway the balance of power in the world. Would it be too much to suppose that this was why she hadn't yet left—she wanted the chance to do something good for her country? After all, her country had been good to her. And she had repaid it with spoiled, selfish behavior. Criminal behavior, not to put too fine a point on it.

Hannah Gray, patriot, she thought, tasting the concept.

If she hadn't been feigning sleep, she would have chuckled aloud. It was, as her father would have said, patented grade-A bullshit. If she stayed around and tried to get a chance at grabbing the book, it would not be for any reason other than selfishness. A priceless military secret could make things easier when it came time to negotiate a plea bargain.

She rubbed unconsciously at the scars inside her wrist. Yes, that would be all. Selfishness. No point in pretending otherwise. *Patriotism,* as Samuel Johnson had said, *is the last refuge of a scoundrel.*

For whatever reason—selfishness, patriotism, stupidity—she was still here, lying in this bed.

Could she get away with her bluff?

She stared at the spiderweb of cracks on the ceiling, and tried to formulate the words she would use in the morning.

The formula, she would say, described an airframe-integrated, scramjet-powered craft. Airflow through the engine would remain supersonic . . .

Meaning what? the man might ask.

It was technical, of course, and neither of them was a scientist. But what it meant, in essence—she strove to picture the article she'd browsed through in the doctor's office; she could almost hear Frank rasping away at the receptionist—what it meant, in essence, was that a new breed of jet would capture oxygen from the atmosphere itself. The vehicle *was* the engine, with the forebody acting as intake for airflow and the aft section serving as a nozzle . . .

. . . ah, but it wouldn't do to go on too long. For if the man felt that he didn't need her anymore, God only knew what he would do.

And at some point, he might let his guard down—even if only for an instant—and she might have her chance at the book.

Hannah Gray, patriot, she thought again, and the idea seemed infinitesimally less ludicrous.

What was in the book? She didn't know.

But whatever it was, she would have it for herself.

SEVENTEEN

I.

"Ow," Henri Jansen said.

Madeleine snorted. "Don't be a baby," she said, and dug her elbows deeper into his back.

Henri's teeth clenched. The massage was passive-aggressive, he thought; somewhere between shiatsu and shish kebab. He put up with it for another thirty seconds, trying not to react visibly. Then he rolled over and pulled Madeleine down for a kiss.

She brushed his lips peremptorily with her own, pushed off him, and went into the bathroom.

Something had gotten into her, he thought. Somehow, since yesterday, she had grown angry with him. Or perhaps she was angry with herself, or with her husband. Whatever the reason for her mood, he resented it. This was for married men—dealing with the vicissitudes of women's tempers. This was not for him. If he had wanted this, he would have gotten married himself.

A scorpion the size of his thumbnail was crawling down the length of the bed. He brushed it onto the floor, looked at it for a second, then sat up and crushed it with his bare heel.

Madeleine came back into the room, still not looking at him. "I'm hungry," she said to the window.

"So let's eat," Henri said.

"There's no food here."

"Of course there is. I went to the market yesterday."

"I want a swim."

"So let's swim," he said.

"I want a drink."

"So . . ."

She turned, and pinned him with her eyes.

"You're fucking Isabella DiMeglio," she said. "Aren't you?"

A moment passed. Henri, with some effort, maintained eye contact.

"Madeleine," he said patiently.

"Yes."

"Don't ask a question if you don't want to know the answer."

"I hate when you say that."

"I'm sorry. But—"

"Oh, forget it." She turned away again, to face the window. "Let's have a drink," she said.

2.

He found one of the last good merlots in the cellar, opened it with a silver corkscrew, then carried it with two glasses to the side of the pool, where Madeleine stood looking out across the fields, naked.

The resentment was still with him as he poured the wine. Now they were going to have a talk, he thought. Like husband and wife. She was in a mood; she was feeling jealous; she wanted reassurances. Henri, on the other hand, wanted none of it.

He poured two glasses, then waited for the opening salvo.

"My husband mentioned you today," Madeleine said casually.

She continued to face the field as she spoke. To the east of the house was raw wilderness: immense fields of purple lavender, distant rocky hills dotted with golden shrub. Behind them, the vast picture windows of the living room reflected the glow of the setting sun.

"Yes?" Henri said.

"He wants you to get him some coke. I told him you don't do that anymore. But he insisted I ask."

"I don't do that anymore," Henri said.

"I told him that. But he wouldn't listen. He wants you to come over to the house."

"It's a waste of time."

"You should come anyway. He knows a lot of important people. It could be worth your while. You could meet some new friends."

He took a sip of wine, and fell into a chair. "Whatever you like," he said emptily.

She came to take a seat near him, reached for her glass, and gave him a tender smile. For a moment, Henri was utterly baffled by that smile. One minute she was furious—and what right did she have to be furious if he was seeing another woman? She was married to another man—and the next, she was tender. During that moment, Henri Jansen felt that he would never understand women, the way they thought and the way they behaved, for as long as he lived.

In the next moment, he saw the answer clear as day. Madeleine had fallen in love with him, of course. That was why she went from angry to tender in the space of a heartbeat.

The thought was troubling. Madeleine's husband, after all, was not a good man to have as an enemy. The man's enemies had a way of disappearing.

But the vulture, Henri was sure, did not know that he and Madeleine had been carrying on together. And there was no reason for him to find out—unless she did something stupid. Until this moment, he had not felt there was any need to fear this. Madeleine wasn't stupid. But if she'd fallen in love . . .

"I love you," she said suddenly.

Henri kept his face impassive; but inside, he clenched.

"You know that, don't you? I've fallen in love with you."

"Madeleine," he said.

"Yes."

"Let's not get crazy."

"No."

"You're a married woman. And I'm . . ."

He trailed off. She snorted laughter.

"Let's get drunk," she said after a minute.

"All right."

"Do you want to hear about my hike today? With the famous American criminal and the Saudi prince?"

"All right."

"Let me get drunk first. Otherwise I might get sad, when I think of how I spent the day, and how you spent the day."

"I spent the day walking."

"And fucking Isabella DiMeglio?"

"Just walking, alone."

"When's the last time you saw her?"

Henri didn't answer.

"Oh, forget it," Madeleine said again. She wiped at the corner of her eye, and raised her glass. "You know—I really couldn't care less."

3.

Madeleine was very drunk.

"And you should have seen his nose," she said with a giggle. "His big Jew nose. This Arab—with his big Jew nose."

Henri was smiling too.

"They're the same, you know," she went on. "The Arabs and the Jews. That's what makes it all so funny."

"It is funny, isn't it?"

"This prince—"

She paused to refill her glass, unsteadily, from the second bottle of wine. The first lay glittering on the concrete by the edge of the pool, empty. "This Saudi prince," she said. "He's a suspect."

"A suspect?"

"You know. Bin Laden."

"Ah."

"My husband says that he launders money for them. He explained it all to me. Offshore finance; that's how they do it. Those little Caribbean islands, those shell companies—that's what they call them, shell companies . . ."

Henri reached for the bottle.

"Nauru," she said. "In the Pacific. Twelve people live there, and there are four hundred banks."

"Your husband told you this?"

"But the real money goes through the big cities. London, New York, Paris, Tokyo. And Switzerland. Of course, Switzerland. It's easier to cover the tracks in a big city. Then you've got your diamonds, your tanzanite and honey, funneling money to Al Qaeda . . ."

She hesitated, as if following some thought of her own.

"I'm hungry," she said then.

Henri pushed himself out of the chaise lounge, took an instant to check his balance, and headed for the house. As he crossed the stone patio, he stumbled and righted himself. He pushed through the front door and into the dark kitchen. The air in there smelled of ripe cheese and fruit. He loaded up a tray with bread, brie, and *saucisson,* then went back to the pool.

But Madeleine was gone.

Henri slowed. He looked across the vista, at the pool, the vineyards, the fields of lavender, the guest houses, the setting sun. Madeleine was nowhere to be seen.

Then his eyes moved back to the pool, and in that moment he knew: She had drowned herself.

Suddenly, he felt almost sober.

It had been half on purpose, he thought. Half suicide, at being put off after her declaration of love; and half accident, a drunken mistake. When he approached the edge of the pool, he would see her body at the bottom like some bizarre sunken treasure.

And what would happen then?

He would report it, of course. And the police would come. And Madeleine's husband would see to it that Henri never received an invitation to be a houseguest anywhere, ever again. If he didn't see to it, then Princess, the owner of this house, would take care of it—for Henri would have smeared her reputation.

Or perhaps it wouldn't end with ostracism. Vladimir Ismayalov, after all, was not a good man to have as an enemy. Perhaps sometime in the next year or two Henri would be the one facedown at the bottom of a swimming pool, his head crushed in, his body slowly bloating . . .

She burst out of the water. "Ah!" she said, and began to paddle in a clumsy sidestroke.

His breath came out in a long, shuddering sigh.

He moved to the edge of the pool and set down the tray in his hands: a thirty-four-year-old man who suddenly felt seventy. He wondered if he was going to faint. It seemed possible.

"Come in," she said. "It's wonderful."

"Get out of there," Henri said. "You're too drunk to swim."

She came out of the pool, naked, and into his arms.

They kissed. "I love you," she said into his throat. "I love you, Henri."

He was not going to faint. It was under control. It had been close—but it had been a false alarm.

But God in Heaven, he thought as she leaned up for a kiss. God in Heaven, how he needed to get out of this business.

EIGHTEEN

I.

As soon as he allowed himself entrance to the apartment, Keyes smelled something rotten.

Not literally—the place was spotless, the only odor a faint trace of lavender oil. Yet something was not right.

He sighed. The flight here had exhausted him. His leg was throbbing. He needed rest, and food. But now he was here; and so he set down the bag in his hand, planted the cane, and doggedly began his search.

The air and the room had the feeling of being on hold. Food and water had been set out for a cat; the lights were hooked up to a timer. The newspaper topping a pile inside the front door was dated five days earlier. So a trip, Keyes surmised, had been undertaken. But on the kitchen counter he saw suntan lotion, a sun visor, flip-flops. If the woman who lived here had gone on a cruise to Greece, why would these have been left behind?

A preliminary tour of the apartment suggested that it belonged not to a young woman, but to a young family. In the master bedroom, he found a king-sized bed surrounded by antique walnut furniture. The next room was a nursery, with a crib, a heap of stuffed animals, a closet filled with puzzles and toys. A dining room featured a glass table with four chairs, one supporting a pink plastic booster seat. The final room was a study, with bookshelves lining the walls, a computer resting on a heavy mahogany desk, and an enviable view of Lake Michigan.

In the bottom drawer of the desk, Keyes found a fireproof box. Inside the box he found three birth certificates: Greg Gordon, Victoria Ludlow, and Margaret Ludlow Gordon. Nowhere in the box were passports, which seemed to confirm his suspicion—a trip had indeed been taken.

But not to the Greek Isles, he thought. Not with the visor and suntan lotion and flip-flops left behind.

He leaned the cane against a wall, sat behind the desk, and switched on the computer. Here were e-mails from Greg Gordon to his work, a law firm in downtown Chicago. Many of the e-mails concerned the impending merger of two British publishing companies. There were also e-mails from the woman, who seemed to run a catering business, to her friends. The woman had many friends. He browsed down the list, looking for something of special interest, finding nothing.

Then he turned his attention to a date book beside the computer. Over the past month, despite having a toddler, the woman seemed to have spent most of her days eating lunch. The lunches blocked out entire afternoons, from one to four. By comparison, he thought, Rachel had been a saint. She'd given up her own career, when Jeremy had come, without complaint. For the entire first year, she hadn't once let him out of her sight.

He put the thought from his mind, and focused on the date book.

A string of days had a line drawn through them, starting five days previously and continuing into the next week. The days of the cruise, Keyes thought. So they had planned on going, as the sun-themed paraphernalia indicated. But then their plans had changed. Where had they gone instead? And who was the woman on board the ship, if not Victoria Ludlow?

Nowhere in the computer or in the date book did he find any mention of Steven Epstein, Francis Dietz, ADS, or anything that seemed to indicate an involvement with physicists or foreign interests—besides the British publishing concerns—of any kind.

He installed the surveillance software anyway. The software would take hundreds of screen shots per minute. Each time the computer connected to the Internet, these would be clandestinely forwarded to ADS. Keyes would possess an ongoing record of everything this computer did, including every stroke registered on the keyboard.

After watching the installation bar creep across the screen for a few moments, he reached for the cane and continued his search.

The apartment, he decided at length, was not a front. People did live here; and he believed they were the husband and wife whose birth certificates he had found in the fireproof box. On a bookshelf in the study was a photo album featuring wedding and baby pictures. In the refrigerator were tofu, springwater, rice salad, organic milk, organic eggs, chopped fruit in Tupperware containers, and gourmet cat food.

Keyes looked at these items with a slight curl to his lip. These people, he thought, did not know what it meant to have obstacles in life. They thought that, as long as they did everything right, fate would reward them. They didn't understand how fragile their house was—a house of cards.

He closed the refrigerator.

He put in a call to Daisy, back in Vermont, and asked her to gain access to the apartment's telephone records. Daisy told him to hold on.

He returned to the bag near the front door, crouched beside it, and withdrew the fingerprint kit. The apartment was spotless; he would need to find latents. On the bathtub spigot, he discovered good prints with ridge details intact. He spritzed them with ninhydrin and lifted them with tape.

Daisy called back with six names, constituting the recipients of the most recent ten calls placed from the telephone in the apartment. Two of the names had local Chicago addresses; the others were in San Francisco, Atlanta, and London. Keyes scribbled them down on a pad by the Ludlow woman's telephone, then carefully removed the sheet beneath the one on which he had written.

The software had finished installing. He removed his disc, then went back to the e-mail account and searched for the names of the locals: a Mr. and Mrs. Fielding, and a Hannah Gray.

The Fieldings, he soon realized, were the woman's sister and brother-in-law. Hannah Gray was a friend. Her e-mails described the breakup of a relationship with a man called Frank. Judging from Victoria's helpful responses—along the lines of *plenty of fish in the sea, plenty of time to reel them in*—Hannah Gray was a fairly young woman.

A young woman, Keyes thought.

A young, single woman.

He scrolled back to an e-mail he had only skimmed the first time. It was possible, the man's law firm said in this correspondence, that Greg Gordon might be tapped at the last minute to travel to London, where he would oversee the merger of the publishing firms personally.

Assume that this had happened, Keyes thought. And so assume that the tickets for the cruise had suddenly been up for grabs. Assume Victoria Ludlow had offered them to her young, newly single friend, suggesting that a trip like this might help her get over the breakup with Frank.

Hannah Gray's high-rise, according to Daisy's information, was less than a half mile away.

Keyes shut down the computer, made sure he had left no evidence of his visit, and let himself out.

2.

He walked the short distance to Hannah Gray's apartment.

He was not the only one hobbling along the lakeside, this afternoon, with the help of a cane. The neighborhood appeared equally split between the wealthy elderly and young, successful professionals; Keyes, falling smack in the middle, fit in well.

He waited outside Hannah Gray's building until a group of six entered the lobby, then followed close behind them. The doorman wore a brass-buttoned coat; his desk was nearly lost beneath a stack of paperback books. He nodded at the group and then looked back down at the crossword puzzle in his lap.

Hannah Gray's apartment was on the fifth floor. Nobody had put a stop to newspaper delivery here; a stack had piled up outside the door. Keyes tried the knob. Locked. He set the cane aside carefully and reached again into his bag of tricks.

The electromechanical pick gun he withdrew looked like a slightly undersized power drill. He chose a stainless-steel needle, affixed it to the front of the gun, and slipped it into the lock. He pulled the gun's trigger. The small motor inside the device vibrated; the cylinder pins bounced into alignment; the lock opened with a soft click.

He stepped inside, closing the door behind himself.

Another empty apartment, abandoned for a trip. Air stale, plants shriveling. He made a cursory first pass. The walk-in closet was filled with Prada shoes and Hermès bags. The bathroom featured Chinese rose soap, bowls of potpourri, propolis, and myrrh toothpaste. More beautiful people, he thought. More people who believed that if they bought the right things, and lived the right way, then life would reward them.

He took fingerprints. He returned to the living room and glanced at a line of photographs neatly arranged on an étagère. The woman he had seen in the bazaar was here: clowning around with another young woman, receiving a diploma with a broad grin, standing arm in arm with an older man who might have been her father. As he looked at the woman's face, the flat expression he assumed when looking at the blackboards in the elevators of ADS crossed his face.

After a few moments, he reached out, took the graduation photo, removed it from the frame, and moved on.

There was a computer in the bedroom, beside a bed covered with pink lace. He switched it on. The motor whirred; then an error message came up. The hard drive had been reformatted, he realized. Someone had been covering her tracks.

He shut it down, wondering if it would be worthwhile to lug the whole thing back to Vermont so ADS technicians could have a go at it.

He found himself standing by the answering machine. A digital *3* blinked softly. He played the messages. The first was from an automated telemarketer, selling a phone plan. The second was from Frank—the ex-boyfriend—saying he hadn't heard from Hannah in a while, and just wanted to check in. Was there something urgent in the man's tone, something being left unsaid? It seemed that there was. But they had recently been a couple. There must have been issues there. It wouldn't do to read too much into the tone of the man's voice.

The third message set his heart racing.

Hi, Hannah Banana. It's me. We're at the Savoy and it's just incredible. Greg is doing so well; we're so proud of him. And Maggie's having the time of her life. I know you're still on the cruise, but I just wanted to make sure you call the second you get back; I can't wait to hear all about it. Maggie and I should be home on the fifteenth. Talk to you soon. Love.

He listened to the message twice. Then he popped the tape from the machine, turned it over thoughtfully in his hand for a moment, and slipped it into his pocket beside the photograph.

3.

Six hours later, back in his office, he stared at the telephone, willing it to ring.

For the moment, he had taken all the action he could. Four DIA agents—the most he had felt he could request without raising too many eyebrows—were watching Dietz's contacts in New York. Casper was running down the Hannah Gray woman, looking for anything on her that might prove of value. Leonard was in Istanbul, ready to be of service. And so there was nothing to do, for the moment, but wait.

Time and again he found himself reaching for the phone, meaning to call Rachel. He would—what? Beg for a second chance? Ridiculous. Calling Rachel would be grasping at straws. It would be the last desperate act of a ruined man.

Yet he was a ruined man, beyond any doubt. The cane leaning against the wall drove the point home.

If only results would come in, Keyes thought, perhaps the cane would not be making him feel this way.

If results would come in, then perhaps, despite being crippled, he would find some hidden reservoir of strength. For the lame could still be strong. Hephaestus, the god of the smith, had been lame, thanks to his ignoble expulsion from Zeus's side. He had tumbled down to earth from Olympus, and his legs had been forever ruined by that tumble. Yet Hephaestus had become a powerful God nevertheless. In his great forge, he had built locks that were resistant even to immortals; he had crafted thunderbolts for use by Zeus himself. He had become the deity of destructive fire, and through activity his lameness had been conquered.

Keyes wondered what Hephaestus might have crafted, in his great smithy, to deal with something like the rat king. A mighty sword; an awesome hammer. He would not have sat back, defeated and hopeless, at the sight of such a horrible tangle. He would have broken that gruesome Gordian knot of tails with a single stroke . . .

He was losing his mind.

If only the damned telephone would ring.

He stared at the telephone; but it was silent.

The waiting was killing him.

He reached for a pencil and began to toy with it. Again, he felt the urge to call Rachel. If he didn't find someone to lean on, in the very near future, then he would pass a point within himself. And once he had passed that point, there would be no going back. A lone man was not meant to deal with this kind of stress. A man could not handle something like this by himself.

If results didn't come within a day, he would give up. He would call off the test, and confess everything to Dick Bierman. He would . . .

The phone rang.

4.

It was David Brown—part of the DIA team covering Dietz's associates from the COURTSHIP days in New York. Brown and his partner were watching, and listening to, a man named Andrei Yurchenko. Yurchenko had just received a rather interesting telephone call . . .

Keyes leaned forward. "Yes?"

"We're in business," Brown said.

The pencil in Keyes's hand snapped in two.

PART THREE

NINETEEN

I.

Inside the Haydarpasa railway station, Leonard found himself faced with a nearly overwhelming amount of activity.

Travelers bustled beneath stained-glass windows, staggered landings, and elaborate foliage cartouches. There was a palpable thrill of tension in the air—thanks, Leonard supposed, to the current situation in the Mideast. Haydarpasa was the portal from Istanbul to the east; those traveling to or from the west used Sirkeci station, on the opposite side of the city. So these people surrounding him were heading into the hornet's nest. It made sense that they would be nervous.

He drifted to one wall, put his back against it, and tried to sift through the crowd.

If Dietz and the woman were here, he couldn't find them.

But they were here. He had seen them board the ferry from Beşiktaş to Haydarpaşa with his own eyes. Perhaps he should have made his move then, he thought. Perhaps he should have followed them onto the ferry and confronted the man there. But how could that have worked to his benefit? If things had turned violent, there would have been nowhere to run. Even if he'd been able to handle Dietz by himself—which he rather doubted—he would have been trapped on the ferry after it was finished, surrounded by locals, with blood on his hands. By now he would be under arrest.

Instead he had waited for the next ferry, fifteen minutes behind the first. Now he found himself doubting that decision. According to the call he'd received from Keyes—

—he'd been shaving at the time; an ironic piece of bad luck, for Leonard needed to shave only once a week, and when the phone had rung, the razor in his hand had jumped and nicked his throat—

—according to the call he'd received from Keyes, this was their last and best chance at regaining Dietz's trail. And by waiting for the next ferry, Leonard might have let it slip through their fingers.

Keyes had sounded very tense. No surprise there; he'd been sitting in his office in Vermont with three phone lines open and valuable seconds ticking away. A call, as expected, had been placed from Dietz to one of his old contacts in New York. The man in New York, called Yurchenko, had indeed provided a name for Dietz, someone to whom he might hawk the secrets he had stolen. But the name had been a code—"the vulture." And so Keyes had been left with nothing concrete, except the results of the lock-in trace his men had placed on Yurchenko's phone.

The trace had given them the name of the hotel from which Dietz had placed his call. Keyes had immediately contacted Leonard, with instructions to get to the hotel and keep Dietz in sight.

Their best chance; their last chance. For if the man slipped away now, then he would vanish into a war-torn section of the world, where keeping on his trail would become difficult to the point of impossibility.

But Leonard would not let him slip away.

He touched the cut on his throat, gingerly.

He kept searching through the crowd, his eyes bright and hungry beneath the visor of his baseball cap.

2.

It was all a matter of timing.

Dietz had been careful about the timing. After hanging up with Yurchenko, he and the woman had gone to their waiting cab. And yet it seemed that Keyes was slow. There had been nobody watching the cab outside the Four Seasons. So Dietz had manufactured an excuse, and trotted back inside the lobby. He had stared out through the windows, waiting for the timing to be just right. At last, he had seen Leonard. He had rushed outside and into the back of the taxi as if he hadn't had a second to spare—

—and then, since Keyes had dutifully dispatched this pursuit, he had asked to be taken to the ferry to Haydarpasa.

Now more good timing was required. For if things went badly, and he was seen taking care of Leonard, there would be trouble with the local authorities. That was the last thing he needed.

He stood with the woman in a circular room in the southeast tower of the station, his eyes raking the crowd. A single American boy would not stand out in this crowd of Western-garbed travelers. Yet Leonard also would be looking for them. So he would be moving; he would show himself.

Patience. Timing.

Dietz's hand, inside his bag, worked at the Hush Puppy.

It was all a matter of timing.

3.

A train was being called.

The crowd jostled, separated. Leonard pushed off the wall and moved forward, still searching. Were Dietz and the woman in this crowd? The train was heading to the south, whereas he expected Dietz to head more directly east. His buyer for the secrets, of course, would be an Arab. The Russians these days were too weak, too scattered, to do anything except sell out to the highest bidder—and these days the highest bidders were Arabs.

But Dietz was a master of deception. He might head south initially, to mislead any possible pursuit, and then circle back around. Why, look how easily he had deceived Leonard—making him feel as if there was some special bond between them.

Perhaps Leonard had made too much of it. If so, he could forgive himself for the mistake. For the first time in longer than he could remember, perhaps for the first time ever, he had thought he had found someone on a similar wavelength to his own.

Even the other carnies, back from the days in the circus, had not made Leonard feel welcome. The alligator girl, the frog boy—people afflicted with ichthyosis and Ehlers-Danlos syndrome, people with whom he should have fit in—had banded together to exclude him. Because every scapegoat needed a scapegoat, he thought now. Everyone who was made feel to worthless found someone even lower, on the societal scale, to abuse.

He had thought that Dietz was different.

But he had thought wrong.

As he approached the swarm heading for the train, he touched the Peskett in his waistband. If things went well, he would find Dietz without being seen. He would follow Dietz and the woman, wherever they might go, and then report back to Keyes. But if Dietz saw him, and it came down to it, then Leonard would defend himself. Part of him would have relished that opportunity—the chance to exact revenge for this latest unexpected betrayal.

The crowd was dissipating. He was left in the center of the room, in plain sight. He quickly turned and melted back toward the wall.

One finger moved again to his throat. He had been in such a hurry, after receiving Keyes's call, that he hadn't even found time to press a square of toilet paper against the wound.

It was bleeding.

4.

Dietz saw him—or, more precisely, he saw the bill of his baseball cap.

Then Leonard was slipping away again. But he had shown himself, and now Dietz had his position. Now it was only a matter of execution.

Yet his timing still needed to be right; for he could not afford to get hung up, here, with the locals.

He turned to the woman, who stood beside him.

"Walk into the center of the station," he said. "Let yourself be seen. Then come back here. But move slowly. Take your time."

Her eyebrows went up. She was not stupid, of course. She understood that he wanted to use her as bait.

But they were in it together, and she seemed to realize this. After a few seconds, she nodded, turned, and walked slowly out into the center of the station.

Dietz watched. Then he began to move in the opposite direction, looping back behind the place where he had seen Leonard.

It should not present a problem, he thought. With the woman as a lure, Leonard would be distracted. Dietz would have his chance. But he had learned, over the years, never to underestimate an enemy. And Leonard, all appearances to the contrary, was a respectable enemy—driven by his anger, Dietz thought; driven and determined. It was a shame that they had met under these circumstances. They had things in common. Perhaps, had things been different . . .

But things were not different. And so it was every man for himself. Leonard would be of more value dead, now, than alive. His body would be left behind as a calling card of sorts, sending a signal to Keyes. The wrong signal. For when Keyes heard that Leonard's corpse had been recovered at Haydarpasa, he would assume that they were heading east.

Then they would head west, to keep their rendezvous with the vulture.

He saw Leonard again: keeping his back against the wall as his eyes tracked the crowd.

He was not to be underestimated. With his back against the wall, he would be difficult to approach. But Dietz, of course, had tricks of his own.

He positioned himself twenty feet from Leonard, shielding himself from view behind a column, and then waited.

Any moment now, Leonard would see the woman. Then he would be torn for a moment, reluctant to take his back from that wall. But at last, he would move forward. He had no choice. He needed to keep on the trail. The bait would be irresistible.

Dietz's thumb, inside the battered leather bag, slipped off the safety of the gun.

Any moment now . . .

Leonard saw her.

He stood for a moment, as expected, torn by doubt.

He began to move forward.

It was a shame, of course. They could have worked well together, he and Leonard, under other circumstances. But life was what life was.

Then a train's arrival was being announced. The station, which had emptied a bit after the most recent departure, suddenly was flooded again with people.

And Leonard, standing barely four feet tall, was lost in the crush.

Dietz left his place behind the column.

5.

Leonard saw the woman.

Twice before, he had seen her—in the tower of Sapienza and leaving the Four Seasons with Dietz. Now she appeared to be alone. She was strolling out into the center of the station, looking around. Had she and Dietz become separated? Or was she bait?

Bait, of course. Dietz was no fool.

But he needed to keep her in sight. He had no other choice.

A moment passed. Then Leonard took his back from the wall, although his every instinct warned against it.

An announcement was being made. Crowds swept into the station. Leonard had the impression of being caught in the midst of the parted Red Sea as the waters came rushing back in. Harried-looking travelers of every persuasion closed in on him in a crush. He lost sight of the woman.

A couple in front of him was being reunited, the man sweeping the woman into his arms as she screamed laughter. A family to his left was bickering as the mother tried to keep her children from wandering. Leonard pushed forward. There she was—looking overwhelmed herself by the sudden influx. He hesitated. If he moved closer, she might see him. But if he stayed here, she might vanish.

Then he became aware of someone coming up behind him. It was an odd awareness, since the space behind him already was filled with people; but this someone was not one of them. This was something else.

He began to tug the Peskett free. But he was too late, and he knew it. Something cool touched the base of his neck. It felt nice, he thought—like an ice cube wrapped in a washcloth applied on a sweltering summer day. Not so bad, Leonard thought. It was not such a bad sensation, with which to leave this cursed life—a cool washcloth on a hot summer day.

He kept trying to pull the Peskett free anyway. But it had caught on the elastic of his shorts. He almost smiled. Just his luck, he thought.

Shitty to the end.

Dietz fired.

TWENTY

I.

For some reason, the Italian detective seemed fond of Keyes.

When he mentioned that he was looking for yet another missing person—this one a man of nearly thirty who appeared, thanks to a condition called hypopituitarism, to be a boy of only twelve—the Italian made a sympathetic sound. He did not ask why Keyes wanted the information, or if it was tied to the other investigation, or how that investigation had turned out. Instead, he said, "Let me look into it. I'll call you back."

Keyes paused. His number had an area code of 802; a New York City Police Department's area code would be 212. "I'm on my way out," he said. "I'll get back to you . . . how's an hour?"

After hanging up, he wondered why the man seemed so kindly disposed toward him. Because of September 11th, perhaps. In certain sections of the world, now, New York City cops enjoyed an unusual amount of goodwill. Or perhaps laconic *bonhomie* was just a character trait of the Italians. He pictured the man sipping wine as he looked into the matter, stopping every few moments to wolf-whistle out his office window at a passing young woman.

In any case, he would not look a gift horse in the mouth. He returned his attention to his computer, where he was searching for any mention of a man who was known by the alias "the vulture." So far, he had come up empty. But there was no cause for alarm. At any moment, he expected a call from Brown, stating that Yurchenko had been arrested. Then the Russian could shed light on the question of the vulture's true identity.

The phone rang. He reached for it. "Keyes."

"He's flown the coop," Brown said.

Keyes put his head into his hands.

Brown sounded defensive. "Two minutes after he got the call, he was out the back door." A pause. "I'd say he had a contingency plan," Brown added, in a manner that struck Keyes as slightly disingenuous.

"'A contingency plan,'" Keyes repeated.

"We'll get him. There's—"

Keyes hung up.

For a few moments, he sat still.

So it had come to this. They couldn't even apprehend a man when they were, at least in theory, two steps ahead.

He felt an anxiety attack coming on. The pressure was too much for one man. His shoulders were too narrow for this burden. He was beginning to shake—not on the surface, but inside, at his core.

Had there ever been a time when he actually had been in control? No, he saw now. Control had been only an illusion. With his career, with his family, with the current situation—he was merely an observer, along for the ride. Sometimes he seemed to be holding the reins, but in reality this horse was in charge of itself.

The fear he felt was a slavering, undeniable thing. It wanted him to give in, to give up . . .

He tried to concentrate on small activities, to distract himself.

He spent the rest of the hour searching his database, to no avail. Was the vulture another Russian? Or someone else, with whom Yurchenko had come into contact during his spying days?

When the hour had gone by, he lifted the phone and dialed his Italian friend again.

"I've found your boy," the Italian reported.

Keyes steeled himself. It would not be good news, of course. God forbid that he ever get some good news.

"His body was discovered an hour ago at the Haydarpasa railway station. Right in the middle of it, as a matter of fact. Someone put a bullet in his head in plain view."

Keyes pursed his lips.

"There's going to be an investigation. I wonder if I can tell my superiors that the case has already been opened on your end . . ."

Keyes hung up.

Then he stared at the phone. The Italian would not be able to trace the call; ADS's security system guaranteed that. Let them do what they would with Leonard's body. It could not be traced back to him.

Yet he was starting to shake again. Haydarpasa, the man had said. So Dietz was heading east. To the Arabs.

It was the rat king. It was worse than he had feared.

A half-dozen determined men breaking into a particle accelerator, with Epstein's results in hand, could do untold damage. These men would be fanatics, after all. They would not pause at the thought of creating a singularity. They would be thinking of the seventy virgins awaiting them on the other side . . . beautiful like rubies, with complexions like diamonds and pearls . . .

He was going to throw up.

He pulled the trash basket out from below his desk and stared into it. His stomach was empty; but it didn't seem to know that. He swallowed painfully. After another few seconds, he had the nausea under control.

He shoved the basket away and leaned back in his chair, looking blankly at the telephone. So much bad news, coming into his life through such a little instrument. Why, he should destroy this thing. He should pull it out of the wall and fling it through the window behind the desk. As if that would change anything.

Keyes watched as his hand reached for the phone.

He watched as his fingers punched out a number. He kept watching, bemused by his hand's action, as he brought the receiver to his ear.

The phone rang twice. "Hello?" a voice said.

He cleared his throat. "Alice?"

"Yes?"

"Um, it's Jim. Jim Keyes. Is Rachel there?"

He could hear the intake of Rachel's mother's breath. Then the phone was set down with a clatter. A few moments passed. The phone was picked up again. "Hello?" Rachel said.

"It's me."

Silence.

"How are you?" he asked.

Silence.

"Listen," he heard himself saying. "I'm, uh. Listen. I'm in Boston. I wondered if you might . . ."

"You're here?"

"Yes. I wondered if you might want to . . . you know . . . um, grab a bite."

More silence.

"Rachel?"

"Yes."

"What do you say?"

"It's not the best time," she said.

"Dinner?"

She paused.

"We could go to the old IHOP. You know, the one we used to go to when we were . . ."

"Jim," she said. "Are you all right?"

He laughed. The sound of the laugh surprised him.

"No," he said. "No—Rachel—I'm not."

2.

Four hours later, he was setting down at Logan Airport.

It was insane to be leaving his office right now. This was not finished, not by a long shot. Yet Keyes himself *was* finished. He couldn't do it anymore.

He took a cab to the International House of Pancakes where he and Rachel had gone on their earliest dates, back when she had still lived with her parents, back when they had been two kids playing at being adults. In those days, he had driven six hours each way just to spend a weekend with Rachel—and none of it in bed.

Almost two decades had passed since his last visit, but the restaurant looked essentially unchanged. The same fragrant Dumpster was still located unfortunately close to the front entrance. The same bicycle rack out front was completely devoid of bikes, as ever. He stepped inside; chimes on the door jangled. The air-conditioning hit him in a blast. A gum-chewing hostess stepped forward with a menu. "One?" she asked.

"I'm meeting someone," Keyes said, and his eyes slid to what had been their usual booth.

Rachel was there, watching him.

Keyes went to join her, lurching along on the cane. He slipped into the booth, accepted the menu from the waitress, and then opened it, concentrating on the laminated choices. "Hi," he said, running an index finger down the list of pancakes.

"Hi," she said.

"Thanks for coming."

She said nothing.

"Same old menu," he said. He forced a chuckle. "Or is this new? Pigs in a blanket. Did they always have that here?" He glanced up. "I don't think they . . ."

Rachel looked spectacular.

She seemed ten years younger than she had at their daughter's wedding: rested, slim, and fit. She wore a simple white halter top, a turquoise necklace, and small silver-and-amber earrings. Her hair had been allowed to achieve its natural shade of graying auburn; her skin was clear and fresh.

". . . my God," he said. "You look terrific."

She looked away, demurely. She reached for her glass of water, sipped it, then carefully wiped lipstick off the rim. They both started to speak at the same time:

"What happened to—"

"How's your—"

"You first."

"No, go ahead."

"What happened to your leg?"

He opened his mouth, then closed it. He opened it again, wondering if he would tell her all of it now—the Project, the betrayals, the accident.

Instead, he heard himself saying, "I miss you."

She smiled.

"I want—we should try again."

She reached for his hand, gave it a gentle squeeze. "Jim," she said.

"It's just a part of life. It's just all part of it, Rachel. I know it's sad, but it doesn't mean we can't be there for each other . . ."

"Jim."

"I'm not saying it wasn't my fault as much as yours. I don't know why it's got to be anyone's fault. I mean, when you consider—when you think of what—"

"Jim."

"Yes."

She shook her head, slowly, and took her hand back.

His tongue scraped over his lips. "Excuse me," he mumbled. He pushed out of the booth, reaching for the cane.

The bathroom was beside a bank of pay phones. He went in and found it mercifully empty. He turned on the cold water, then leaned both hands against the sink. The tears were coming. He looked in the mirror and saw his face screwing up like a child's. His lip was quivering; he was about to blubber. He reached for the water and splashed two bracing handfuls across his face. Better. He turned off the tap, tore a paper towel from the dispenser, and patted viciously at his cheeks.

Before returning to the restaurant, he looked at himself in the mirror again. His color was high. His eyes were bloodshot. His cheekbones were stunningly clean. He looked like a corpse, or like a man on a hunger strike. How had he lost so much weight without realizing it?

After a moment, he went back to Rachel. "Sorry," he said, clambering into the booth with less grace than the first time.

She was looking at him sadly.

"So," he said. "You don't think, um . . ."

"I think," she said quietly, "that things happen for a reason."

"A reason?"

The waitress sidled up to the table. "Ready to order now?"

"Just coffee, thanks," Keyes said.

"Coffee. Thank you," Rachel said.

The waitress rolled her eyes, took the menus, and turned away.

"What does that mean—things happen for a reason?"

Rachel produced a wad of Kleenex. She set it on the table, at the ready.

"I think," she said slowly, "that God did what He did for a reason, Jim."

Keyes blinked.

"He called Jeremy back to Him for a reason. We can't hope to understand what that reason is. But He does. And if we'd been meant to stay together, then we would have. But we didn't. He has a plan, Jim. We need to trust in that—to trust in Him."

A moment passed.

"You've got to be fucking kidding," Keyes said.

The waitress brought their coffee, snapping her gum.

"Rachel," he started again, when she had gone.

"Yes."

"I'm . . . Please listen."

"I'm listening."

"I need you. When it comes down to it, we need each other. We're in this together, aren't we?"

A strand of hair fell from behind her ear; she pushed it back.

"We're in this together," he said again. He heard the tone of his own

voice—desperate, cracking—but was unable to change it. "I mean . . .
do you remember Jeremy's report? I thought—I didn't know what to
think. I didn't think anything. But now I see. I think I see. It's not
just . . . there are things bigger than us, that we can't understand. And
when he wrote about all the tails being tied up together, he was . . ."

"The tails?"

"The rat king. His report?"

Rachel looked confused. She shook her head, very slightly.

"You were upset by it," he said. "Well—it doesn't matter."

The tears were coming again; he wiped at his nose.

"Was it my fault?" he asked. "I should have gotten the car
checked? Is that what you think? But I did. Every five thousand miles,
a full checkup, oil change, the whole thing. Like clockwork. Two
weeks before the accident, I had it checked. I never told you that. But
that turn signal should have been working. It *was* working. It wasn't
my fault."

"I know."

"It wasn't."

"I know."

He lifted his coffee, looked at the oily slick on the surface, and set
it down again. "Honey," he said. "If you don't . . . if you won't come
back, then I'm . . . afraid of what I might do."

"What you might do," she echoed.

He nodded.

"What do you mean?"

"I don't even know."

A family in the next booth was listening. Because he was crying, of
course. He forced the tears down. He leaned forward, lowering his
voice. "I'm scared," he said plaintively. "That's all."

"I've got to go. I can't do this anymore. I'm sorry."

"Listen," he said. "Let's go away. Remember our honeymoon?

Remember that little stretch of beach? Let's go there. Let's go tonight—right now."

"Jim . . ."

"Please. Rachel. I'm so scared—"

"I'm seeing someone," she said.

3.

She pecked a kiss on his cheek. "I'm sorry," she said, then slipped behind the wheel of her car and fired the ignition.

He watched the car roll to the exit of the parking lot. Then he leaned against the Dumpster, enveloped in the smell of rot. He would have liked to cry again. If he could cry, maybe he could get some of the bad feeling inside him out. But he couldn't cry. The chance had passed. The feeling was inside him for good.

He found himself looking at the restaurant's sign: IHOP. Yet another acronym. He hated acronyms. They were meaningless. IHOP. What did that mean? *International House of Pancakes*, it meant. But what did *that* mean? The words were nonsense. *International House of Pancakes*. Was it really international? Was it really a house made of pancakes? No. It made no sense.

None of it made any sense.

Rachel's car was idling at the exit of the parking lot. She was trying to make a left turn into rush-hour traffic. Good luck, he thought.

I'm seeing someone.

He set the cane, and moved toward the car. He rapped on the passenger-side window. She looked over, surprised. Keyes opened the door and slipped inside. The interior of the car smelled of pine.

"Jim," she said. Now *she* was crying, he noticed. Lucky her. *She* got to cry; *she* got to get it out. She got to be weak, while he always had to be strong.

"Rachel," he said.

"I'm so sorry."

He reached out one hand, and began to massage the back of her neck.

"I miss you," she said. "I miss him. But I just can't do it anymore."

The traffic zipped past them. She would never be able to make a left turn into that, he thought coldly.

"When it first—for a while I thought—oh, God." She reached for the parking brake and pulled it, then began to look through her pockets for another wad of Kleenex. "For a while I thought we might still have a chance. But now I just . . . I can't do it anymore."

She opened her purse, still looking for Kleenex. His hand was still massaging the back of her neck, gently.

When he slammed her head into the steering wheel, the horn gave a startled bleat.

He pulled her head back and slammed it forward again. He saw a small piece of molding come off of the wheel. It was faux wood grain, he noticed. It had come off with barely a provocation. Piece-of-shit car, he thought.

Then he slammed her head into the window. The glass cracked. He did it again. The window became a web of soft, broken fragments; but it didn't fall out of the frame.

He put both hands around her throat and began to squeeze.

Rachel's face was turning purple. She didn't look ten years younger than her age anymore, he thought. Now she looked her age—older. He throttled her, shaking her head back and forth. Her temple was bleeding from the contact with the window. The traffic kept zipping past them, oblivious.

Her breath was hissing. Her hands were coming up, clawing at his face. He sneered, and squeezed harder.

She began to kick. Her feet connected with the bottom of the dashboard, twice, three times. He wondered if any of the molding would come off.

Then her struggles were weakening. After another moment, she was still.

He looked at her. His own breath was rasping in and out, burning his lungs.

Rachel was a rag doll, limp.

"I'm seeing someone," he mimicked. His voice was a high, cracking falsetto. "I'm seeing someone. I'm seeing someone."

Rachel didn't answer.

The traffic keep whizzing past.

Keyes sat without moving for what seemed like a very long time. Then he opened his door and stepped out of the car. He leaned against the cane, trying to catch his breath.

Soon he had caught it. He lurched around to the driver's side, shoved Rachel into the passenger's seat, sat down, and took off the parking brake.

He turned right, merging *with* the traffic instead of trying to turn against it, as any sane person would do.

TWENTY-ONE

I.

The two-berth sleeping car was clean and carpeted, with its own private washbasin and two beds that folded up, during the day, to transform the space into a sitting room.

Hannah had no memory of the first night, between Istanbul and Bucharest. As soon as the train pulled out of Sirkeci station, at a few minutes past eleven, she fell sound asleep in the lower berth. When she awoke the next morning, the Bosfor express was navigating the sunny river valleys of Bulgaria. The man had visited the dining car; a breakfast of bread, jam, and hot tea was waiting for her. He sat facing the rolling green landscape past the window, a newspaper held unopened in his lap.

As she ate, Hannah marveled at the fact that she had been able to sleep at all. In one way, she supposed, she'd had no choice. Her body had demanded rest. But if she had truly felt unsafe around the man, she would have found a way to avoid sleep. He had returned her purse to her, and there were pills in the purse that could have kept her awake. For the time being, however, she supposed he couldn't hurt her. He needed her to deliver the technical details that he thought were in her head. When—and if—the meeting with his contact occurred; when—and if—she was able to follow her charade through to the end, and convince the man that the secrets in the book were valuable—then she would need to watch herself.

But before that, if things went well, she would have the book. And then she would be long gone.

During the meal, her eyes kept moving to the dull knife with which she'd spread the jam. Did she have what it took to pick up that knife, as the man's attention was focused through the window, and . . .

. . . and what?

Lunge toward him, and bury the knife in his throat?

She did not.

They spent the day in the compartment, exchanging no more than a dozen words. The man slept for a time, again using his bag with the book inside as a pillow. She sat watching him, wondering if she could pick up the knife and do it now. She was still watching, still wondering, when he sat up, rubbed his eyes with his knuckles, and reached again for the newspaper, groggily.

In late afternoon, he visited the dining car again, and returned with sandwiches and a fresh thermos of tea. They ate in silence, watching the sun drop slowly behind the low hills in the distance.

That night, she slept less well. Her body had become accustomed to the motion of the boat: rolling, pitching, yawing, up and down, forward and back. The train, by comparison, was a side-to-side phenomenon, jiggling her like dice in a rack. When she did manage to fall asleep, the slumber was fitful. She felt in all too much motion: side to side on a train that was speeding forward, on a planet that rotated on two axes, circling a sun that circled the center of a galaxy that was itself in dizzying, never-ending motion.

Some time after midnight, the train stopped moving.

Hannah blinked awake. The man had left his own berth to look out the window. A moment later, a knock came at the door. Hannah's heart moved to her throat; her eyes found the man's. He nodded once, although she didn't know just what that meant.

They filed off the train with the other passengers, then stood in a line in the chilly predawn as their passports were checked by armed soldiers. Once again, the job she had done on her forgery passed inspection; and whatever passport the man was using did the same. They returned to their compartment in the small hours of the morning, and presently the train began to move again.

Hannah dozed.

2.

The third morning found the landscape changed: The greens had deepened and thickened, indicating an approach to western Europe.

They folded up the beds and then sat down to breakfast. It seemed to Hannah, judging from the new landscape, that they must be nearing their destination. And so the man, she supposed, might soon begin to dig for more details. She had given him only the briefest sketch of her burgeoning lie—enough to let him pique his contact's interest, but not enough to make Hannah herself unnecessary.

Sure enough, as the meal was finishing he said: "I've been wondering about something."

Hannah looked up. She popped the crust of bread she'd been holding into her mouth, and chewed.

"The formula," he said. "It describes the engine itself? Or the propulsion method used by the engine?"

She bought herself a few moments by chewing, then by swallowing, then by dabbing at her lips with a napkin. Her pulse thrummed lightly in her throat.

"There's really no difference," she said then.

"The craft *is* the engine."

"Right."

"I'm not sure I understand."

She considered elaborating for his benefit: painting a picture of the ramjet sucking down oxygen, turning the oxygen into fuel, the fuel into speed, creating a never-ending, always-increasing loop.

Instead, she summoned her courage. She set down the napkin and said: "I'm not sure I have a problem with that."

His brow creased.

"I like you needing me," she said flatly. "Because I need you. And fair's fair."

For a moment, she thought that she had pressed the wrong button. She remembered the man putting his hands on her, in the suburbs outside of Istanbul. If he came for her now, how would she defend herself? Her fingers moved a fraction of an inch toward the haft of the dull knife. If she had to, she could do it. If she had to, despite the fact that he outweighed her by eighty pounds . . .

Then he relaxed—once again just a laid-back, harmless man nearing the far side of middle age. His eyes twinkled, distantly amused.

"I think," he said mildly, "you should learn to trust a little more."

"I haven't told you all of it, you know. Without the rest, you'll be about ten percent short of a working blueprint."

A few moments passed in silence. Then he reached for his pack of cigarettes. He lit one and tapped an ash onto his plate. The ash began to shiver, jigging along with motion of the train.

"You're not the only one who needs to trust," he said. "For all I know, you're with Keyes."

"I'm not."

"But I have no way of knowing that."

"I'm only with myself."

"And with Frank," he said. Again, his eyes glinted. "Whoever that is."

She exhaled—hoping to imply impatience.

"Frank," she said, "is my ex-husband. He works for NASA, on the Pegasus rocket booster. That's used to launch the X-forty-three."

"The what?"

"I told you. You don't know all of it."

He considered. "And NASA is working with ADS?"

Hannah nodded, although she didn't know what ADS was. Then it occurred to her that the man might have been testing her. And she—in her eagerness to drive home the fact that she was still necessary to him—may have failed the test.

She watched him, wondering if it had been a trick.

He was still considering.

Her eyes moved to the knife again. If it happened, it would happen fast.

Half a minute passed. The train rocked back and forth, clattering the silverware against the china teapot, shivering the ash.

"Trust," he said once more. "There's no need for either of us to be suspicious. As long as no one gets greedy . . ."

He offered his hand.

Another few seconds passed; she reached for it. They shook.

Then she looked out the window again. The man smoked his cigarette. The train chugged on, racing with the sun.

TWENTY-TWO

I.

Jeremy was in fine form today.

Keyes liked to think that he bore some responsibility for Jeremy's performance: two runs, here in the third inning, with the promise of more to come. He had taught the boy how to choke up, after all. And the choking up was the main reason Jeremy was doing so well today. He kept finding the sweetheart part of the bat, and clubbing them out deep into left field . . .

Choking. Choking up.

The phone was ringing.

The call was on his direct line. But he couldn't take any more bad news. He would collapse . . . dissolve . . . implode. He answered the phone anyway. "Yes," he said dimly.

It was Brown, the DIA agent. "We've got him," Brown said.

He was out of breath. Keyes could hear traffic in the background. The man was calling from outside, by a highway.

"He went to his sister's ex-husband's house, in Jersey. We made the arrest five minutes ago."

"Bring him here," Keyes said.

"All right. But he wants to know what he's charged with. And he wants an attorney."

"Put a blindfold on. Gag him. Bring him here."

There was an uncomfortable silence.

"Do it," Keyes said.

"All right." Brown sounded uncertain. "But—"

Keyes hung up.

2.

"By the way," the man said as he took the turn.

Hannah glanced at him. He looked almost comically cramped, in the driver's seat of the little rental car, with his knees sticking up on either side of the steering wheel.

"From what I understand, Ismayalov's a tough customer. If he thinks he can cut us out of the loop and take the book for himself, he won't hesitate."

Meaning, Hannah thought, that she wasn't to provide enough details on the formula to make the two of them dispensable. *Way ahead of you*, she thought darkly.

"I don't want you to run him around too much—but I do want to leave some things unsaid. Make it clear that the deal comes with us, or it doesn't come at all. And when it comes time to doing the actual bargaining, leave it to me."

"Fair enough," she said, and looked out her window again.

The colonial-style mansion they were approaching was shaded by eucalyptus trees, set far back from the road. Blue sky unrolled above it, speckled with white clouds. As they drew closer, Hannah saw a woman working in a garden out front. She stood, taking off her gloves, and came to meet them. She was in her thirties, brunette and quite beautiful, with a joyless smile on her sun-browned face.

A man appeared at the mansion's front door: twice the woman's age, with a sharp nose and a crooked mouth. "Madeleine," he called. "Get us something to drink."

The woman bowed her head. She slipped away as the man came forward. He considered his visitors without much apparent interest. "You made good time," he said.

"We were on the road when I called."

"Come inside. I'm eager to hear how Andrei's doing."

He swept an arm cordially toward the mansion; they moved inside, with Hannah in the lead.

3.

The elevator opened into subbasement three.

Keyes stepped out, moving cautiously so as not to drop anything. One hand held the cane, the other a briefcase; in the crook of his arm was a thick manila file. He moved slowly down the corridor, following a yellow line painted on the concrete floor. Overhead, the fluorescents flickered and buzzed.

David Brown was standing outside detention area B-14: a large, bearish man with thick shoulders and a high widow's peak. When he saw Keyes, he rushed forward to relieve him of the briefcase. Keyes rearranged the file under his arm. Then he looked at Brown and nodded. Brown reached for the knob on the door and twisted it.

Andrei Yurchenko sat behind a featureless white table, the blindfold still covering his eyes.

He wore a limp linen suit, and kept both hands clearly visible on the table. He was a tall, gaunt man in his mid-fifties, with a thin neck grizzled from overshaving. His demeanor was that of a motorist pulled aside by an overeager state trooper—innocent, but more than willing to go through the rigmarole of due process, perfectly confident that he would come out in the clear.

Keyes and Brown exchanged a glance. They moved to the two chairs opposite the table from Yurchenko. Keyes set the file down on the table, and went to remove the blindfold; Brown set down the briefcase and took a seat.

Inside the briefcase was a Psychological Stress Evaluator—a polygraph, which used a pneumograph tube across the subject's chest and a blood pressure pulse cuff around the subject's arm to monitor reactions to questions. Impulses were then recorded by a needle on a moving graph paper. In truth, the PSE was not the most effective polygraph on ADS grounds. The Voice Stress Analyzer, which detected micro-tremors in the subject's speech, was a more accurate lie detector. But the VSA used columns of LED lights to display its results, and in Keyes's opinion, the old-fashioned moving graph paper possessed greater visual impact. Visual impact was all he was concerned with. There was no time left for games, for half-truths. Yurchenko would be broken, and would cooperate completely, or he would not cooperate at all.

Similarly, the thick file, which had Yurchenko's name typed in capitals on the identifying leaf, consisted almost entirely of blank pages. The actual FBI file on Yurchenko was eight pages long. Keyes had added another three dozen sheets of paper, hoping to send a clear signal: They knew everything there was to know about Yurchenko, and more; resistance would be futile.

He pulled the blindfold away with a small, theatrical flourish.

Then he moved around to the other side of the table and sat. Yurchenko reached up and rubbed at his eyes. Slowly, he absorbed the room: the cinder-block walls, the cement floor, the plastic table, the windowless door. His eyes moved over the file and the briefcase, moved up to Keyes's and Brown's faces, then moved back to the file and the briefcase.

Brown reached into his pocket, withdrew a portable tape recorder, depressed a button, and set it on the table. "August fourth," he said. "Subject Yurchenko, Andrei. Present are David Brown and James—"

Keyes reached out and shut off the tape recorder.

Two pairs of eyes turned to his face.

"This is off the record," Keyes said quietly.

Yurchenko guffawed. Keyes looked at him. The man spread his arms apologetically, and said, "I'm sorry."

"Is something funny?"

"No. It's just . . ."

Keyes waited.

"Good cop, bad cop," Yurchenko said. "You know. He puts out the recorder, you turn it off . . ."

"Ah."

"He protects my civil rights, you trample on them . . ."

"I see."

"'We have ways of making you talk,'" Yurchenko said, smiling. There was only the slightest hint of a Russian accent in his voice. He turned to Brown. "Then he says, 'Wait a minute. Take it easy.' Then you say . . ."

"You've got it all figured out," Keyes said.

Yurchenko kept smiling, without much humor, and shrugged modestly.

A few seconds passed. Then Brown took the tape recorder and returned it to his pocket. Keyes reached for the folder. He opened it and flipped some pages. He looked over the top of the file at Yurchenko, significantly. He flipped some more pages, then closed the folder and set it on the table.

"Well," he said. "Where would you like to start?"

4.

The sad-eyed, beautiful woman—Madeleine, Hannah remembered —set down a tray of water with lemon. Then she quickly removed herself, before her husband could send her away.

Ismayalov took a glass and squeezed a slice of lemon into it. "So," he said.

Hannah nodded. She leaned forward again on the couch. The room around them was cool, done in stone and antique furniture. On the coffee table between them sat the book, unopened.

"Mach 8," she repeated. "A flight that takes twenty-four hours would be cut to two. But of course, the real applications are military. Hypersonic bombers, cruise missiles . . ."

"And it's a NASA project?"

"NASA is one of the agencies involved."

"So what we've got here"—he indicated the book—"is a blue-print."

"Not precisely a blueprint. A formula, which describes the workings of the engine."

He reached for the book, opened to the back cover, looked at the chicken-scratch there, and closed it. "Hm," he said.

"Andrei seemed to think you might know of a buyer," said the man by the window.

"I might," Ismayalov said reflectively. "I might at that."

"Of course, you'd be compensated for your efforts. Say, five percent of whatever figure is decided upon?"

Ismayalov frowned.

Hannah looked from one man to the other. Her role in this, it seemed, already was finished.

"The usual figure, for an introduction such as this, is fifteen," Ismayalov said.

The man turned from the window. "Fifteen."

"Open to negotiation, of course. But yes. I think fifteen would be the usual."

"You see my problem with that. Andrei introduces me to you; you introduce me to a buyer; and if everyone along the way nips fifteen percent, my associate and I are left with precious little."

"Hm," Ismayalov said.

"Not that I'm not open to a compromise . . ."

5.

A phone was ringing.

The men looked at each other. "It's not me," Brown said.

Keyes reached for his cell phone. Indeed, it was he. He used the cane to lever himself to his feet, then stepped out into the corridor and brought the phone to his ear. "Yes."

It was Daisy; her voice was shaking. "Jim. You'd better come up here."

"Why?"

"You just got a call from a, uh, from a cop in Belmont, Massachusetts . . ."

He looked at the fluorescents. Was it right that they were buzzing so loudly?

". . . he wants to talk to you. He's got news, I guess."

"What kind of news?" Keyes asked calmly.

"I think, um . . . I think you'd better come up here and . . ."

He realized that she was on the verge of tears. "Daisy," he said in a monotone. "What is it?"

"You'd better just come up here. I think that would be best."

"I can't right now," Keyes said.

"It has to do with Rachel . . ."

"Tell her I'll call her back."

"No—you don't understand. It's . . ."

"I'm in the middle of something," he said, and terminated the connection.

Before opening the door again, he took a moment. His breathing was even. His hands were steady. But they would not be for much longer. Time was ticking away. And Rachel had been found; police were calling his office. *Time,* he thought. That was what it all came down to, wasn't it? There was never enough time.

He opened the door and beckoned Brown to join him in the hall.

"What is it?" Brown asked, as the door closed behind him.

"There's a call for you. In my office."

"A call?"

"Your wife," Keyes said. "Daisy's got her on hold. It sounds like an emergency. You'd better run."

Brown scowled. Then he turned, and began to follow the yellow line toward the elevator at a trot.

Keyes moved back into the cell. Yurchenko was looking up at

him blankly. Something about the man's face made Keyes suspect that he had glanced at his own file, when Brown had left the room, and discovered the empty pages. He almost thought he could see a single yellow canary feather falling from the corner of the man's mouth.

Keyes remained standing, so that he towered over Yurchenko. "Where were we?" he asked.

"I don't remember."

"Francis Dietz. You gave him a name."

"Ah . . . yes. So you said."

"The name was 'the vulture.'"

"I told you already," Yurchenko said. "You've made a mistake. You've confused me with someone else."

Keyes looked at the man, icily.

"And I've told you already," Yurchenko said, "that I'm not going to say another word without a lawyer."

"There's no time for that."

"What country is this? The last time I checked—"

"I," Keyes said clearly, "have no more time for this."

6.

"Madeleine," Ismayalov called.

A moment passed. Then the woman appeared in the shadowed doorway of the living room. She had been back in the garden; the heavy work gloves were on her hands again, and a floppy sun hat had been added to the ensemble.

"Darling," Ismayalov said. "I wonder if you could do me a favor."

Hannah watched from the couch. The man by the window was

looking into his glass of water, as if the proceedings in the room could not have interested him less.

"My friends here," Ismayalov said, "are going to meet with the prince. They have a business proposition that I think may interest him. But I'd rather not have such business conducted in my home. One never knows who's watching."

Madeleine nodded warily.

"I was thinking," Ismayalov said. "You have that friend—house-sitting for the Americans, yes?"

She blinked. "Henri Jansen," she said. "Yes."

"Can he keep his mouth shut?"

"I think so."

"Do you think he'd be willing to host a meeting?"

Madeleine shrugged. "I could ask."

"Please do."

She nodded, turned, and began to leave.

"Madeleine," he called.

She turned back.

"Encourage him," Ismayalov said. "You might mention that I know he's been consorting with some of the wives, in the area, when the husbands aren't around."

Hannah thought she saw some color drain from the woman's face; but she couldn't be sure.

"All right, Vladimir."

"Tomorrow evening would be good, I think. If he's willing."

"All right."

"And our friends will be spending the night here. Could you make up a guest room?"

She bowed, then vanished.

Ismayalov watched her go. He looked at Hannah, then leaned forward and picked up the book. He opened to the back cover and looked closely at the equations there, as if he understood their significance.

By the window, the man raised his glass and tilted it back, letting the last drop of water slide slowly into his throat.

7.

Keyes felt himself drifting again.

He remained vaguely conscious of what he was doing to Yurchenko—but in his mind, he was back at the Little League game. The splintered bleachers, the burning sun. Jeremy was stepping to the plate again. People were clapping and cheering. Jeremy turned to look at his father, and smiled. Keyes smiled back. He stood up, clapping louder than anyone.

Yurchenko's face was lost behind a mask of blood. He was trying to speak.

Jeremy had a bee sting on his hand. But he wasn't letting it slow him down. He was taking his stance, choking up on the bat, just as Keyes had shown him. That was one hell of a boy, Keyes thought. For this boy he would do anything. For this boy he would give it all.

"Ismayalov," Yurchenko was saying.

He was struggling to draw a breath. The breath bubbled. "Vladimir Ismayalov. In the name of Christ, please . . ."

Keyes stood up. He straightened his shirt. He looked down at Yurchenko, then dropped the piece of wood in his hand. Where had the piece of wood come from? He couldn't remember. Then he looked for his cane, and it came back to him. The cane had snapped when he had struck Yurchenko with it; that was where the wood had come from.

He hobbled to the door. As soon as he had stepped into the hallway, he ran into David Brown. Brown was saying something, calling after him. But Keyes ignored him, limping off down the hall.

He had a name. Ismayalov. And as soon as he got back to his office, he would find a file to go with the name.

Brown was still calling, his voice echoing hollowly down the corridor. Keyes reached the elevator, hit the button, and waited.

Ismayalov. The vulture.

The elevator door opened, and he stepped inside.

TWENTY-THREE

I.

The mistral was blowing again.

Henri Jansen looked up from his camera, at the waving trees on the front lawn. The trees were bowing hard to the south. It was too early in the year, he thought, for the mistral to announce itself with such authority. This was, doubtless, a false alarm.

But he recapped the lens—he'd snapped a few quick pictures already, to make sure the damned thing still worked—and then went inside to shutter the windows, just to be on the safe side.

In the living room, he found a pair of scorpions scuttling along the edge of the fireplace. He looked at them with a frown tugging at his lips. Perhaps this *was* the real mistral, a little early, after all. Animals were more in touch with weather than people, and something had stirred up their nest.

After looking at the scorpions for a moment, he crossed the room and picked up a trash basket tucked beneath the piano. He carried it back to the fireplace, swept the scorpions inside with a magazine, and then brought the basket outside to dump them.

Madeleine Ismayalov's car was rolling down the long driveway, kicking up twin plumes of dust.

He watched the Audi approach, still frowning. Why was Madeleine visiting now? He'd agreed to offer the house for her husband's meeting that evening—a fine chance to meet the man, to make sure that Henri ended up being counted as a friend, to the vulture, instead of as an enemy—but it was still only early afternoon.

The car jerked to a stop. The door opened, and Madeleine came out. "Henri," she said. "I couldn't say it on the phone, with my husband in the room . . ."

Her eyes were wildly, nervously active. Her hands were in fluttery, frightened motion. Henri felt something cold close around his heart.

"I don't have much time. I told him I was going to the market. We need to—"

"Calm down," Henri said.

"I think he knows," she said.

The icy vise around his heart tightened.

"Calm down," he said again. His voice sounded empty, powerless. "Come inside."

She followed him over the patio, through the front door. "Maybe I'm wrong. But he made some comment, about how you and some of the married women in the area . . ."

"He what?"

"I don't know if he meant me. I don't think so. But I don't know."

"What did he say?"

"Just that. About you and some of the married women. Oh, but I think he knows. He knows, Henri."

He led her to the kitchen. She sat on a tall stool by the counter. He uncorked a bottle, filled a glass for her, and passed it over. Then he raised the bottle and drank directly from the mouth.

She was near hysteria. That wasn't surprising. He felt near hysteria himself. Ismayalov knew. He knew, and now one—or both—of them would pay a price.

"Henri," she moaned.

"Let's not jump to any conclusions," Henri said. "What did he say exactly?"

"He said, tell him I know about him and some of the wives."

Henri raised the bottle, and drank again.

"We could go away," she said. "I have money. I've been saving it. We could get right in my car and go to the airport and go anyplace, anyplace in the world . . ."

"What about tonight?"

"It doesn't matter. Where would you like to go, Henri? Anyplace you want. I'll pay for it. I've got enough to keep us fine for a few years, at least . . ."

"Baby," he said. "Come here."

She immediately set down the wine and came off the stool, into his arms. He hugged her tightly, but with as little intimacy as he could manage. He needed to end it now, immediately. If it wasn't already too late . . .

"Madeleine," he said.

"Yes," she said.

"We can't go away."

"Yes, we can."

"No. Go where? He'd find us."

"Anywhere—"

"You're talking crazy."

She buried her head in his shoulder. "I know," she said.

A few moments passed. Her body shuddered against his. He was surprised, when she leaned away, to see that her eyes were still dry.

He let the embrace break, and took a step backward. For a few seconds, they stood awkwardly facing each other. She looked at him imploringly, desperate for a sign of warmth.

Henri turned away, to shutter the kitchen windows.

When he turned around again, Madeleine was gone.

Her glass of wine sat on the counter; he could see a smudge where her hands had encircled it. He moved back through the foyer and stepped outside in time to see her getting into the Audi. Now she *was* crying—her face gleaming with tears through the windshield.

She twisted the key, ground the gears, and spun the car around. Henri watched without moving to stop her. What would be the point? She would need to face reality sooner or later. The relationship was finished. If he could make it through tonight's meeting with Ismayalov in one piece, he would not jeopardize anything by seeing her again.

Perhaps Ismayalov, he thought, didn't even know.

A moment later, the car was roaring off down the driveway, lost behind a cloud of dust that was swiftly taken by the wind and shredded.

2.

Brown handed the photograph back to Keyes without a word.

Before returning it to his bag, Keyes spent a moment looking at the woman's face. Was it possible that she really was an innocent, who had gotten wrapped up in this out of sheer bad luck? It boggled the mind—yet it seemed to be the truth.

Then he put the photograph back into his bag, and kicked the bag back under the seat in front of him.

The flight attendant was coming down the aisle, offering them menus. Brown took one; Keyes shrugged it off. His entire nervous system was humming. If he tried to put food into his body, it would end up on his shoes. Brown didn't seem to have much of an appetite either. When the flight attendant returned, he asked for a Diet Coke and nothing else.

As he handed the menu back, he avoided looking at Keyes. For the entire flight, he had been avoiding looking at Keyes.

Keyes could live with that. As long as he had the additional man-power, he was satisfied. They had a name for the vulture; they had the man's address in southern France. Dietz, in all likelihood, was at that address at this very moment, trying to sell the formula.

He stared at the back of the seat in front of him, and kept his mind assiduously focused on the job at hand.

3.

Dietz checked the gun for a final time, then slipped it into his bag beside the book.

Suddenly, he turned. The woman had come into the bedroom behind him.

She gave a lackluster smile. "I don't suppose you've got one of those for me," she said.

It was Dietz's turn to smile, very slightly.

"Don't worry," he said. "I've got your back."

The wind was still picking up, keening through the valley. She moved to look out at the shivering trees, fingering one earring absently.

"Trust," Dietz said. "Remember?"

The woman didn't answer. She kept her back facing him, her narrow shoulder blades carefully and perfectly still.

Dietz picked up the bag and went to stand next to her.

"Come on," he said softly.

A moment passed. Then she turned, and followed him from the room.

TWENTY-FOUR

I.

The first car arrived at five minutes past seven.

Henri Jansen was setting down a tray of hors d'oeuvres when he caught the sound of the engine. He straightened, and then looked around the living room, taking this last minute of solitude to make sure everything was in order. What did one serve for an occasion such as this? He had opted for simplicity—brie and bread, celery sticks and mushroom caps. Four bottles of wine were set on the coffee table, alongside eight glasses and a silver corkscrew; the bar by the fireplace had been opened.

He wondered fleetingly, as he checked the spread, if Madeleine had been right about her husband. He wondered if the man would have words for him—or, perhaps, something stronger than words.

Then the car's engine was dying, and there was no more time for wondering. He straightened his jacket and went to meet his first guest, trying to reassure himself as he walked. It would be fine. Madeleine was mistaken; Ismayalov did not know. There was no need for concern.

The Rolls-Royce was the latest model: a Silver Seraph. The driver was an olive-complexioned man in a black chauffeur's uniform, standing a few inches over six feet tall. Henri watched from the doorway as he left the driver's seat and went to open the car's back door.

The man who emerged was short—perhaps five foot seven—wearing a blue business suit, a mustache and goatee, and tinted glasses. He looked familiar. Then Henri had it. Put the man in Bedouin garb and he would have been instantly recognizable from the media: flamboyantly spending his millions with hollow-cheeked models on hundred-foot yachts, winning Kentucky Derbies, making conspicuous investments in American high-technology companies. Yet now he was dressed like any other businessman, and seemed very much at ease.

"Welcome," Henri said, not certain if he should address himself to the man or to his driver, instead sending his words directly between them.

The man in the blue business suit gave a slight but cordial bow.

The driver preceded his charge into the house. He stepped over the threshold and peered left, toward the kitchen, then right, toward the sunken living room. Henri stood to one side, waiting. When the man had satisfied himself that no ambush was waiting, he nodded at the prince, who stepped forward with a pleasant half smile on his face.

"A beautiful house," he said. He was soft-spoken, almost shy, and surprisingly young. His English was excellent, with an added trill. "How long have you been here?"

"Only since the beginning of the season. I'm looking after it for a friend."

The man kept smiling, but looked vaguely disappointed.

They moved into the living room. The driver—who doubled as a bodyguard, Henri was gathering—positioned himself by the entrance, where he stood ramrod straight. The prince walked around the space leisurely, examining the sculptures and the paintings on the walls, inspecting the solidly wrought antique poker by the fireplace.

"Wine?" Henri said, moving toward the table.

"Absinthe martini, please. Thank you."

Henri detoured to the bar. As he splashed vodka into a glass, he heard the hum of another engine. He quickly added vermouth and absinthe, then handed over the drink before returning to the front patio.

This car was a black Mercedes: polished to a high shine, engine murmuring. Vladimir Ismayalov's car. It pulled up beside the Rolls, moving slowly, and the engine died.

As Henri waited for the door to open, his right eyelid began to twitch. What if Madeleine had been right? What if Ismayalov had orchestrated this evening as part of some complicated revenge?

No. Ismayalov didn't know.

He hoped.

He recognized the man from Madeleine's photographs: hunched, dark, beetle browed. He had driven himself. He stepped out of the car and looked at Henri. "You're the house-sitter," he said.

Henri drew himself up a little straighter, and nodded. "Henri Jansen."

"Vladimir Ismayalov. Madeleine's husband."

The handshake was all too strong; Ismayalov made a point of taking Henri's hand slightly off center, and then squeezing the bones together. *He knows,* Henri thought.

Ismayalov crunched Henri's bones together for a few seconds, then took his hand back. "My friends are a minute behind," he said.

Henri led Ismayalov inside. The bodyguard/driver was still positioned by the entrance to the living room, his arms folded imperiously. The prince was sitting on a low couch. As Ismayalov entered the room, he stood. "Vladimir!"

Ismayalov grinned. "There you are! Recovered yet?"

"Halfway," the young prince said. He turned to Henri. "Most people go for a walk. Vladimir goes for a marathon."

"He complains, but he loves it. He needs the exercise."

"He's full of shit. Look at us. Which one needs exercise?"

Henri smiled. His eyelid was still twitching. "What are you drinking?" he asked Ismayalov.

"Whatever he's having."

Henri went to fix the drink. Once again, the sound of an engine caught his ear. That would be the friends—the last to arrive.

He handed the glass to Ismayalov and went to meet them.

The final car was a Mini, small and cheap and cramped. A rental, Henri thought. A man was behind the wheel, a woman in the passenger seat. As they parked, the wind gusted strongly. Henri's hands went to his hair, trying to pat it back into place.

The man was a typical oversized American, both wide and tall. The woman was pretty and poised, a few years younger than Henri, dressed well. His eyes ran up and down her body of their own accord. "Welcome," he said.

Neither answered. Henri gestured them inside.

Before following, he paused to look up at the sky.

The sun hung low, like an overripe plum. The sky was clear; there would be no rain tonight. Yet the wind was blowing harder than ever.

He looked up for another moment, and then followed his guests into the house.

2.

"Ever fire a gun?"

Keyes, who had been watching the pastures outside his window turn orange, looked over. "No," he said. "Well—at summer camp, once. When I was a boy. A twenty-two."

"Reach into my bag, there."

Keyes turned to the back seat of the 4X4. He found Brown's bag and dragged it around into his lap. He opened it and found a tangle of leather harnesses. Attached to the harnesses were holsters; instead the holsters were guns, black and squat and ugly.

"Your basic Glock," Brown said, keeping his eyes on the road. "Easy to shoot. Internal safety, so you don't need to worry about that. Seventeen rounds in the clip."

Keyes turned the weapon over in his hands, surprised at its weight.

"Just point and squeeze. But be ready for the recoil; use both hands. Your hands are going to be shaking anyway. And be prepared for the noise. It's loud."

Keyes slipped his finger over the trigger, and practiced sighting on a tangle of passing brush.

"Aim for the body," Brown said. "Two shots at a time. Keep shooting until he goes down."

Keyes grunted acknowledgment.

He returned the gun to his lap, and returned his attention to the view outside his window. They passed vineyards and fields, shallow wandering creeks, climbing rock formations. Every quarter mile or so, a smaller road led off into wilderness.

Five minutes passed. "Think we missed it?" Brown asked then.

The road on which Ismayalov had his house, he meant. Keyes

didn't think they had. But he opened the glove compartment and took out the map as Brown eased the 4X4 to the side of the road.

They both bent over the crackling paper, studying the web of roads in the dimming light. "We're here," Brown said, pointing. "And we want to be . . ."

"Up here."

Less than a quarter mile away, if he read the key correctly. Suddenly he felt slack inside, and hot; his chest tightened painfully.

Brown leaned back into his seat and resumed driving.

When they reached the driveway, Brown pulled over again. They left the car and checked their weapons. Then they took off toward a distant colonial-style mansion. Keyes limped along without the help of a cane. The ground was muddy, sucking at his shoes. The night breeze smelled of eucalyptus and lilac.

Aim for the body, he thought. *Aim for the body. Two shots at a time.*

A single car was parked outside the house, an Audi. The two men paused, listening. The front door of the house, between trellises of ivy, was cracked open. A radio was playing something gnawingly familiar—Billy Joel.

Brown looked at the door, looked at Keyes, and began to move again. He put himself to one side of the cracked-open door and peered inside the house. He pushed the door open another inch. Then he was gone, leaving Keyes alone on the patio.

Keyes found his courage. He followed, clutching the Glock tightly with both hands.

A dim, damp foyer. Van Gogh and Chagall on the wall—originals, Keyes sensed. Several arched doorways opened off this front hall. All were dark except the last doorway on the left. The same doorway from which the music was coming.

Brown moved toward it, cautiously.

Two shots, Keyes thought. *Aim for the body.*

The room was a kitchen.

A woman sat at a low table, crying. On the table before her was a half-empty bottle of wine and an overflowing ashtray. On the counter, a bowl of fruit and the radio. Hanging from the ceiling were heavy skillets and pots. Nestled beside the refrigerator was a cat, who looked back at Keyes jadedly.

When the two armed men stepped into the kitchen, the woman looked up. She wiped a hand across her nose. A bitter smile crossed her face.

"You're looking for Vladimir?" she asked.

3.

Once again, Brown pulled to the side of the road.

Twilight whispered around them as a strong wind stirred the fields. Brown had taken a pair of binoculars from his bag; now he was training them to the east, the direction in which the long driveway led.

Keyes, with his bare eyes, could make out the house that the woman had described. There were smaller structures around the house—bungalows, or outbuildings. Past the house were more vineyards, purple with lavender.

"Three cars," Brown said. "One's a Rolls, I think."

"Let me see."

Brown handed over the binoculars. It took Keyes a moment to find the cars and focus on them. One was a station wagon, parked almost behind the house, looking unoccupied. Another was a black Mercedes. Beside the black Mercedes, as Brown had reported, was a silver Rolls-Royce.

"Don't look now," Brown said softly. "Company."

Keyes swept the binoculars to the right. Another car was heading down the driveway, raising dust. For a moment, he thought it would be the Audi; the woman had managed to escape from her bonds, and had come to warn her husband. But it was a Mini. He followed it, his thumb working on the focus wheel. As the car parked, a man came out of the house to greet it. Keyes didn't recognize the man: in his mid-thirties, handsome and confident of carriage, nattily dressed.

But he recognized the people who came from the Mini to meet the man. One was the woman. The other was Dietz.

He lowered the binoculars, and looked over at Brown.

4.

As the sun went down, the windows turned into mirrors.

Henri watched as the swimming pool, by degrees, became a reflection of the sunken living room. The process took about twenty minutes, and was not really all that interesting. But he focused on it anyway, because he didn't want to hear what the people around him were saying. To hear what they were saying seemed like a very bad idea.

Hosting this event in the first place was starting to seem like a very bad idea.

But it was too late to back out. He couldn't suddenly refuse his hospitality; nor could he leave the room, not when he was required to empty ashtrays and refill drinks. All he could do was stand, staring fixedly out the window, pretending not to hear.

"—a variety of offers," the American was saying. "I'm a pragmatist, gentlemen. It makes no difference to me where this ends up. But I do prefer to conduct business with trustworthy people, and Vladimir assures me that you qualify. So I'm glad to have the opportunity to give you this chance . . ."

He was standing before the fireplace, hands folded behind his back, making his pitch. His voice was confident, low, almost musical. Vladimir and the woman and the prince sat on the low couches, listening attentively. The bodyguard/driver stood in the doorway, motionless.

"Of course I understand the need for prudence. Yet time is of the essence. We have another meeting in forty-eight hours, with certain parties who shall remain nameless. What I'd like to do is write down a figure . . ."

He was looking around for a piece of paper. Henri moved to the piano, reached behind a songbook on the shelf, and found a pad. He carried it to the American. At the same time, Ismayalov reached into a pocket and produced a ballpoint pen.

". . . and we can go from there."

The American took the pad, took the pen, and wrote down his figure. He took two steps and set the pad, facedown, on the table. The Saudi reached forward and picked it up. He read it, his face expressionless.

A moment passed, and then another.

He was opening his mouth to speak when suddenly a dog began to bark, from very close to the house.

The prince looked at his bodyguard, then at Henri.

"It's the neighbor's dog," Henri said. "It's nothing."

Nobody seemed reassured.

"I'll take care of it," Henri said, and slipped out of the room past the bodyguard, heading for the front door.

5.

It was the wind, he thought as he stepped outside; nothing more.

But the little terrier's timing couldn't have been worse. Tensions were running high. The evening had been moving along nicely, drawing toward a close. And now Sylvie, with a single string of hoarse barks, had put everybody on edge.

For some reason, she had stopped barking. Because the wind was dying down again, Henri guessed. But he would find her anyway, and shoo her back to her own property. For the wind might pick up again, and if the dog started barking every time that happened, these people would never finish their goddamned business . . .

He moved around the house, approached the swimming pool. From here he could see inside the brightly lit living room, although they couldn't see out. The living room looked like a fishbowl; five pairs of eyes stared blindly at the glass.

"Sylvie," he called. He snapped his fingers, peering into the night. "Come here, girl."

A movement from the far side of the pool—a short rustling. He walked in that direction.

"Don't be that way," he said. "It's me. Henri."

There she was—standing in tall grass, her tail wagging.

Somebody was standing behind her. Two somebodys.

As he looked at them, his mouth went dry.

One was raising a gun.

After that, things happened very quickly.

TWENTY-FIVE

I.

Keyes raised the gun with shaking hands.

If he fired, he would give away their presence. But their presence would be given away anyway; for the man was looking right at them.

Brown, beside him, was starting to move. He was circling around behind the man. Perhaps he could take care of it without making noise. Look how easily he had calmed the dog.

Yet Brown was too late. For even now the man was backpedaling, turning, breaking into a run. Heading back toward the house, where Keyes could see the five people pinned, in the bright light, like statues in a museum exhibit.

Aim for the body, he thought.

He fired.

At first he thought the gun had exploded in his hands. His wrists bent back painfully; the sound seemed impossibly loud. Then he realized that the gun had not exploded at all. That was the recoil, the noise of which Brown had warned him. How on earth could one fire two shots at a time, Keyes wondered, when even a single shot produced such a violent reaction?

The man stopped running.

He paused. His legs buckled.

Keyes watched, staring.

The man tumbled into the pool with a terrific splash.

The five people in the house scattered.

2.

At the sound of the shot, fear closed Hannah's throat.

She found herself staring at her own wavering reflection in the mirror-windows, struggling to draw a breath. The people around her were similarly frozen, in tableau: the Saudi sitting on the couch, the Russian standing, the man with whom she had traveled halfway around the world in the process of standing—all staring at the glass, trying in vain to look through themselves into the night beyond.

In the next instant, they were scattering.

The bodyguard in the doorway was the first to move. He was coming toward the couch, reaching for his charge. And the Saudi was moving to meet him, as if some elemental force were bringing them together. The taller man was wrapping his body itself around the smaller one, enveloping him, dragging him toward the front door.

The Russian was also moving—but aimlessly, stepping toward the piano and then pausing, lost.

Her eyes flicked to the American, her traveling companion. He was sinking. To Hannah, he looked like a balloon with the air leaking out. It took a moment for her brain to process what she was seeing: a trained man dropping to the floor, out of the range of fire.

She tried to do the same. But the fear was also paralysis, and she couldn't move.

There came the sound of a splash.

The dog was barking again.

Where was the book?

In the man's bag, of course. And the bag was on the couch, where he had been sitting. For the first time, he and the book had become separated.

Move, she thought.

Now the American was slithering across the floor. He was going for the light switch, Hannah realized. The Russian was still lost, walking in circles. The bodyguard and the Saudi prince were already gone.

She looked from the bag to the Russian to the man reaching for the light switch. Her eyes kept moving and rested on the fireplace, on the wrought-iron poker leaning up against it.

Her paralysis broke; she reached for the poker.

The lights went out.

3.

Brown was racing around to the front of the house.

Keyes stayed where he was, aiming the gun across the top of the pool at the living room. The people there had scattered—except for the woman. She was petrified, looking blankly out at him goggle-eyed. He sighted on her. His hands were still shaking. He tried to take aim. *Aim for the body.* To his left, the dog was letting loose a volley of hoarse, panicked barks. He ignored it.

His finger tightened on the trigger.

The lights went out.

He lowered the gun, blinking.

In a moment, his eyes would adjust to the starlight. But for now all he could see was flickering ghost images, the remnants of the lights inside the house. He could hear the surface of the pool, hissing softly and somehow luridly.

He stepped to his right, away from the dog, moving far enough that he wouldn't fall in the pool. Then he lurched forward, following in Brown's footsteps.

4.

Something was coming at Dietz.

After hitting the light, he became aware of the thing rushing in his direction. He fell back into a combat stance, from instinct. But the shape was rushing past him, clumsy in the darkness, making for the front door. It was the Russian, Ismayalov.

He passed Dietz, knocked into something—the something fell to the floor, shattered loudly—and kept going.

So close, Dietz thought.

They had been within minutes of making the deal. He had been within minutes of securing his future, of putting it all behind himself and escaping somewhere with Elizabeth Webster. And now it was falling apart: the Saudi already gone, the Russian going; intruders outside. Armed. Who were they? Keyes? Ford?

But it was not too late. As long as he had the book, he could still make things right.

Yet the room was pitch-black. In a few seconds, his vision would adjust. But for now he could see nothing but shapes. Better than being under bright lights, offering himself as a target. But frustrating nevertheless. For he had had to let go of the book. And the woman—

—where was the woman?

He was conscious of a shape, in the place where she had been. The shape was moving. Something heavy dragged along the floor, rasping. Dietz reached for his pistol. But the pistol was in the bag; the bag was on the couch.

He stepped forward. His shins rapped against the coffee table, painfully.

To his right, whistling up into the air and then coming down . . .

5.

Hannah heard the man walk into the coffee table.

She hefted the poker. She raised it above her head. She thought of the suburbs outside of Istanbul, the way the man had put his hands on her.

She swung the poker down with all the strength she could muster.

Her first thought was that she had missed. There had been only a quiet sound, after all; whatever the poker had hit had a lot of give. It was not the solid rap she would have expected, at putting the poker against the man's skull. Instead, it felt as if the heavy iron had sunk into the pulpy flesh of a watermelon.

She tried to raise it again, to take another swing, and was surprised when the poker refused to rise.

It was stuck in something. Then the something it was stuck in was folding, collapsing, and the poker was torn from her hands.

She backed up until she hit the cool stone of the fireplace. Then she stood, listening to her own shallow breathing. Except for her breathing, the room was silent.

Slowly, her eyes began to filter out shapes in the black.

First she saw the piano. Then the coffee table, closer. A lump was half on, half off the coffee table. The lump, she realized, was the man she had hit with the poker—motionless.

The book was beyond him, in the bag on the sofa. But she couldn't make herself move forward, within reach of that lump. Instead she began to tiptoe in the other direction, toward the foyer. Her feet found the steps. She climbed them backward, still staring into the gloom.

Outside, an engine was starting.

The dog kept barking.

Then she was in the foyer. The front door was open; silver light trickled in. She was moving for it when a sudden rattle of shots came from directly outside.

She screamed, and backed up again.

Up the stairs, to the second floor? But she would be trapped there. In the other direction, deeper into the house? Or back into the living room?

She went back to the living room, the echoes of her scream ringing in her ears. Now she could see more clearly. The man was still slumped over the table, still motionless. The poker protruded from his head.

She moved around him, toward the couch. One foot slipped in something wet. She lost her balance, caught it again. Then the bag was there, right in front of her. She grabbed it and hugged it to her chest.

A car was pulling away. She listened as the sound of the engine dwindled.

Quiet descended on the house. The dog's barks were receding; the engine sound was gone.

Hannah reached into the bag. She found the book, dug past it. Her fingers closed around the grip of the gun. She withdrew it, moving the bag to her other hand.

Silence.

She stood in the darkness, her heart pounding in her throat.

6.

Keyes came around the front of the house, and hesitated.

Brown was there: feet spread, aiming the gun in his hands at the windshield of the oncoming Mercedes. Beyond him, another car was disappearing down the driveway. The men in the house, Keyes thought, had reached their cars. The disappearing Rolls belonged to the slight man who had been the first to move, with his bodyguard. And the Mercedes must have belonged to the other, stockier one: the Russian.

As Keyes watched, Brown began to fire. He squeezed the trigger in bursts of two. Somehow he managed to absorb each recoil, to keep holding the gun level. He fired deliberately, as if enough deliberation might somehow stop the Mercedes from running him down; with each shot his wrists flicked up gracefully. *One-two; three-four; five-six.*

But the car didn't slow.

It took Brown full-on.

Keyes saw his body roll over the hood, over the windshield, soaring up into the air. A long, lissome moment passed before he hit the ground again. The thud sounded dull and meaty.

The Mercedes screamed off down the driveway.

Keyes moved forward. But he knew even before he'd crouched beside Brown that the man was dead. He started to search for a pulse, then took his hand back when he saw the angle of the neck for which he was reaching.

The engine revved throatily, then diminished. Nothing rose to replace it except the eerie whistle of the wind.

Presently, Keyes gained his feet. After all the noise, the silence seemed preternatural, suffocating. He looked at the door of the house. The door was ajar.

He licked his lips.

He stepped toward the door.

The foyer was quietly, coldly empty. He pushed his way in. The house creaked around him. Before him, a staircase led up. To his right was the room in which the meeting had been going on. That was where they would be, he thought; however many of *them* there were.

He considered turning, leaving, limping back down the driveway to the 4X4. But he had come too far to give up now. Instead, he stepped cautiously into the living room. There was cold all through him. His heart itself seemed to have turned to ice; it beat clumsily, thuddingly.

He stood, staring at the room before him, and his eyes began to pick out details.

To his left: a body slumped over a low table. To his right: the piano, hulking in the dimness. And directly before him: a figure.

The figure held something, trained on his chest.

Keyes started to bring up the gun, to wrap both hands around it, preparing himself to absorb the recoil with a flick of his wrists, as he had seen Brown do.

Then the something whispered.

7.

Hannah squeezed the trigger.

There was only the smallest, thinnest sound. Perhaps the safety was on, she thought distantly. Perhaps that was why the gun hadn't fired. And yet there had been an impact, in the fine bones of her wrist. Before she even realized how strong the impact had been, she had dropped the gun.

The man standing before her gasped.

He staggered backward. Something heavy fell from his hand, making a wet sound as it hit a puddle on the floor.

He reached out a hand to support himself. He leaned against one wall, shakily.

Hannah cradled her right wrist into her body. The wrist throbbed. She had broken a bone there, she thought. So the gun had fired, after all.

The man kept leaning against the wall. Gingerly, he began to lower himself toward the floor. She could hear a rattle in his breath. He slipped; then he was lying on his side, curling into a fetal position.

A moment passed. His breathing slowed, rasping.

She waited.

The time between breaths lengthened. At last, he gave a long, agonized inhalation. Five seconds passed, and the breath had not come out. Ten seconds; twenty.

There was no sound but the wind.

Hannah raised a hand, shuddering, and covered her eyes.

TWENTY-SIX

I.

The lake was in eastern Maine and the cabins were in the trees on its bank, screened from view by balsam and pine.

As Roger Ford approached the cabins, he inhaled appreciatively. The trees were pungent, sharp and clean in a way that artificial pine scent could never be. It occurred to him that he didn't spend nearly enough time out of the city anymore. There had been a time, he remembered, when he had managed to get away almost every other weekend—hiking or camping or fishing with old friends. Now he spent all his weekends in the office, or so it seemed; and the old friends had fallen by the wayside, or so it seemed, dropping off the face of the earth one by one.

He gave his head a small shake, and checked his watch. In an hour, they needed to be back at his car in the parking lot on the far side of the lake. A half hour after that, they needed to be aboard the private Gulfstream that would return them to Langley. So now was not the time for reverie.

He kept moving, picking his way carefully over the forest floor. It was autumn and the leaves underfoot were turning to mulch. In his Italian loafers and tailored business suit, Ford was hardly dressed for this. He was thirty pounds overweight and ten years past his prime; as he moved, his breath started coming harder. Perhaps this was why he never found the time to get away anymore, he thought. Wilderness only threw his physical limitations into sharp relief.

The woman was sitting in a rocking chair on the cabin's porch, holding a closed book in her lap.

She looked well, Ford thought as he drew closer. Her hair had been cut short and her body had achieved a slight softness. When he had first seen the woman, her body had been too hard, too angular, from a lifetime of strict diets and regular visits to the gym. Now, after a month by the lake, she had grown more natural—more at ease with herself, he thought, although of course he couldn't truly know how she felt.

He couldn't know, but he could hope. If she was satisfied with her situation, after all, her future with them would be that much easier.

The woman's choices had been made the moment she had delivered herself to the American embassy in Paris. At the time, she may not have realized this. By handing in the book, and herself, she may have thought that she had discharged her responsibility to her country. She'd thrown herself on their mercy, and had claimed not to expect anything in return for the secrets she'd delivered. But in truth, he thought, she had expected to be pardoned for her crimes. Perhaps she'd even expected a reward.

She had probably held on to this notion all through the flight back to America, and all through the long drive up into Maine, to this cabin. She had probably held on to it right up until the moment that Ford had disabused her of it—the moment when he had explained that, rather than providing a service to her country, she had done just the opposite. She had ruined the operation that he had put together with such care, and now it was up to her to set things right again.

He hadn't told her all of it; there was no reason for her to know the details. He'd simply explained that the situation into which she'd stumbled was not as simple as it might have seemed at first blush. He had revealed that Dietz and Leonard had been working for Ford before they'd been working for Keyes, and during. He had mentioned that he'd never intended to let the book fall into enemy hands. The question that had concerned him was what hands *were* enemy hands— who would be interested in gaining possession of a secret like the one in the book.

He'd given her only the slightest inkling of the reasons he had chosen to play the game the way he had. Verisimilitude, in his business, was the top priority. Had Ford manufactured a secret himself, to be put up for bids through the remnants of Dietz's COURTSHIP network, then his enemies might have sensed a fake. So Keyes had provided the perfect opportunity, although the man hadn't realized it at the time.

The secret had been real, and Dietz had proceeded as if he truly intended to sell it to the highest bidder. In fact, Dietz may even have planned on going farther with the masquerade than his plan with Ford had dictated. He had not kept Ford informed, as promised; he had taken matters into his own hands. Perhaps, had things gone through to the end, Dietz would have sold his prize and then vanished forever. Ford would have been left frustrated.

Or perhaps that had not been the man's intention. With Dietz gone, Ford had no way of knowing for certain.

And now it hardly mattered. By turning herself in at the embassy, the woman had brought Ford back into the loop. And the Saudi had taken the bait. Yet the prince was not the final link in the chain. There was someone above him, and that was the someone whom Ford wanted now.

At the sound of his approach, she lifted her head. She gave a quiet smile as he moved to sit in the rocking chair beside her.

A few moments passed. They looked out across the lake, at the dancing trees.

"I'm here to take you back," Ford said then.

"'Back,'" she echoed.

"To Langley. We're going to move ahead—soon, now."

She considered. "When do we go?"

"As soon as you can get your things together."

"I was just going to make myself a sandwich. Do we have time?"

He shrugged, then followed her inside.

The cabin was nearly as fragrant as the forest: piquant wood-smell and vanishing summer. The woman had kept it neat and simple. As they crossed through the living room, Ford saw a small pile of books and a writing desk with which he assumed she had been filling her time. They entered the kitchen, and she waved him to a chair by a low wooden table.

"Join me?" she said, as she opened the refrigerator.

"No, thank you."

"Something to drink?"

He shook his head.

"I'm making a pot of tea," she announced.

She spread the ingredients of a sandwich on the counter, put a kettle on the stove, and began to fix herself lunch.

Ford, watching, felt a bit of dark amusement. She was a tough one, he thought. Surely she wondered why they were taking her away from this place now. Yet she wouldn't give him the satisfaction of asking. Instead she would play along, waiting, leaving the ball in his court.

He rearranged himself in the chair, and cleared his throat.

"He's coming into the country this week. He'll be here for most of the month—visiting friends, doing business. You'll be ready and waiting, whenever we get the chance to make contact."

Hannah closed her sandwich, picked up a knife, and cut it in half without answering.

"Unless," Ford added, "you've had second thoughts."

She turned and looked at him.

"Do I have a choice?" she asked.

He didn't answer.

After a moment, she moved into the next room. Ford stayed at the table, listening. She was sifting through things. When she came back into the kitchen she held two envelopes. She set them on the table before him. He looked at the addresses without picking up the envelopes. One was addressed to her father in Baltimore; the other, to Victoria Ludlow in Chicago. "Can you mail these for me?"

He grunted. The kettle whistled; she went to take it off the burner. She poured the tea with her back facing him. Then she moved to the table, set down the mugs, picked up her sandwich, and came to join him. Ford was looking at the envelopes, wondering what she had written. Before mailing them, of course, he would find out.

"Assuming this works," Hannah said, "and I make contact, and the deal goes ahead . . ."

Ford reached for a cup of tea, and sipped.

". . . what happens to me then?"

"That depends on a lot of things, I'd expect."

"Such as?"

"Such as what you want, for starters. Also, such as what we consider to be in the best interests of security—considering what you know."

She pursed her lips.

"But don't worry about that," he said quickly. "We trust you."

It was nearly true.

She had turned herself in, after all, when there had been nothing compelling her to do so. But perhaps she had expected leniency, and had grown disenchanted by their treatment of her. For that reason, Ford had placed her under surveillance—the cabins on either side of Hannah's were occupied by agents on his payroll.

Yet even if she escaped from this place, she had nowhere to go. Her finances were frozen. She was with them, whether she liked it or not; for all her other roads led to dead ends.

She took a bite of her sandwich, and he drank more of his tea.

"Nice watch," she remarked.

"Hm? Thank you."

"Rolex?"

"Yes. My wife gave it to me."

"I used to have a Rolex."

He leaned forward.

"And you may again," Ford said. "If this works out, we may be able to find a permanent place for you. If, as I said, you're interested."

She said nothing.

"In the meantime . . ."

He reached into his jacket and withdrew an envelope, which he set alongside the other two on the table.

"I'd like you to take a look at that, over the next few days. It provides some background that you'll want to have memorized before you meet the prince again. We've built upon the story you came up with. Your husband worked for NASA on the scramjet; when you discovered his infidelity, you raided his computer. You met Dietz at a function in Washington nearly a year ago, and he set you on this current track."

She looked at the envelope, chewing.

"When it comes time to make the rendezvous, we won't have much warning. You'll need to be ready."

"All right," she said neutrally.

Ford reached for the mug again and drained it. The tea made him feel very relaxed. Some kind of herbal something, he thought; some kind of natural, gentle tranquilizer.

For a few moments, they sat in silence. The woman finished her sandwich. The wind outside picked up, soughing through the trees.

"Well," he said then. He was starting to feel all too at ease. Because he didn't get out of the city often enough, he thought. Nature was casting its spell. But he wasn't on vacation, and he needed to remember that. "We should get going."

She nodded, and brought her empty plate to the sink.

2.

As they left the cabin, he saw one of the agents next door, stacking wood. The man glanced in their direction, saw that Hannah was with Ford, and bent himself again to his task.

They walked around the lake. Ford almost felt himself floating, now, with relaxation. The lake whispered secretly. There was a cool nip in the air, which only made the glow inside him feel hotter. He would need to make an active effort to get out of the city on a regular basis, he thought. Look how wonderful he felt: he was having a physical reaction to the environment.

Or perhaps his reaction was due to satisfaction. Despite the fumbled operation, things had turned out well enough. They'd made some headway, in identifying the prince, and now they would continue to press the investigation, with the woman's help.

In a way, the whole snarled situation had been a blessing in disguise. For if things had not ended up this way, then Keyes's mismanagement of ADS might never have come to light. Keyes, his judgment skewed by grief, had been taking all too many chances with the Project. He had ordered the death of Chen. His own wife had died under mysterious circumstances. Without the recent snafu just passed, the man might have continued to run ADS without attracting attention. And if he'd been able to press far enough ahead, the results could have been disastrous.

Now, of course, Ford had stepped in. Dick Bierman had been placed in charge of ADS. He would slow things down, and proceed with due caution. Ed Greenwich had been censured, and the censure would likely lead to something worse. So things had turned out well enough, if not exactly the way Ford had initially planned.

Something flashed just beneath the surface of the water. Pickerel, or trout. He could almost feel the fishing rod in his hands, the warm sun beating down on the back of his neck.

"Good fishing here, I bet," he said.

His voice was a softer murmur than he had expected. The woman, strolling beside him, didn't answer.

They kept walking. The sun overhead was a glowing nimbus, fuzzy at the edges. Suddenly Ford didn't feel like walking anymore. The woman's bag seemed heavier than it had a moment before, as if by some strange alchemy its contents had turned to lead. He wanted to sit down, here at the edge of the lake, and let the afternoon warmly pass him by.

When he came to a stop, the woman took his elbow. "What is it?"

He shook his head. "Let's . . . sit down for a second."

"No, I see your car. We're almost there."

She took the bag from his hand, and urged him forward.

Now he could see the car himself, glittering under the afternoon sun. But the effort required to reach it was beyond him. His legs had turned to jelly. Over the next few steps, he leaned more and more weight against the woman, until she was supporting him.

"I . . . let's stop," he said.

"No. We're almost there."

They kept moving.

When she had gone into the other room, he thought, to get the letters. Then when she had poured the tea, her back facing him . . .

They reached the car.

Hannah leaned him against it, and reached into his pocket. His keys were there. She took them out, and then gently lowered him to the asphalt on the edge of the lot. Except for the cars belonging to the agents, the lot was empty; they were alone.

Ford tried to protest, but he felt all too sleepy. His eyes were closing.

"Relax," she said. "You'll be okay. Sleep it off."

He shook his head. He struggled to keep his eyes open. *What are you doing?* he tried to ask.

But he knew what she was doing. She was taking his wallet. Then she was taking his watch.

"Nothing personal," she murmured into his ear.

His skull was pounding. His eyelids fluttered, pressed together.

He lay his head down on the asphalt. He heard the door of the car open and close; then the engine starting.

Stop, he thought.

But his lips weren't working.

The engine was revving, then moving away. The sun beat down. His eyes stayed closed.

He lay on his back, and the afternoon warmly passed him by.

EPILOGUE

I.

The Greyhound carried Hannah west.

She stared blankly through her reflection at the sights of the highway: interchangeable motels, strip malls, fast-food joints, and gas stations. Not far past Buffalo, the sky turned a toneless gray. Soon after, snow began to fall. Arcs of dirty slush spun past the window. She stared through these, too.

The man beside her was snoring. With each passing minute, his head moved closer to her shoulder. She drew into herself, leaning toward the window, trying to avoid contact.

She was starving.

Presently she reached into her bag. Her hand brushed past the pawn shop ticket—she had considered leaving it in Ford's car, by the

bus station in Portland, and had then decided not to do him the favor—and found a package of pretzels. She opened it and put one into
her mouth, chewing without tasting.

Beneath the pawnshop ticket was her wallet, which contained the
six hundred dollars she'd gotten for the watch, plus the three hundred
and twenty dollars she'd taken from Ford. Beneath that was precious
little else: a pen and a notebook, a tube of lipstick and a compact, two
more bags of pretzels, and the envelope Ford had given her. In the bag
in the overhead compartment was her modest wardrobe. Together,
the two bags contained all her worldly possessions.

After a moment, she took out the envelope, opened it, and read the
contents. As promised, the paper contained the details she was to have
told the prince—the story she had started herself, on a train halfway
around the world from here, which had been finished by some CIA
analyst in some basement office in Washington.

When she had finished reading, she folded the paper, returned it to
the envelope, and returned the envelope to the purse.

She looked out the window again, thinking. They wouldn't reach
Chicago for another eleven hours. So she had some time in which to
decide her future.

Not much time, all things considered; but some.

2.

"Frank," she called.

He turned, saw her, and blinked.

He looked the same as ever—dressed in a seersucker suit with his
hair heavily gelled, holding a leather briefcase in one hand. He
blinked again, and then took a step toward her. Around them, the
building's lobby swirled with a lunch-hour rush.

"Hannah," he said.

He moved to hug her; she pulled back.

"Let's talk," she said.

3.

They sat in the same old TGIF, salads untouched before them.

When Frank finished speaking, a few moments passed in silence. He avoided looking Hannah in the eye. For that, she couldn't blame him. He had just told her, after all, that he had indeed turned on her—that a warrant was out for her arrest, and that Frank himself had been let off with a slap on the wrist. Had their positions been reversed, she wouldn't have been able to look him in the eye, either.

Finally, he stirred. "Listen," he said. "I feel horrible about this." Hannah nodded remotely.

"I don't know if you . . . What I mean is, if you think you're not going to turn yourself in . . . if you need a little money . . ."

For an instant, she was surprised by the offer. Frank Anderson, in her experience, was not a generous man. In the next instant, her surprise passed. Of course he didn't want her to turn herself in. If she did, she would tell the truth; the case might be reopened; the blame might be more evenly parceled between them.

She thought about it. "How much?"

"How much would you need? I could get . . . five hundred?"

She smiled.

"A thousand?" he said hopefully.

Hannah let a few moments pass.

"Ten thousand," she said then, "is the most you can take from a bank without their notifying anyone. Count yourself lucky. You're getting off easy."

He blanched.

"Pooh Bear . . ."

"Don't call me that."

"Hannah . . . I can't do ten."

She reached out, and put a hand on his.

"You'll find a way," she said sweetly.

4.

She stood beside him as he accepted the money from the teller. They moved outside, to the sidewalk, and he handed her the brown envelope.

"Hannah," he started. "I feel just . . ."

"Shh," she said.

She touched an index finger to his lips, then turned on her heel and walked away.

Halfway down the block, she caught sight of a cab. She hailed it, and gave the address of her old building.

The doorman seemed surprised to see her. "Ms. Gray," he said, coming quickly to his feet behind his desk. The gold buttons on his coat glimmered; a pile of untouched books was stacked on the counter.

"Craig. How're things?"

"Can't complain. Can't complain. I didn't expect to see you again. After . . ."

His words trailed off. After the government agents had come to search her apartment, he had been about to say. After they had no doubt told the managing company that she wouldn't be returning, and that if she did show her face, she was to be reported to the police.

Instead, he fumbled, and finished lamely: ". . . after so long."

"I'm just passing through," she said vaguely. "I was wondering if you got the gift I sent you."

He brightened. "The book!" he said. "I've got it right here. Thank you, Ms. Gray. That was awfully thoughtful of you. Usually I don't get gifts from the tenants except during the holiday season. It's sure nice to be remembered . . ."

"May I see it?"

He leaned over the intercom buttons at his station, and examined the spines of the books stacked on the desk. He found the paperback she had mailed—*The Chronicles of the Crusades*—and handed it to her.

"It's a nice one," he said gravely. "Thanks again. I'm really looking forward to reading it."

Hannah smiled, and flipped to the last page. The doorman hadn't opened the book, and wouldn't for months. She had gambled on that. During her entire tenure in the building, she had never once seen him reading any of the books he kept stacked on his desk; they were only for show.

"I just want to copy something down," she said, and reached into her purse for the pad and ballpoint pen.

The formula was a few short paragraphs of equations and text. She copied it down and then carefully drew lines through the writing in the book. After drawing careful lines, she went back and drew second careful lines, until the writing was lost.

Then she flipped to the midpoint of the book, to the bookmark she had inserted at page one hundred, took it out, then handed the book back. The doorman took it, looking curious.

"Thanks, Craig," she said, and turned again on her heel. She left the lobby without looking back.

5.

What was it?

She didn't know. But whatever it was, she had the only copy. The book she had handed in at the embassy, *Paula,* by Isabel Allende, had been scavenged from a bookshelf in the house in Provence. The formula she had written in the back was inaccurate. She had omitted one line completely, and in another she had changed x to c, 1.4 to .14, a square to a cube.

What should she do with it?

That was the question now.

She rode another Greyhound. Outside was night. She looked at her reflection in the window, instead of through it, as she turned the question over in her mind.

Several answers occurred to her. Yet most of them, she dismissed immediately. She would not try to profit from possession of the book. She would not squander this second chance, as soon as she'd received it. Nor would she destroy the formula, not when she didn't know what it truly was. What if she carried the cure for cancer, in this paperback book?

But she wouldn't return it to Ford, either. Ford had shown that he was playing games. And she was through with games.

She looked at her fellow passengers. They were drowsing, paying no attention to her.

One thing she knew for certain. She could not trust anyone else for help. Frank, Dietz, Ford, her father; they had all taken advantage of her, in one way or another. From now on, she would depend only on herself. Hannah Gray.

No. Not Hannah Gray.

She reached into her bag and removed the bookmark she'd taken from the copy of *Chronicles*. She opened it and then considered it, in the dim light.

The passport was in the name of Maya Willis. She didn't know who the woman in the photograph was—perhaps a decade older than Hannah, with similar bone structure and dirty-blond hair. But she guessed that the woman, whoever she was, was called something else. Dietz had carried many forged passports in his bag, half of them featuring his face, half featuring this one, all of them with different names.

But Maya Willis would do just fine.

Life threw one curveballs, she thought. A year ago, she never could have imagined herself here. And yet here she was. It was as her grandmother had always said: *We live life on life's terms.*

Yet she didn't need to accept those terms blindly. There was some small room for negotiation.

It sounded all right, she thought, looking out the window at the sun beginning to rise.

It sounded just a little better than all right.

ACKNOWLEDGMENTS

Once again, thanks are owed to my agent, Richard Curtis, for his insight and guidance, and to my editor, Neil Nyren, whose contributions to this book are too many to count, and too valuable for words.

I went to Jonathon Poritz with some simple questions about physics. By the time he'd finished answering them, I had a whole new round of questions. He shared with me not only his knowledge and his time, but also his ideas, his ideals, and his language. I am deeply indebted.

The following people also contributed: David Maddux, Ian Sowers, Joellyn Weingourt, Alison Brower, and Chris Robertson.

Thanks to Sarah Silbert; Robert, Jane, and Jennifer Altman; and Rachel and Benjamin Edelson.